WISHING ON A STAR

BOOKS IN THE STELLAR GUILD SERIES

WISHING ON A STAR

JODY LYNN NYE

WITH
ANGELINA ADAMS

THE STELLAR GUILD SERIES
TEAM-UPS WITH BESTSELLING AUTHORS

MIKE RESNICK
SERIES EDITOR

an imprint of

Rockville, Maryland

Series edited by Mike Resnick.

ISBN: 978-1-61242-264-0

www.PhoenixPick.com
Great Science Fiction & Fantasy
Free Ebook every month

Published by Phoenix Pick
an imprint of Arc Manor
P. O. Box 10339
Rockville, MD 20849-0339
www.ArcManor.com

CONTENTS

Welcome to another Stellar Guild book, the ultimate pay-it-forward science fiction series. Most of the field's superstars can't pay back the people who helped them when they were starting out; those people are rich, or dead, or both. So, in this field more than in any other, it has become an honored tradition to pay forward.

Stellar Guild was created for just that purpose. Each book in the series consists of a novella by one of the field's superstars, plus a novelette by a protégé of the star's own choosing, said novelette being a sequel, a prequel, or a companion piece to the star's novella.

The first book in the series was by Kevin J. Anderson and his protégé, and it won the very first "Lifeboat to the Stars" Award. Since then Stellar Guild has featured books by Mercedes Lackey, Harry Turtledove, Robert Silverberg, Nancy Kress, Eric Flint, and Larry Niven – and, of course, their protégés.

Jody Lynn Nye has written more than 40 novels, alone and in collaboration with both Anne McCaffrey and Robert Asprin, and well over 100 stories. I invited her to say a few words about the book you hold in your hands.

Mike Resnick

WISHING ON A STAR

Book One
BEST WISHES

JODY LYNN NYE

CHAPTER 1

The little white boy with the missing front tooth eyed Raymond Crandall up and down with suspicion in his round blue eyes. He had handled the concept of a six-foot tall African-American teenager in a shirt and tie walking through the wall to his bedroom, six stories up, but he just couldn't seem to accept the reason for Ray's appearance.

"You got to be kidding me," he said. "There's no such thing as fairy godmothers! And how come you aren't a girl?"

Ray was glad for the moment that his mentor, Rose Feinstein, wasn't in the room to hear. She had remained outside the apartment building, standing on the air six stories up while he had followed the need string he had sensed to this very angry child. He pulled himself to his full six feet while still trying to keep kindness and patience uppermost in his heart. He was, after all, there to help. Something in this child's soul cried out to him. Ray was determined to grant his wish and make him happy. He tapped the blue, arm-length, star-topped wand on the palm of his hand. Ray just wished he wasn't so tired. His new college schedule was eating his life, but he couldn't give up fairy-godparenting for anything. He tried to think what Rose would say. She could handle it on her head, but this was his task.

"Look," Ray reasoned, crouching down to the boy's level. The child's name was Jacob. The magic told him that, but not how to help him. "How do you think I found you? You really needed someone to listen to you."

Jacob snorted, looking far older than his years. "You don't look like Dr. Phil."

"Nope, I'm not," Ray said. This kid was determined not to let anyone in. He'd had days like that himself when he was that age, and nothing would enrage Jacob more than having him say so. "You want something badly. I could feel it all the way up the street. What's on your mind?"

The boy's nose turned red, proving he was suppressing anger. "Get lost!"

"No," Ray said. With a mental apology to Rose, who was standing outside in the dark in the middle of a snowy Chicago winter, he sat down on the floor and crossed his legs. "Not going until you tell me what's got you so miserable that every fairy godparent on the north side is homing in on you?"

Suddenly, Jacob looked terrified. His eyes flicked to every wall, as if expecting a horde of strangers to walk in the way Ray had.

"They're eavesdropping on me?" he whispered.

Ray cursed himself.

"No, I mean, they want to help you! We can't read your mind. All we want to do is help you to be happy."

"You can't make me do anything!"

"True," Ray said. He sighed. It was his fourth call of the night. He knew he was getting punchy. "Look, I have home-work to do. I bet you do, too. If you tell me what is bugging you, I'll take care of it, and get out of your space."

Jacob's blue eyes filled with tears. "Okay, if you have some-thing better to do, maybe you should go and do it!" He turned and plunked himself down so he was facing the corner of the room.

Chemistry 101 suddenly took a back seat to this unhappy child. Ray went to sit down beside Jacob. The child radiated hurt.

"Jacob, there is nothing more important than you, right here and right now," Ray said. "I'll do whatever it takes to fix your problem."

"You can't do that."

"Maybe not, but I'll do my best. I can't promise you better than that."

The blue eyes slewed sideways.

The boy glanced back, a sly look on his face.

"First, you gotta prove you're really a fairy godfather," he said.

Fifteen minutes later, Ray scrambled out through the wall, failing even to enjoy the raspy, cool sensation of the drywall and scratchy feeling of the faux brick façade on his face, one of the perks of the job. He came to a windmilling halt on the patch of thin air just beyond the eaves of the elderly Lake Shore apartment building. Rose Feinstein, a short, plump woman with a blunt nose and warm brown eyes and whose bun of salt-and-pepper hair was tucked into a knitted bobble cap made of thick red yarn, took his arm and steadied him.

"That was like Shakespeare's 'exit, pursued by a bear,'" she said. "Are you all right? The need string vanished, just like that! You must have done a great job. How did it go?"

Ray shook his head.

"I don't want to talk about it," he said.

Rose's arched eyebrows rose into the brim of her cap.

"Hard case?" she asked.

Ray glanced over his shoulder at the wall.

"That kid is going to be a major politician one day," he said. "I just know I'm done with him."

"He wanted you to prove what you were," Rose guessed. Sometimes Ray hated the way she could read his mind. "I had one little pisher who made me do a little dance and sing a song about how I helped little children. In the end, all she wanted was someone to take her seriously. Her parents were too busy for her. You know the kind." Ray nodded. "I didn't even grant a wish for her that day. It was four years later when she finally called me."

"That's the way it was with this kid," Ray said. "He's really just unhappy. Then it all flooded back to him how humiliated he felt at that moment for having to manifest a pair of blue wings on his back and flit around the room like Tinkerbell, and he felt his face flush. "I said I didn't want to talk about it!

Rose's eyes twinkled, as though she could see his thoughts.

"Be thankful he's only unhappy," she said. "You know plenty of children who would give anything only to be unhappy. And don't be so hard on yourself. You made a judgment call."

"Yeah," Ray said, struggling to find the words. "But what if he really needed a wish and I didn't help him?"

"You do the best you can with what you have, with the knowledge you have at that moment," Rose said, taking him by the arm. "None of us can do more than that. Come on. It's cold. I could use a cup of hot chocolate. With whipped cream. How does that sound?"

Ray allowed himself to be escorted down to earth. Next to actually getting to grant wishes, flying was still the most awesome thing about being a fairy godfather. Hot chocolate wasn't bad, either.

"Good," Rose said, as they sank down toward the shadowy pavement beside the apartment building. "Did I ever tell you about the little girl who made me sing the whole song of "Happy Talk" before she'd let me grant her wish? And I'm nobody's idea of a singer, either. She was just making me jump through hoops. Sometimes making yourself vulnerable is the only way to make a child in need feel as if he's not the only person in the world someone's made a fool out of. I felt like a complete nebbish at the time, but it was worth it in the long run. I did my job, and that is the only thing that counts."

CHAPTER 2

Her words were on Ray's mind the next day as he sat surrounded by fellow volunteers in the raked stands in the studio at WPBS-TV. He wasn't a famous doctor, yet, or a rich philanthropist, yet, so all he had to offer the people who could do good in the world was his time. He and a number of his fellow fairy godparents had signed up to answer phones, write tweets, and fulfill CrowdPleaser online pledges for Selane's Kids, a charity that funded research for Spaulding's syndrome.

The appeal was scheduled to run an entire month. It put Ray in a bind, timewise, with regard to studying for his upcoming first-semester finals at Northwestern University, but he really wanted to be a part of the cure. Besides, he got to watch Selane herself doing her stuff live. His little sister, eleven-year-old Chanel, was emerald green with envy.

"Get me an autographed picture!" she demanded every morning when he left the house to catch the El to the studio. "See if she'll let me come in and meet her! She could sign my CDs! I'm her biggest fan in the world, Ray. You know that!"

He knew it. Chanel and fifty million other people, who bought Selane's albums, saw her movies, and paid huge bucks to attend her sold-out concerts, were each her biggest fan in the world. He might be able to wangle an autograph by the end of the month, but bringing in his sister was out of the question. No matter how many times he had explained to Chanel what he was really doing and how things really were at a televised charitable appeal, she paid no attention. It wasn't glamorous at all.

Warbling tones in the earpiece tucked over his left ear told him he had a call. He punched the numbered square flashing on his keypad to answer it. He spoke into the microphone of the headset, careful to keep his voice upbeat.

"Hello! Thank you for calling to help Selane's Kids! This is Ray. How much would you like to donate today?"

"Uh, I dunno." The male voice sounded hesitant in his ear. "How much is a good donation?"

"Well, fifty bucks is what most people give," Ray offered. He ran his finger down the touch screen in front of him, scanning the list of donations during his segment of the telethon, to make sure he was telling the truth.

"That sounds like a lot."

Ray got an immediate mental picture of the man on the other end of the line: an older person, probably white, but you couldn't be a hundred percent sure, who grew up when fifty dollars bought more than it did today. Still, the dude was calling to offer. Not that Ray himself had a whole lot of money to throw around himself.

"It is kind of a lot of money, but it's a good cause," he said. "You donate whatever you want. It all goes into the fund to pay for treatment for Spaulding's syndrome. The kids are grateful to every single person, no matter what you give."

"What does Selane's Kids do with the money?"

After six days answering that same question, Ray had the information on the tip of his tongue. He began to recite the number of studies being run on Spaulding's syndrome, the increased awareness that led to early detection, physical therapy to help kids cope with the symptoms of the neurological disorder, the many drugs going into trial, all funded by donations and corporate sponsorships.

"Well… would twenty-five be okay?"

"Sure!" Ray said. His long fingers tapped number keys at the top of the keyboard. "Credit or debit card?"

"Credit."

Ray took the information down almost automatically. He had become pretty adept at touch-typing in the last year. His senior year at high school he could have gotten away with his old system of two-finger hunt-and-peck, but there was so much homework for a freshman in pre-med that he gave up and took an online course in speed typing. He dropped his eyes to the keyboard to make sure he was putting in the credit card information correctly, but the rest was so easy that he glanced around him while the man dictated his name, address, phone, and e-mail addresses.

A buzz of other voices surrounded him, as the other volunteers gathered pledges just as he was doing, but there were plenty of other noises. The rows of operator desks, raked like stadium seats but with a table across each row for the computer terminals, were at the rear of a huge studio. Some of the volunteers were there to answer phone calls from donors, but this appeal was more than a telethon. Every kind of social media was represented, up to and including instant photography and texting. The slim, dark-skinned girl with the long neck and flat-ironed hair brushed back to show off her high cheekbones three seats down from him was answering tweets and entering status updates on FaceBook, Google+, Instagram, and other sites. Everyone was publicizing, entreating, encouraging, chatting about, and outright asking for donations.

At the heart of the Spaulding's Syndrome Appeal was a woman with a nanowatt personality, a celebrity that other celebs deferred to: Selane.

The lady herself stood clutching a microphone in both hands as though it was a torch to light the way to glory. She looked like an angel, her cloud of sable hair an aura touched here and there with the sparkle of diamonds, which also hung around her neck in a V-shaped blaze. A narrow white dress that contrasted with her warm, golden skin clung to her famous, voluptuous curves. The hem of the skirt danced around her bejeweled high-heeled sandals. Her big, hazel-brown eyes, framed in black lashes, seemed to look into people's souls. She was beautiful, and she had what Rose called 'charisma' by the ton. She was speaking earnestly into the mike, beseeching those who were listening to pay heed to the cause that was in her heart.

At the front of the enormous room was a studio audience, maybe four hundred people. It wasn't the kind of crowd that Selane normally played to. She could sell out Soldier Field in twenty minutes. The real audience for her performance was the millions, maybe even billions of people, checking in across the world. All around the room, her image was repeated on huge flat screen monitors. The big one on the wall to Ray's left was the output from master control. He saw the logos on the others that denoted on what websites and television stations across the globe the feed was being carried. Selane knew how to work the camera. She gazed into it with a warm, confident expression that made Ray feel as if he, and anyone else watching, was one of her best friends in the world. Too bad the reality was so far from the truth.

"Why do you need my e-mail?" the man said suddenly. Ray's attention flew back to his caller.

"Well, sir, Selane has some online promotions going for people who donate. You're probably watching us on television, but we've got a web channel going, too. If you would like to see what kind of progress the doctors have been making with the kids, there are some interviews on the FundChannel and CrowdPleaser sites. In your thank-you letter, you'll get links you can click to watch videos, or read some excerpts from the research you helped fund. Most of them are pretty easy to understand."

The man let out a rueful chuckle. "All except the link part. You're a nice kid. You've been patient with an old man, a lot more than my grandchildren. Sure you wouldn't like to come over and explain my computer to me?"

"You running the latest version of the operating system?" Ray countered. "Even I don't get that yet. I'm waiting for my little brother to explain it to me."

The caller laughed. "Thanks a lot, kid."

"No, sir," Ray said. "Thank you. Selane's Kids appreciate it."

He heard a descending musical tone that indicated the call had ended, and an ascending one that meant another caller was on the line. He reached for the 'answer' key, when a large man in a dark, greeny-gray suit appeared at his side and put his big hand over the console. Ray looked up in surprise.

"You're not supposed to talk with them," he said, sternly. "You're taking too long. Just get their information and go onto the next call."

Ray dared to meet his eyes. The guy must have stood six foot eight, with shoulders like a linebacker. His suit was cut to outline a slim waist. The effect only served to make him more threatening. Like Ray, he was African-American, but much lighter in complexion. The bronze skin of his shaved head gleamed in the spotlights like real metal. He was one of Selane's 'enforcers,' there to do the star's bidding. Her goons were always watching the volunteers, only talking to the phone squad or tweeters to enforce the long list of rules. Ray suspected that the enforcers carried concealed weaponry, but they didn't need it. No one who wanted to go home in one piece would try and get to Selane past them.

Ray kept his voice and eyes level. He refused to let the man intimidate him, but he didn't want to get thrown out, either.

"Yes, sir," he said. "I got that."

"That's one. You get three. Then you're gone." The enforcer shoved his face closer to him, just for a second, then withdrew. He had said his piece. Ray would comply. He had seen other volunteers heaved out for similar minor infractions. He didn't want to get bounced. He *had* to stay. He wanted to be there.

The musclemen were the only part of the star's huge entourage who associated with the 'little people,' and they didn't mean the kind of fairy godmothers Ray had met who stood just over a foot high. Selane had come to smile at the volunteers just once since the appeal had started, five days before. Since then, she'd remained in the circle of her coterie except when she interacted with the studio audience or the children.

They all adored her, of course. The viewers who had been approved to watch her in person applauded everything she said, and burst into rapturous cheers when she sang. Ray had to admit her thrilling alto reached into his soul in a way he couldn't explain. Maybe she had some kind of magic, like the Sirens in Greek mythology. He wanted to be near her, to have her fix that jewel-bright gaze on him. It was what had made her an international superstar. He wished she knew his name.

She didn't, of course. He doubted that she even knew he was there. None of the volunteers who were answering the phones or sitting with the Spaulding's syndrome kids or helping seat the rotating audience were allowed to associate with the star. Outside the studio on one of the side streets was the most elaborate trailer he had ever seen, with a guard in dark shades and a huge camel hair coat standing near the door. Selane had a fancy buffet spread at one end of the studio, prepared by one of Chicago's finest chefs, a sweet little white lady with light brown curls, who looked proud to be associated with a big star like Selane. Ray assumed the food tasted as good as it looked and smelled. He was sure he'd never know. The volunteers had a table at the exact opposite side of the room laden with generic cookies, no-name pop, and huge urns of coffee that smelled like it had been passed through a cat.

"I heard that the refreshments were paid for from the donations," one of the other volunteers had whispered. It made everyone feel guilty about partaking, knowing that the money for their snacks could have gone to help more kids.

No one thought their treatment was fair. Still, no one had quit. Like Ray, they enjoyed the frisson of being insiders, however temporary, on a world-shaking event. They got to see what happened behind the scenes. It was like something out of a movie. Every time the feed cut away from Selane making her personal appeals, one of the enforcers brought out a chair for the lady. Selane settled into it like a soap bubble alighting. Three women in pink smocks ran onto the set from the sidelines. One of them fluffed out the star's hair while another dabbed at Selane's face with brushes and sponges. The third woman held a mirror so the lady could see herself. It was just like all the backstage stuff that they showed in the movies.

While short documentary footage rolled, talking about the fundraiser and the premiums that a donor could receive, burly men moved parts of the set around or adjusted lights. Ray had been a little disappointed that the director was an ordinary, middle-aged Hispanic-looking guy in a checked shirt and Dockers, instead of an imperious Englishman wearing a beret and jodhpurs. He talked into a little microphone-earpiece a lot like the one Ray was wearing, instead of shouting through a megaphone.

A couple of technicians in blue jeans and black t-shirts with cameras balanced on their shoulders ran up and down the front of the audience, getting their reactions to the live show going on. The focus of their attention was the small knot of children in wheelchairs, of all different races and ages, all of them bent over sideways or in some kind of contorted position that made Ray just ache for them. They were the reason that he was there. They all had Spaulding's syndrome, a skeletal disorder that rendered children so fragile that even a sudden movement could break their bones. Over time, the children's muscles atrophied because they couldn't exercise. The body aged like that of a centenarian, but their minds continued to develop. It was a grim disease, like juvenile osteoporosis. The kids knew what was happening to them. They were careful, relying on super lightweight support braces and deeply padded seats, but it had to feel like being in a prison. Ray knew if it had happened to him he would be frustrated as hell every day of his life. He checked the balance of brownie points in his mental piggy bank. The nine bright sparks in it leaped up and down. They were dying to help, but there just weren't enough of them. When Ray tried to figure out how many it would take to cure just one of those kids, the rows of black holes in his mind's eye went on into infinity. To give them credit, the kids handled the situation better than their parents did. They accepted the inevitable. He was glad to be able to give them any little measure of help he could.

"Well, I don't really understand these Kickstarter things any better than you do," Rose's cheerful voice came from behind him, "but if a regular donation doesn't work for you, they're making a special DVD of Selane's duets just for the online fundraiser. Oh, yes, all sorts of celebrities singing with her. I saw some of it the other night. They're very good. It would be worth the extra money to have it. You can see a preview and order it right off the website. Let me read you the url thing."

"That's U.R.L.," murmured a woman's voice. Ray recognized it as belonging to Alexandra Sennett, the president of the local FGU chapter. A few apprentices like him were among the patient call-takers, but most of the volunteers were adult rank-and-file of the Local 263.

"*Yerl*, right, sorry, honey. Right, you got that? Good! We look forward to seeing your order. Bye, now!"

The heartfelt violin and flute music coming from the speakers cut out suddenly. The voice of the director broke in over the speaker.

"Coming back to you in ten!"

"Places!" shouted the floor manager. He held out a polite hand, palm up. "Miss Selane, if you don't mind."

The minions scattered to their stations off stage. Selane rose from her throne, and the stagehand removed it from the set. A girl in a peach-colored Spaulding's Syndrome Appeal t-shirt brought back the lady's microphone, then retreated swiftly. Selane took her place on the white star painted on the floor, bowed her head, and waited. The spotlight hit her, and she raised her face to the camera.

"Thank you, all you wonderful people across the world who are helping to combat this terrible disease! We're lucky to have with us today a number of the children who are bravely dealing with Spaulding's Syndrome. I would sure like to have you meet them."

The spotlights on the kids lit up. A little blond girl, who still had some substance in her bones, straightened up and beamed at the audience. The others did their best to react. All but one little boy, a skinny child with long dark hair and lashes, hollow cheeks and long, slender wrists who listed at a sharp angle in his all-enveloping wheelchair. His name was Francisco. He looked about six years old, but Ray had read the biographies the volunteers had been issued on all of the kids, and knew Francisco was almost eleven. He had been diagnosed with Spaulding's when he was only two years old. He had never been able to play outside, or go to school, or even go to the bathroom without help in case he broke something. Ray had seen him on the Appeal broadcasts for years. Francisco had pretty much grown up in the public eye. Unlike the others, he didn't interact with the audience or any of his fellow patients. Except for his caregiver, a brisk, small-boned Filipina in her fifties, and his desperate, loving parents who waited in the shadows on the edge of the stage, he had eyes only for Selane. He lived for those moments like that one.

The star came to crouch down beside his wheelchair and put an infinitely gentle hand on his forearm. He leaned toward her. Selane addressed the camera.

"Everybody, I want you to meet Francisco. He's a survivor. In spite of his condition, he has over two million Twitter followers and Facebook friends. He posts every day about his struggles. He's my hero. He should be yours, too. Aren't you, honey?" She glanced down briefly. Francisco gazed up at her, his large eyes fixed on her.

"I love you," he said.

The busy room went silent, except for the hums and screeches of the machinery. Everybody was touched by the boy's declaration, delivered with soul-crunching sincerity, except its object. His words bounced off Selane's hide like raindrops. She smiled and turned back to the cameras.

"He means he loves all of you for giving freely to help him and his fellow sufferers. Keep on giving to this boy. Whatever you can, all of us will be grateful. Thank you."

Pity welled up in Ray's heart. All right, so Selane probably got thousands of messages and letters every day professing undying love to her. She must have become inured to the words. Couldn't she see that the boy really idolized her, and it meant something special to him to have her close by?

You wouldn't have been able to tell by the way she acted. The second the red light on the cameras faded, she rose and stalked back to her spot off stage. Her staff clustered around her. Francisco watched her go. Tears welled up in those big, dark eyes. His caregiver hurried to blot them away.

On the far side of the room, the lights went up in a small set that had a backdrop painted with a pattern of cinder-block bricks. An ancient, scrawny African-American man with close-clipped white hair seated on a wooden stool with a guitar slung around his neck leaned into his microphone.

"Hey, folks, how ya doin'? I'm awful grateful to Miss Selane for lettin' me be wit' you here today. Got a special song I hope a bunch o' ya remember."

He struck up a blues number and began a throaty wail of a lament about lost love and memories. Ray wished he could listen, but he had another call coming in.

CHAPTER 3

The old man drew his forefinger down across his guitar strings, then clapped his hand over them to still the vibration.

"Thanks, folks. And don't forget to donate to Selane's Kids!"

Ray joined the others in clapping like mad. The red light on the camera facing him died, but more on the other side of the big studio blazed into life. A hip-hop group took the stage among tossing spotlights and a shower of glitter. Half a dozen dancers, slender women in wisps of spandex, gyrated and body-popped behind the singers, all young black men in their twenties. Ray couldn't keep his hands from dancing over his console to the driving beat.

The floor manager, a brown-haired and bearded man in blue jeans, came over to tell the volunteers to take a break. Gratefully, Ray took off his earpiece. Rose appeared at his side. Her eyes twinkled with mischief.

"They're rearranging us again," she said. "Putting all the out of date or used merchandise in the back so you handsome young people are up front."

"Come on, Rose, that's not true," Ray protested, although he knew after a week's experience that it was. When the volunteers showed up early in the morning, half an hour before the video portion was to go live, they were allowed to take refreshments from the sorry tables on their side and to sit wherever they wanted. After the first break of the day, the floor manager came over, always with an apologetic look on his long face, and made everyone sit in a different location.

"It's so our viewers think we have hundreds of people answering the phone," the manager explained, looking sheepish. No one believed it was true.

"Never mind. I'm going to visit with the kiddies," Rose said.

"I'll come with you," Ray volunteered.

"I'll come, too," said George Aldeanueva, a short, stocky man with bowed legs who was the secretary of the union. He brandished an accordion folder. "My grandchildren made get-well cards for all of them."

"They're good kids," Rose said. "You should be proud of them."

George puffed up his chest.

"Por supuesto, Rose. I wouldn't be able to call myself a grandfather if I wasn't proud of them."

One little girl with blond braids raised shining eyes at their approach. She was seven years old, but could have been a hundred with that pinched face and claw-like hands.

"Hi, Grandma Rose," she said. "Hi, Ray. Hi, Abuelo George."

"Hello, Celeste," George said, with a warm smile. "Here's something for you from my Teresita and my Guillermo." He put a card down on her tray and moved over to the African-American boy in the next wheelchair.

"Good morning, Celeste," Rose said, squatting down beside her. "You look lovely today." The girl's caretaker, a young woman with brown hair pulled back in a ponytail, pulled over a chair. Rose settled down on it. Ray hovered at her shoulder. His heart always went out to the kids, but he wasn't so good at approaching them as she was. Not yet, anyhow. Rose promised him he had all the skills, but he just didn't feel confident in using them yet.

"Charlotte braided my hair," Celeste said, touching the end of one plait with a gnarled forefinger.

"Well, she did a great job. I brought you something for today," Rose said. She reached into her purse and pulled out a colorful book. Ray recognized it as a graphic novel, for a series that was aimed more at his little sister's age than his. The book was used, but Celeste took it in her feeble, slender fingers with an expression of joy on her face like she had been given a treasure chest.

"Thanks! You didn't have to."

"Oh, I know. But you like Jewel Bears. I thought you could read it to me later."

Celeste giggled.

"You can read!"

"Oh, but I wouldn't do it as well as you do," Rose said. "You know all their names and their voices. That one that sounds squeaky, I can never remember which one he is."

Ray relaxed a little. The tingle in the air that he could feel with his wand, resting concealed in his shirt pocket, assured him that none of the kids needed a fairy godparent. All they wanted was a little kindness and attention. On his rounds he was used to following a child's desperate need for a wish. These kids were surprisingly at peace with their condition.

The wand tingled lightly. He was used to feeling the desperation of a child in need. These were the sickest kids he had ever met, but their need strings broadcast a kind of modified contentment. He respected them for accepting their situation. It made him want to please them all the more.

Francisco sat all alone at the front of the stage. As soon as the lights were turned off, his caretaker turned him so he was facing away from the audience. Ray knew he hated the looks of pity. Who wouldn't? All the volunteers felt for him. The long-necked black girl who had been tweeting the event beside Ray in the phone banks was already kneeling beside Francisco, trying to cheer him up. Ray felt a twinge of need lance out to him from that direction. He wanted to go over and find out what the boy wanted so badly, but he didn't want to interfere while the child already had a visitor. Particularly not one who belonged to a rival organization. She was part of the contingent of Sandmen who were also working the charity event.

Though there was a bar in the Glenwood neighborhood not far from where Ray lived that catered to all the magical unions and guilds on the north side, the groups didn't mix much. The Tooth Fairies spoke chiefly with other Tooth Fairies. The Guardian Angels who talked loudly among themselves about their exploits, weren't even the Angels who really mattered. The real ones, like his girlfriend Antoinette and her uncle, were usually out doing good deeds and protecting the helpless, not knocking back beers and bragging. There weren't any members of the Demons, Djinni and Efreets Guild left in the area after the events of the previous summer. The House Brownies socialized with everybody, but they were usually busy. The Sandmen came in early and left about the time the Fairy Godmothers Union arrived. Ray supposed it was logical, since his folks dealt with kids while they were awake, and the Sandmen visited their clients once they fell asleep, or were trying to go to sleep. He had read the FGU manual cover to cover and knew their history and responsibilities, but he had no good take on the duties of the other disciplines. When he tried to make friends with some of the Sandmen in the studio to find out more about them, they pretty much blew him off. Too bad, because that girl near Francisco was a fox.

Rose left Celeste with the comic book, and went to visit with another child. She caught Ray's eyes on the little boy.

"Why don't you go and talk to him?" she asked Ray. Her face told him she felt the longing, too. "He needs a friend."

"I tried," Ray said. "He ignores me. All he wants is her." He nodded toward Selane.

"Young crushes are hard," Rose said, with a sigh. "Poor little guy. She's there for him, but not in the way he hopes. You and I, we can't do anything about that. Hearts' desires don't make people act against their will. All we can do is grant that wish when he finally knows what he wants."

The girl rose to her feet and went back to her keyboard. She didn't make eye contact with Ray or Rose as she passed them.

The desperate yearning faded. The caretaker had Francisco rearranged in his chair so the boy seemed less uncomfortable.

She set down a lidded plastic cup of juice with an attached plastic straw within range of his right hand. She went off into the darkened area where Francisco's parents hovered.

Francisco tried to pick up the cup, his long fingers fumbling on its orange-peel-textured surface. It looked as though it was just out of his reach. Ray ached for him. The boy tried again and again to grasp it.

Ray couldn't help it. He went over and put the cup into the curve of the boy's skinny hand. Instead of being grateful, Francisco glared at him. With his eyes fixed on Ray's he deliberately pushed the cup off the edge of his tray just as the camera operators came around with their gear on their shoulders to get some reaction shots. Ray jumped back, trying not to get splatters on his best pair of kicks. Francisco turned a pathetic gaze in the direction of the cameras, who homed in tight. His caretaker came running in from the side with a paper towel and a loud exclamation of dismay. The little brat had made it look like Ray spilled his juice! Ray tried to protest, but no one would have believed him. He retreated, feeling stung. Francisco shot him a triumphant sneer.

Rose came over and put an arm around his shoulders.

"Don't feel bad. You might be that bitter if your body started lying to you, like his does."

"I probably would be worse," Ray said. At least the painful aching need had dissipated. All of the fairy godparents in the room had to be going crazy, wanting to respond to it. Sooner or later someone would be able to grant his wish.

Once again in the spotlight, Selane thanked the musical group, giving each of them a one-armed hug. As they left stage right, she held out her hand to the opposite side. A special fanfare played, drawing everyone's attention.

From Ray's point of view, an assistant director came over pushing a cart on which sat a big, turquoise-blue pillow, suitable for a sheik to lounge on, dripping with gold fringes on the corners, although on camera he and the cart remained invisible. Beside the assistant was an elderly woman with short, bleached blond curls, wearing a velour track suit and orthopedic shoes. The camera zoomed in so everything around it was invisible. All the worldwide audience could see was the ivory-colored embossed china vase cradled in the blue velvet nest. Selane lifted the vase in her fingers as though it was made of sighs and moonlight, and turned it for the camera.

With the air of letting the viewers in on a great secret, she leaned close to the lens.

"This is one of my newest 'finds'," she said. "It's a gift to Selane's Kids from Nadine, here." The camera moved back to show them both. "Now, you may see an old, discarded piece of *junk* that you wouldn't give to your auntie, but I see a treasure. I see such treasures everywhere, just like these precious children. I would never discard them, just as I would never discard one of these wonderful objects, set aside, forgotten, neglected and alone in the back of a dusty cupboard or on a shelf so high you never, ever look at it, or in a little shop where it has been forgotten about for years, never knowing its value."

Beside her, the woman in the track suit started to protest. The assistant director held up a hand to forestall her outburst. Nadine subsided, but she looked stricken and a little angry. Selane continued to croon to the camera.

"...But if you learn to see the beauty in those little finds, as I do, you will be enriched like you never could believe. These would otherwise be neglected or ignored, just as these precious children have been. And just like my darling little friends there, getting to know these finds will bring you joy. Now, look at this vase and see how pretty it was. I hate to let it go, but I am sure that out there is somebody who will love this and cherish it even more than I do. Reach into your souls and think if you would enjoy having this in your house, bid for it. The bidding is now open, both on the phones and over the Internet. I can't wait to thank you for your donation to Selane's Kids! Ready, get set, go!"

She put the vase upright on the pillow and stroked it with one hand, waiting.

The phones began to buzz loudly. Ray punched the button on his console.

"Twenty!" an excited female voice bawled in his ear.

"Twenty!" Ray sang out, but he was too late. Morry Garner, an older man in the Fairy Godmothers Union two rows behind him, had beaten him by a split second.

"Twenty-five," the woman cried.

Ray echoed it, joining a chorus of others who were taking calls from phone bidders.

"Oh, that's so nice of you," Selane said, with an encouraging smile for the camera.

On the screens all around the room, the highest bid appeared across the bottom of the pillow. The price soon exceeded what the woman on the line with him could afford. She was replaced by a hoarse-sounding man who made a one-time three-figure offer, then hung up when he was outbid. A grandmotherly woman offered a thousand. For the life of him, Ray couldn't see paying a thousand dollars for a piece of junk from an antique store, but they weren't buying the vase per se. They were sharing a 'find' with Selane.

Within a minute or two, the bidding slowed down to jumps of five dollars. An elderly Asian man taking Internet offers closed it down at $2,255. Selane tapped her microphone on the vase. It rang softly.

"Sold," she said. "And what is the name of this very generous buyer?"

"Mary McNulty, of Nashville, Tennessee," the man called out.

"Well, Miss Mary of Nashville, Selane is grateful to you. You go ahead and give my wonderful volunteer all your information, and this beautiful thing will be going out to you tonight. And all my darling Kids thank you, too." The lights went on over the knot of children. A couple of them nodded vigorously. Francisco looked longingly at Selane, and mustered a feeble tilt of his head. "I'll also be including you in my Gratitude Lullaby later on tonight. Be sure and tune in to listen. Now, we all need a little cheering up, so let me introduce you to Emmett White! Don't laugh so hard you forget to keep calling and sending in your donations. My helpful volunteers are standing by to hear from you." The cameramen appeared before Ray and the others, and their images popped up on the multiple screens. They plastered on eager smiles. The picture changed in an instant to the Selane's Kids logo, then dissolved to reveal a black comedian in an oversized sweater and tight, shiny trousers standing at an upright microphone halfway across the studio.

CHAPTER 4

The cluster of spotlights faded. Selane handed her microphone to the stagehand and stalked off the stage. Nadine trotted after her.

"That wasn't a piece of junk!" the elderly woman protested, hurt. "That vase is Royal Worcester china. I had it appraised just last month. It's worth five times what you just auctioned it off for!"

Selane turned and regarded the older woman with a distracted air. She focused on the frowning face.

"Oh, you can't pay attention to the words I use, honey," she said, sweetly. "The folks at home don't know anything about that. I want them to reach into their hearts and offer all they can for one of my finds."

"You could have told them what it really was. You'd have gotten more!"

Selane glanced toward her coterie for help. She shouldn't have to be arguing with a donor! Her manager, Dennis Folger, came bustling over. A tall, slim Brit with a long nose and heavy-lidded blue eyes that gave him an ironic look, he always knew how to keep a friendly face on things. He put his arm around Nadine and drew her away from Selane.

"This isn't eBay, sweetheart," he said, confidentially. "We're not here to sell goods. The focus has to be on the kiddos. We don't want people talking tonight about this event being the one where we sold a Royal Worcester vase; we want it to be the one where everybody in the world came together to help fight a terrible disease. It's the *story*, my love. None of your grandchildren have Spaulding's Syndrome, do they?"

"Well, no," Nadine said. Her indignation faded, replaced by concern.

"Count yourself lucky, darling," Dennis said, leaning closer to her. He coaxed her to look into his eyes. "Anyhow, thanks a million for the beautiful vase. Selane doesn't make a big fuss because she doesn't want to embarrass the people who don't have a lot to give, like you do. If the most that that phone bidder could afford was two grand, then that's five days of treatment for a child at the Spaulding's Clinic in Rochester. That's what you did today. Isn't that worth a little white lie?"

By then, Nadine was beaming. Selane gave a sigh of relief. Dennis was worth more than the fortune she already paid him. She retreated into the circle of her coterie and collapsed into her waiting chair. The makeup and hair girls clustered close, ready to give her a touchup.

"Not yet, girls," she said, waving them back. "I need refreshments."

Dennis's second-in-command, Morgan, a whip-thin African-American with the longest eyelashes that Selane had ever seen, raised a hand and beckoned to the air.

Against the far wall, the celebrity chef, a plump little woman with brown curls – now, what was her name? – acknowledged the gesture with an eager nod. She turned to the rows of small pots and warming trays, gathering things onto a moonlight-white china plate. She poured a glass of wine and brought both to Selane. Her enforcers, bless them, gave the chef the once-over as though they had never seen her before, even though this was day six of the Appeal. They never left anything to chance. No stranger could ever get close to Selane. That was the way she needed it.

Selane waved the chef over. She was hungry after all the work she had done, but she never wanted to seem too eager. The chef held out her platter, then whisked the top off as though revealing a magic trick. Selane surveyed the dainties with a cautious eye.

"That looks just delicious," she said. "Now you do remember that I'm lactose intolerant."

"Of course, Miss Selane," the chef said, patiently. "Nothing here will upset your stomach. I am very careful not to include any foods that you dislike or have an intolerance for."

Selane put a dainty finger under her chin and fluttered her eyelids playfully.

"I am never intolerant," she said, coyly. "Those foods just don't like me. I can't think why. I never did a thing to them!"

The chef laughed nervously. Selane smiled. She liked keeping people on the edge. She reached for a little pink morsel of fish wrapped in nori paper, then changed her mind. Maybe something hot first?

"Miss Selane?" The floor manager approached her.

Selane waved a hand toward her personal manager. Dennis stepped forward, interposing himself between his employer and the intruder.

"Yes, Mr. Race?" he asked. The man tried to look past him, then gave up.

"We have a skid of small items for Miss Selane to look over, Mr. Folger. For your 'finds.' Half the staff have been combing antique shops and little out-of-the-way places all week." Race gestured behind him at a small knot of young people, all hovering in hopes of getting a smile or some other acknowledgement from Selane. "Because you asked them to."

All those shining young people, so eager to serve. Selane didn't trust them an inch. They all wanted something. She couldn't give to everybody who demanded from her. She just couldn't. Why couldn't they just be grateful to be there? But she rose to her feet and turned on the charm.

"You're all so generous to give your time to my Kids," she said over Race's shoulder. "Thank you all for helping. I can't wait to see what you brought me."

The volunteers smiled at her.

"About the purchases," Race began. "I added up the receipts. It comes to about $1,400. I itemized a list by everyone's name."

"Well, they can take the cost off their tax return," Selane said, settling down again. "It's a charity. Each of their donations is tax deductible. There's a brochure on the website with a copy of the form. Dennis can tell you how to find it."

"But that's not what you..." Race tried again. Dennis put an arm around the floor manager's shoulder and steered him away. Selane ignored them. It didn't matter what Dennis said, as long as she didn't have to deal with it. That's why she paid all of these people, to keep the pain out.

Selane sat down heavily on the padded chair. No one in this whole place really knew a thing about her. There were rumors, but there were always rumors. People thought she was a selfish bitch whose lovers only knew she had ditched them when they found their key cards wouldn't open the door of her mansion any longer. They thought she demanded isolation because it made her look more exotic to the public. Nothing could be farther than the truth! She concentrated on her career, her business interests, and these kids because they kept her mind off her own life, and how miserable it was. Who cared about all the trappings and beautiful things? They meant nothing in the long run.

Hungry as she was, she stopped to say a silent prayer over the food. The girl she had been not that many years ago could never have hoped for dainty little morsels like those. She had done too many months eating nothing but ramen and macaroni and cheese to get by. The hardscrabble diet had kept her figure slim enough so she looked just right when a producer saw her singing in a small hotel club. Since then, she had never so much as looked at a package of ramen. Anything but hand-rolled noodles was banned from her table forevermore.

The first bite, a tiny white dumpling, was a gift from heaven. The chopped meat inside was flavored with a tangy sauce. She closed her eyes to enjoy it.

When she opened her eyes, her staff turned away hastily. Selane glared at them. They had been watching her. She felt a surge of temper. They wanted her food. But they couldn't have it. Selane's things belonged to Selane.

Dennis bustled over and spread a silk napkin over her lap.

"You'll kick me if you get a spot on that dress," he said.

"You're right, I will," Selane said. She dabbed her fingertips clean and took up a baked mushroom cap filled with green paste and topped with a single, perfect shrimp.

"Would it kill you to say thank you to the donors?" he asked.

"I'm going to sing her name in the Grateful Song," Selane said, surprised at him. She bit into the canapé. The lemony tang in the sauce made her mouth sing. So good. It was a pity that more than a few mini-meals per day made her blow up like a balloon.

"A bird in the hand is worth a whole poem later on, baby." Dennis wasn't going to let it go.

Selane waved a hand dismissively.

"She knew what she was going to get. I don't like it when people ask for too much."

"Fine, love," Dennis said. "They know that. They'll do whatever you want. You know you have all the influence."

Selane leaned forward, letting the ambient noise cover her words. She didn't want to sound too anxious.

"Did anyone call back yet?"

"No, love," Dennis said, his brows twisting in sympathy. "It's a Monday. You would be dreaming if you thought any of them came into the office with their weekend hangovers."

He sounded confident, but he looked uneasy. Selane knew he was lying. Why was no one returning her calls? They were treating her like poison! It had been more than two months. How could she have known that the national leader, who flew her to central Africa to perform a birthday concert, had paid her in blood diamonds? Was she supposed to read the news? She *was* news. That was why she paid people. The researcher who hadn't informed her about the bad reputation of the leader had been tossed off her staff. But repairing the damage was just so tiresome.

She had to get back into the producers' good graces somehow. She had an album to promote, concerts to perform, maybe even a movie to star in. All those beautiful things had dried up and blown away. Didn't heading an international charity count for anything?

"Did you tell them what we're doing here?" Selane demanded, waving a hand. "We've got millions of people watching on TV and the Internet!"

"Or course I have, love," Dennis assured her. "They'll call. I'll try a few more. I haven't exhausted everyone in your address book. Look. We've got about eighteen minutes before that musical act winds down. Come and look at your new finds. We need something for the four o'clock break."

Selane contemplated the last bite on the china plate: a tiny filo shell filled with two kinds of caviar. She wanted it, but she didn't want people to think that she had to eat everything they gave her. On the other hand, if she left it, someone might take it. No guarantee the taker would wolf it down. Her leavings had sometimes ended up on eBay, gone for money she could have had for herself. Sometimes, people just plain creeped her out. She picked up the thimble-sized morsel and popped it into her mouth. Her hairdresser handed her a clean napkin to wipe her fingers. Selane gave her a brief but puzzled smile. Shouldn't that have been the chef's job? Why was that woman back across the room? Never mind; it just wasn't important.

"All right," she said, offering Dennis a delicate hand. "I'm ready."

CHAPTER 5

"Sorry, ma'am," said the big black man in the dark green overalls, blocking her as she reached for a small, white-painted box. "Don't touch that."

Selane pouted her lower lip and presented the man with big, sad eyes.

"I just wanted to see."

"I'll get that for you if you want it." He picked up the box and handed it to her. "You have to follow the rules, ma'am."

Selane snatched it from him with little grace. These union stagehands wouldn't let her take things off the skid by herself. It was irritating. Some kind of regulation always seemed to prevent the most natural actions in the world. Selane considered all of those rules such a bother. On the other hand, it was easier for one of them to risk his or her life reaching for the item she wanted to examine than for her to mess up her priceless couture gown. The rough, dirty wooden platform had been stacked high with boxes, trays and cartons like a giant Jenga puzzle. Better that they fell on him instead of her. Dennis stood a few feet away, his ear to his tiny cell phone. The rest of her staff knew to keep their distance unless a real crisis was brewing. Nothing must interfere with her contemplation of her next find.

Selane peeked into the small box. Another Hummel figurine. God, did anyone even care about those anymore? She held it out in her left hand at arm's length, and Dennis ran to catch it before she dropped it. A reject. There had to be some-thing that she could tell a story about.

She stood before the tiered cartons, considering what to examine next. Mr. Race's volunteers must have cleared out the shelves in every hole-in-the-wall, knickknack shop from here to the Indiana state line. Most of it was hopeless junk. Selane didn't want to touch it, let alone show it off on international television. She automatically dismissed anything mass-pro-duced, like Beanie Babies, cartoon soda glasses from fast-food restaurants, and comic books that weren't in acid-free plas-tic bags with a cardboard stiffener. China Kewpie dolls, cut crystal candlesticks, Murano paperweights, antique porcelain-faced dolls all had some style, but not enough cachet to excite her imagination. She had to feel the item to know whether it was worthy of *her*.

She flipped open the lid of the painted box, and a skinny ballerina doll with pink skin and a real cloth tutu sprang up. Tinny music played as the ballerina turned in place. It was an old-fashioned jewelry box for a little girl. The box smelled of aged metal and sawdust. A slip of yellowed paper had been folded into one of the ring slots. Selane winkled it out with a long fingernail. On the slip, beautiful handwriting in faded blue ink proclaimed, "Happy Birthday, Katie! April 16, 1920. Love from Mother and Father."

Selane smiled, warmly satisfied. There was her story, right there. She closed the lid and held the box out to the right. She didn't have to look. Dennis sprang forward and retrieved the box with his free hand. He knew their code. This one was a winner. He would see to it that it was set aside safely until the next auction.

She considered several choices from the mass of open car-tons. A glint of gold-colored metal caught her eye from a box at waist level. Between the swathes of a white macramé plant holder and a faded yellow teddy bear, she saw the tip of a spout.

"That, right there. No, not that!" she protested, as the stage-hand picked up one wrong item after another. "That yellow metal thing."

The man looked as exasperated at her as she was with him, but eventually she steered him to the right place. With thumb and forefinger, he extracted a brass object like a sauce boat, only it had a lid. No, it wasn't a sauceboat. It was an antique-style lamp shaped like a pointed slipper, just like the kind that Aladdin had in all the movies!

Selane seized it from the stage hand. He protested, but she ignored him. She cradled the object in her arm, admiring its loop handle, the disk-shaped pedestal, and the engravings all over the surface that reminded her of leaves and vines. About a foot long and made entirely of brass, the lamp looked ancient. That didn't mean a thing, of course. She had been offered perfect replicas of Egyptian tomb treasures, Chinese Ming vases and Faberge eggs, none of them worth more than their materials. But the story behind each of them that she told brought in a fortune for her charity. She could picture just how she would unfold this tale for the cameras.

Remember Aladdin? she would ask the unseen audience. *How he rubbed the lamp, and got his heart's desire from the genie who appeared to do his bidding? Well, you can do that too, if you only reach into your heart for Selane's Kids.*

The little lamp felt strange in her hands. She had had these dreams as a child of finding a magic lamp. And this was just that kind, like Aladdin would have had in his poor, pathetic little room in wherever the fairy tale took place. She had heard it was actually a Chinese fable, but who believed anything you read in Wikipedia these days? She threw her head back defiantly. The image would make a great photo for her Instagram followers. She caressed the side of the lamp with her palm, feeling the cool metal tickle her skin.

And almost dropped it.

A stream of smoke issued from the spout like steam from a kettle. Instead of floating away and dissipating, the smoke gathered in a column in front of Selane.

Selane's eyes widened. Her heart banged against her ribcage as if it had to escape this terrifying unknown. She wanted to throw the lamp away, to run, to scream out her fear, but she didn't dare move. She trembled, wondering if she was going crazy, or if this was some kind of joke the crew was playing on her.

The smoke thickened, took on color and substance. In moments, it had coalesced into a shape. A human shape. She expected a huge, tawny-skinned man clad in silk harem pants and a turban. Instead, she got a girl. A young girl with disheveled, light brown hair, milk-white skin and big, hazel eyes. She wore a cropped top that bared a skinny midriff. At least she had the harem pants, although the moss green trousers weren't made of silk. On her wrists was a pair of tight-fitting, gunmetal blue cuffs. Selane looked around her, but she couldn't see how the trick was being done. She looked at the black stagehand for an explanation, but he stood with his mouth open, too.

The girl put her hands together under her chin.

"What is your will, my mistress?"

It took Selane a couple of pounding heartbeats to gather her wits. Instead of replying to the girl, she turned to the stagehand. This was the kind of disrespect that had been brewing under the surface for days.

"Is this some kind of joke?" she demanded, her voice shrill as the anger welled up inside her like a geyser. "Are you people making *fun* of me? Did you set this up for a laugh? Do I look like I'm laughing?"

"Ma'am, no, ma'am, nobody's making fun," he said, his voice shaking. His eyes were stretched so wide his eyeballs could have popped out of his head. "Ain't nobody set nothing up! I... did she just...? I got to go."

He backed away from her and scooted into the shadows. Selane gathered her dignity and waited, fully expecting someone from *Punk'd* or one of the other practical-joke reality shows to jump out and stick a microphone under her nose.

The girl stayed where she was, her eyes fixed worshipfully on Selane. The star advanced on her, putting her face an inch from the girl's nose.

"Who are you? Just who the hell do you think you are?"

"I'm your genie," the girl said, eagerly. "You've got my lamp there. You rubbed it. Now I have to grant you three wishes. What's your first wish?"

"That your name? Jeannie?"

"No, mistress, my name's Vickie."

"Don't call me mistress!" Selane said, her voice ringing up to the rafters. Dennis turned around in the middle of his phone call and frowned. She waved him away. She didn't need his help to deal with one disrespectful little teenager.

"What shall I call you, ma'am?" the girl asked. She seemed polite enough, but Selane wasn't ready to let go of her mad yet.

"Don't you know who I am?"

"Sorry, no," Vickie said, with an apologetic grin. "I don't get out much. What year is it?"

Selane was taken aback. Someone who didn't know who she was? Or pretending that she didn't know? She struck a pose, the same one she had used on the cover of *Rolling Stone* that had sold a couple million copies.

"You may call me Miss Selane."

The girl's slightly vacant expression didn't change. Clearly, she wasn't as impressed as she ought to be. What the hell was wrong with her? Was she mentally deficient?

"Yes, Miss Selane. What's your first wish?"

A wish?

Really?

Well, what harm would it do?

Selane sort of believed in magic. She had always wished on stars and wishbones and things like that. She had a collection of amulets and lucky pieces she counted on to help her from having bad things happen to her. She would never go on stage without having petted the teddy bear she had had since she was a baby. It was in her trailer at that very moment. What if the girl's assertion was true? What if, against everything she had ever been told, that magic was real? What if this girl *was* a genie? The people answering her phones right now claimed to be things like fairy godmothers and tooth fairies, not that she had seen them do spells or grant wishes. What if she had really just found a genie? She glanced toward Dennis.

"…Look, angel, I know you have him on speakerphone. He's sitting right there where he can hear me. Selane is money in the bank," Dennis said. He ran his hand up his forehead, shoving his gelled blond hair into a rooster's comb. "She's got about to go to the studio to record her new album. The songs are absolutely excellent. When the record hits, you'll wish you were on the crazy train with us. She read your script for *Little Girl Lost* and fell in love with it. The part of Sophia is her, darling. A rising tide lifts all boats. …Eh? Well, I'll try again later. Right. Thanks, angel. I owe you a dinner next time I'm in LA."

His shoulders slumped. He slid his fancy phone into his pocket and stared out at the musicians performing on the set. He couldn't face her. Selane didn't need to have heard the other side of the conversation to know he had failed again. He was supposed to be the best of the best! He had to get her a starring role somewhere! She had been in such demand only a few months ago. People were falling all over themselves to get her to endorse this, or star in that. The resentment welled up in her stomach.

"I wish the producers were pounding down my door for the Selane experience," she said. "I wish they needed me the way they used to."

"Is that your first wish?" Vickie asked brightly. "That sounds really cool."

Selane turned to the girl and stared at her. Vickie didn't look ironic or sarcastic. In fact, she looked eager. A tiny measure of hope rose in the star's chest.

"Can you do that? I mean, can you really do anything?"

"Sure, mistress. I mean, Miss Selane. To hear is to obey!"

Vickie held out her folded arms at shoulder level and closed her eyes. A cloud of muddy-colored smoke formed a cocoon around her, concealing her from sight. Little lights like LED bulbs twinkled in the murk. Selane stared at it, still trying to work out how it was being done. The cocoon began to turn like a tornado, faster and faster. The lights smeared into bright streaks. Then the cloud exploded outward. Selane felt part of it as it burst through her. She touched her midsection, expecting the priceless pearl gown to be covered with mud-colored mist, but nothing was there. The girl stood before her just as she had before, looking ordinary and a little shabby.

"Now, what?" Selane asked.

"Your wish has been granted," Vickie said, simply.

"How will I know that?"

"You'll know."

Dennis's phone rang. He snatched it from his pocket. Selane strained to hear over the other noises in the room.

"Dennis Folger." His voice rose an octave and took on a musical lilt. "Well, hello, my darling. So nice to hear your voice. What can I do for you?" He listened for a while. "I thought you might like to get in touch with us. Yes? Well, what do you have in mind?" He spun on his heel so he was facing Selane. His mouth twisted into a wry but triumphant grin, and he closed his fist with one thumb pointed up. "Naturally we want to hear all about it. When are you coming into Chicago? Really. Yes, she's staying at the Four Seasons, of course. We'll see you there." He blew Selane a kiss. As soon as he hit the 'call end' button with his thumb, he began to scroll down the phone screen. "We're in business, sweetheart!" he shouted. "Got to call your publicity right this moment! Hello, Bob, it's Dennis. Yes. Well, listen, I've got some smashing news for you...." He wandered away with the phone to his ear.

"That's not magic," Selane said, her heart full of hope but her mind full of doubt. "They just changed their minds, that's all. They can't keep an important person like me waiting."

Vickie nodded, not disagreeing. Selane wondered if the girl was just a little slow.

A few moments later, Dennis returned, his eyes glowing.

"We've got one, my darling," he said, holding out the phone like a beacon. "Neil Karburg is coming in to talk to you about his movie. He's flying out tonight. He thinks you'll be perfect in the role of Roxanne in *Ten Days' Wonder*. He's up for a co-op program to publicize it alongside your album. Ten weeks production shooting in Barbados, first-class everything. All he wants is to come out and hear you read for him."

Selane shook her head.

"I do not read for people," she said automatically. "He either trusts in my performance, or he does not."

Dennis took her hand and curled it into both of his. He kissed her knuckles.

"It's a little late for that, my darling. He turned me down just a couple of days ago. I mean, flat. I gave him my best pleading voice, but it fell upon deaf ears. I have no idea what changed his mind, but let's go with it. Indulge me, darling. We can't fail again."

She tossed her head.

"I can't fail at all, Dennis. It's going to work for me now, I know it."

His blue eyes narrowed, and he tilted his head.

"Why do you say that, love?"

Selane cradled the lamp in her arm.

"Magic," she said. "This is just the beginning."

"What magic?" he asked. "That lamp? And who's the girl?"

"She's my genie."

"Your what? Selane…" The phone in Dennis's hand erupted, playing a different ring tone than before. He glanced down at the screen, his face a mask of astonishment. "Her? Dammit, I have to take this. Excuse me a minute." He moved a few feet away.

"What's your second wish, Miss Selane?" Vickie asked. Selane waved her to silence. She couldn't hear Dennis over the fanfare of music that suddenly blared out over the speakers, but the animation in his movements told him that the call was good news. Selane hugged the lamp to her.

"Come on, magic," she murmured. Vickie waited motionless beside her.

Dennis all but danced back to them. He gestured at the tiny phone.

"That was Rochelle Cox. She wants to cast you in the next "Celebrity Survivor"! I never expected *her* to call us again after the scandal, but she was gushing like she had never given that interview to *People* calling you a money-worshiping whore who couldn't see the blood dripping out of the jewels around your neck. She was positively babbling your praises. She's hopping a private jet to come talk to you tonight. She cannot wait to speak with you. It's like…"

"…Magic?" Selane asked.

"It has to be," Dennis said. "Now, what's this nonsense about a genie?"

"She is," Selane said, nodding toward Vickie.

"That girl? Where did she come from?"

"From this lamp," Selane said. "It was in one of those boxes of junk. I just thought of the Aladdin story. I rubbed the lamp, and she appeared."

"This girl?" Dennis asked. He pinched Vickie's arm.

"Ow!" Vickie recoiled, rubbing her skin. Selane batted at his hand.

"Let her alone, Dennis. She granted my wish! You'll see. This is just the beginning."

Dennis tilted his head and peered closely at Selane.

"You think she's a genie? You really believe in that kind of thing?"

"She appeared in a puff of smoke, Dennis. I'm not imagining it! One of the stagehands saw it, too!"

Dennis put his arm around her.

"Darling, you have been working your fingers to the bone. Don't you think you might have imagined it?"

Selane tossed her head. "Hell, no. There is no one who could have made that happen in front of my living eyes. No special effects. No cameras or host waiting to jump out and make me feel like an idiot."

"Well, I didn't see it. You'll have to make me a believer before I lend credulity to such an outrageous statement."

Selane turned to Vickie.

"Prove it. Prove you're a genie. And that doesn't count as a wish."

"I hear and obey, Miss Selane," Vickie said. She put her crossed arms up, and turned into a column of smoke.

Selane wanted to watch what she did, but she enjoyed much more seeing the expression on Dennis's face. At the typical genie pose, his long face assumed a grimace of open derision. But the moment the girl dematerialized and became a beige cloud, his mouth gaped. The colored steam seeped into the spout of the lamp. Selane held it out to him. Dennis looked at the lamp, up at her and at the lamp again.

"Well, dress me in drag and call me Shirley," Dennis said. "That's impossible!"

"Now what do you say?" Selane asked. "You saw it. How could she disappear like that? Unless we're both hypnotized."

"I'm a rotten subject," Dennis said. "Make sure. Can she do it again?"

Selane knocked on the lamp. "Come on out, genie girl."

A finger of smoke issued from the spout and gathered into the familiar shape of the girl. She wore a happy grin.

"That's new," she said, cheerfully. "No one ever knocks."

"That is unbelievable," Dennis said, touching Vickie on the shoulder to make sure she was really solid. "How is that even possible?"

"It looks like at least some of those fairy tales I read as a kid are real," Selane said.

"Flat out ridiculous. What's your deal, pet? What's your name?"

Vickie smiled at him.

"I'm Vickie. Just the usual deal. I grant Miss Selane three wishes. Then my obligation to her is finished. Pretty traditional."

Dennis turned to Selane, his brow furrowed with concern. His hand flew to his mouth, and his eyes darted from side to side. The hand flashed out and pointed a forefinger at Selane.

"Don't make a wish yet. We have to run the wording through Legal. Don't commit to anything right away. I want you to get the absolute maximum mileage out of this situation."

"I did make a wish," Selane admitted. Dennis clutched his hair, ruffling it still further.

"Oh, no, darling! What did you ask for? A new car? A facelift?"

She glared at him. Sometimes he treated her like such a child!

"I wanted success again. I wanted the producers to beat down my door."

Dennis looked at his phone. "And they did. They started calling. Just like that."

"Just like that."

"Amazing. But what's the catch?" He turned to Vickie. "What's the obligation to Miss Selane?"

"Nothing," Vickie said, patiently. "She gets three wishes. That's all. She can't use one wish to wish for more wishes. I can't bring anyone back from the dead. I can try to do something impossible, but it doesn't always take. You have to be careful how you word stuff, though. The powers are pretty literal. Personally, I don't know about any real catches. That's not my scene."

"We have to make this last as long as we can," Dennis said, tapping a forefinger on his lower lip. "There has to be a source of information I can find, to see if there are down sides to making wishes."

"Maybe we ought to ask someone," Selane said.

"Who?"

Selane waved a hand toward the phone banks. "Well, those people think they're fairy godmothers. Maybe you can ask one of them. They say they grant wishes all the time. Maybe they're real. I mean, if genies are, why not fairy godmothers?"

Dennis shook his head. "I prefer not to be laughed at. It reflects back on you, my love."

Selane could have stamped her foot, but people were watching.

"Ask them in a general sort of way if there is such a thing as a genie. You don't have to sound like you believe it. Even after we both watched her turn into a cloud of smoke. Which we did."

Dennis nodded. A broad smile crossed his face at the memory. He nodded sharply.

"The president of the local chapter seems like a sensible woman. I'll run it past her. In a casual sort of way. In the meantime, your first wish is doing great guns. I'll sit down with you this evening and run through the proposals we've already had. But don't do anything rash! And no more wishes!"

"I won't! Lord Jesus, you are so annoying."

He grinned suddenly. It made his long face handsome. "That's what you pay me for, Selane."

He sauntered away, his hands in his jacket pockets.

A production assistant, a young Asian woman with long black hair in a ponytail under the usual headset, came toward them. Two of her security men headed her off. The girl stuck her head between their shoulders, undaunted by the wall of muscle.

"Ten minutes until we need you, Miss Selane. Hair and makeup coming your way in two."

"Thanks," Selane said. She felt buoyed to the skies. Just when her life was crashing down around her feet, God sent a miracle to raise it up again. She couldn't believe it, but it was all happening again. And she had more wonders to look forward to!

"So, what's your second wish?" Vickie asked.

"Not now, child!" Selane said, waving an impatient hand. "I want to enjoy my first one for a while!"

"Whatever you say." Vickie sat down on the floor with her legs folded. "I'll wait."

"No!" Selane said, horrified. "Get up! Were you raised in a barn or something?"

"Kind of," Vickie said. "I was in a commune with my sister for a couple of years." But she rose to her feet. "What do you want me to do?"

"Nothing! Go somewhere else."

"Okay. Where?"

"Anywhere. But stay in the building."

Vickie looked hopeful.

"Is there anything to eat around here? Maybe some juice?"

"My chef has juice. Over there." Selane cocked a finger. Minnie, a motherly woman who saw to her wardrobe, came running.

"What can I do for you, dear?" she asked. Selane pointed at Vickie.

"She wants something to eat. Take her to the chef."

"This way, honey," Minnie said, putting her arm around Vickie. The girl looked back at Selane.

"Thanks!"

Selane frowned, impatient to get rid of her.

"Just go."

"Yes, Miss Selane."

"You need me to keep an eye on her?" Minnie asked.

"No. I have this." Selane patted the lamp. "She won't go anywhere I don't want her to."

CHAPTER 6

It was quiet in the studio at that moment. An orchestra on the other side of the world was playing a medley of Selane's greatest hits. The caretakers helped make the kids more comfortable, taking the ones who needed it away for bathroom breaks. A young man and woman in matching leotards supervised the stagehands who were putting together some kind of rig made of metal poles and blue ropes. Ray tried to figure out their act by the apparatus. Aerialists? Acrobats? Something like Cirque du Soleil? Wouldn't that be fantastic? He'd never seen them.

A sharp poke in the back distracted him from his speculation. He glanced over his shoulder at Rose.

"I hate it when you do that," he said. He looked down at his console. At least nobody was calling. He didn't want a second demerit. He wanted to stay, for the kids' sake. And maybe to get that autograph for his sister Chanel.

"Look," Rose whispered. "That girl's heading for Her Royal Majesty's lunch counter."

Ray glanced across the room. A white girl in a cutoff blouse and bare feet whom he had never seen before was heading toward Selane's personal catering station. She must have been freezing in the cold studio.

"How'd she get in here?" he asked.

"I don't know," Rose said. "I didn't see her come in. Maybe she sneaked in through the loading dock. Poor thing. She might be homeless. You'd better head her off before she gets a scolding."

"Why me?" Ray asked.

"Because you can move a lot faster than an old lady like me," Rose said. "Get going. We'll take her to our snack table."

Before Ray could disentangle himself from his headset, the girl reached the velvet rope.

To their amazement, one of Selane's assistants spoke to the enforcer on duty. The large black man raised the white rope and waved the girl inside.

"She did it!" Rose exclaimed.

"I wonder who she is," said Ray. "She has to be some kind of celebrity herself to get that kind of treatment."

"Not a celebrity," Fred Lincoln said, leaning close over Rose's shoulder. "Miss Selane's manager just had a little talk with Alexandra. He asked questions in a general sort of way about genies."

"Genies?" Morry Garner asked, his wrinkled face contorting. "I thought we were rid of the whole DDEG!"

"We were," Rose said. "All the bad seeds are gone. Maybe she's a newcomer. You can't automatically assume the worst. She might be a good djin."

"Oh, no, not that again! When you can prove to me that there are good djinni, I'll stop being paranoid, Rose. I don't need another episode like with that Albert Froister!"

"Well, I'll find out," Ray said. The floor manager signaled for a break. All the volunteers in the phone bank rose from their places and stood up to stretch. He put his headset down and walked out around the perimeter of the stage area.

By then, the girl had emerged from the cordoned enclosure with a bunch of bananas under one arm, a pile of sandwiches in the crook of her elbow, and a whole pitcher of orange juice clutched to her thin chest.

"She can have all that?" Ray heard the enforcer ask as he got closer.

"She gets what she wants," Selane's assistant assured him.

"But that was special squeezed by the chef for Miss Selane!"

"The chef can squeeze some more. Have her make two pitchers from now on. That's what *she* said."

There was no doubt in Ray's mind or any of the employees' who *she* was.

The girl took her booty and scurried off the side of the set into a dark corner. Ray followed. She sat cross-legged on the floor and began to eat as though she was starving. Ray felt sorry for her. He put his hand to his shirt pocket and tested the air ahead of him for need strings. She didn't seem to need anything. In fact, she seemed happy. Her clothing said 'homeless,' but her attitude said, 'little friend to all the world,' like Rudyard Kipling's Kim.

He opened his stride, his eyes fixed on the girl, who had broken a banana in two and was eating from one half, then the other.

Weird. Who eats a banana from the middle?

Ray was so fixed on her strange behavior that he didn't see what he slammed into with his left shoulder.

"Ow! Hey!"

Ray halted suddenly. He reached out to steady the tall girl with the long neck.

"Man, I'm sorry!" he exclaimed. "I didn't see you."

"No kidding!" she said, her dark eyes flashing. She smoothed her black, knee-length skirt.

"Are you all right?" Ray asked.

"No thanks to you, but yes."

"Sorry," he said again. He put out his hand. "I'm Ray Crandall."

"I know." Her eyes lost their angry light as she got herself under control. She extended her hand, and they shook. Her slender fingers were dry and cool. "Ayosha Gilbert. Excuse me."

"Nice to meet you," Ray said. Man, she was pretty! That oval face was just about perfect, with fine, high cheekbones and smooth skin. She had nice curves, too.

"You're going to talk to that girl? Our group heard some rumors about this girl, that she might be a genie, and I wanted to check out if they were true." Her voice had a southern lilt.

"Me, too," Ray said. "The Fairy Godmothers Union had some trouble with the DDEG over the summer. Just wanted to check and see that it wasn't going to start up again."

Ayosha eyed him up and down, not disapprovingly, or so it seemed to Ray.

"I can't stop you. Come on."

Ray fell into step with her.

"So, you're a Sandman?" He stopped himself. That didn't sound respectful. "Uh, Sandgirl? Sandwoman?"

She tilted her head and gave him a wry half-grin.

"Sandman," she said. "If you can handle being called a Fairy Godmother, I can handle Sandman."

Ray felt a modicum of hope. Most of the Sandmen manning the phone lines made it clear that they didn't approve of the FGU. He had heard they felt they ought to be in charge of all magical service organizations in the Chicago area – in fact, everywhere. But she seemed nice enough. Maybe they weren't all like the ones who had given him the cold shoulder.

"So you know who we are? I'd like to talk to you about your group some time," he said, keeping the hope out of his voice.

"Yes, maybe later. Hey, there."

Ayosha's voice became gentle as she squatted down beside the thin girl.

"Hi!" the girl said, turning her wide hazel eyes up to them. "Come and sit down. Do you want some lunch?"

"No, thanks, they fed us," Ayosha said. "I'm Ayosha. This is Ray."

"My name's Vickie," the girl said. She had a sweet, open face. Ray automatically felt protective toward her. She looked like she might be fifteen years old.

"Where are you from?" he asked, sitting down on the floor beside her. Vickie grabbed up the banana skins from the floor an inch from his high-top sneakers and threw them into the air. They vanished in a puff of smoke. Sure looked like magic to him.

"California," Vickie said. "Where am I now?"

"Chicago," Ayosha said. "I thought genies always know where their lamps are."

Vickie's grin widened.

"So you can tell I'm a genie? Hardly anyone believes me right off the bat."

"The bracelets give it away," Ray said, nodding toward the steel-blue bands on her wrists. He knew from previous experience that they were bonded on by the oathbound spell that made the wearer a genie. "I'm a fairy godfather." He took his wand out of his breast pocket. He was glad that he had graduated in the last month to a fifteen-inch dark blue stick with a solid silver star the size of a half-dollar at the top. Still a journeyman's wand, but a vast improvement on the eight-inch, baby blue training wand he had started with.

"I'm a sandman," Ayosha added. She pulled up a chain that hung around her neck and showed a silver bag. Ray did his best not to stare. It was the size of a baseball, but had been absolutely invisible under her thin orange silk sweater until she produced it. Vickie looked impressed at both symbols of office.

"Cool! I am totally into dream interpretation. I'd love to share dreams with you."

"I'd be honored," Ayosha said. She looked as if she meant it.

"What are you doing here?" Ray asked Vickie.

"Oh, I dunno," Vickie said, with a vague wave over her shoulder. "I used to hang out in this coffee shop in Fresno. Really easygoing kind of place. I played the guitar and cleaned up in exchange for meals. No hassle. Been a while since anyone rubbed my lamp." She looked around. "I guess they must have gone out of business. I wasn't really paying attention. I do deep-theta meditation. Time gets away from you, you know? But I'm really getting into my inner mind."

"Where's your family?" Ray asked.

"I dunno. They're always so busy."

For someone packing food away as fast as she was, Vickie swallowed her mouthful before she spoke. Ray's grandmother would approve. Grandma Eustatia absolutely came down like a ton of bricks on anyone who talked with their mouth full.

Vickie reached into the air and came out with a gold cup encrusted with big, square-cut gems. Ray gawked. It was the kind of thing that kings used at Renaissance Fairs, but this looked like real gold and jewels. She filled it with juice from the pitcher. She glanced up and noticed their keen gaze on the cup.

"You guys want some? I've got more glasses."

"Uh, no, thanks," Ray said, although he felt a little thrill at the idea of drinking from a sultan's goblet. "So, you're new to Chicago, huh?"

"Is that where I am?"

"Yes," Ayosha said. "We just told you. Don't you know?"

For answer, Vickie put down the goblet and stretched her arms out. She twisted her shoulders and shook her head vigorously.

"Sorry. I think I've been asleep a long time. I do that, in between masters." She looked a little uncomfortable. "The real world zones me out, you know?"

"Don't you go to school?" Ray asked. "How old are you?"

"Oh, I don't know," Vickie said. "What year is this?"

Ayosha's mouth twisted in a wry smile.

"Now you're putting us on. No genie I ever met just zoned out. They all took advantage of the magic to go places when they weren't on assignment. They have jobs or families, or other interests."

Vickie shrugged, a little uncomfortably. "I'm okay this way. I meditate a lot."

Ray's inner alarm went off. He didn't know too many people who were so disengaged with life, but all of them had had some terrible thing happen to them to make them withdraw like that.

"What were you doing in a commune?" he asked. "I didn't know there were any more around."

Vickie seemed pleased at his interest.

"Well, a bunch of us joined because it seemed so cool. There were about fifty of us, I think. We all had jobs to do. I liked it. Living close to the earth is so grounding, you know? It was nice not to have to make any decisions. I had… a lot of stuff going on I needed to get away from."

"Like what?" Ray asked, one brow drawn down.

"You know. Stuff." Vickie squirmed and took a big gulp of juice.

"What kind of stuff?"

Ayosha made a cutting gesture with one hand. Ray frowned at her. Who was she to tell him what to do? Then she shot him a glance that appealed for his cooperation. All right, in the interests of peace with the Sandmen, he promised himself he'd cool down.

"So who rubbed your lamp?" Ray asked.

"Miss Selane did," Vickie said. "I think it'll be fun granting wishes for her. They're not like anything anyone ever asked before."

"What did she ask you to do?" Ayosha asked.

"Uh, I kinda can't tell you," Vickie said, apologetically.

"Client confidentiality?" Ayosha asked, with a wry smile.

"Yeah, that's it." The young genie looked relieved that they weren't going to push the issue.

"Well, we'll leave you to finish your lunch," Ayosha said, rising gracefully. She signed to Ray to follow her. "Nice to meet you."

"What was that back there?" Ray asked. "Cutting me off like that."

"It was too much, too soon," the tall girl said. "Looked to me like a case of abuse, or something else bad."

"I got that impression, too," Ray said. "I wasn't trying to push her. Just taking an interest. She sounds like she's troubled about something. I thought I could get her to open up."

"She'll trust us more later on if we give her space," Ayosha said. "All the case histories I've helped work on give an edge to backing off earlier in favor of a more intense approach later on."

Ray raised an eyebrow.

"Clinical research?"

"Yes. I work as an intern with a research psychologist for credit hours. That's my major."

Ray peered at her. "I thought maybe I'd seen you before," he said. "On campus. You go to NU, too."

Her eyebrows went up.

"You're a student there?"

"Freshman," Ray said, feeling the surge of pride that he experienced every time he stepped onto the century-old Evanston campus. "Pre-med."

"Nice," Ayosha said. "Your insights are on track, as far as I can tell. She's doing a lot of deflecting, and not just because what we're asking might be none of our business. I've talked to runaways who sound just like her. Have you even started Psych 101?"

"No. Next semester. I just figure out things about people. It's in their auras or something. Part of the deal with being a fairy godfather. My grandmother got me involved in it."

"You'd have to have a natural affinity for people or they wouldn't take you."

She sounded as if she had had a lot more experience than he had. Ray felt his heart swell with pride.

"What year are you in at NU?" he asked.

"Junior."

Before the summer, talking with an upperclassman might have made him feel at a disadvantage, but being accepted as a member of the FGU had given him a lot more confidence. Still, Ayosha wasn't a fairy godmother. Experience he had gleaned from growing up in the city was that letting himself be too vulnerable would leave him open to being a victim. He just nodded.

Ayosha glanced back over her shoulder. Ray followed her gaze. Vickie had torn through all the sandwiches on the plate, and was carefully picking up all the crumbs with a fingertip. Ayosha shook her head.

"The guildmaster says this girl's not on any of our lists. We have no idea where she came from."

"Your lists?" Ray asked. "Your group keeps track of other people like… us?"

She waved a hand. "We don't have to worry about fairy godparents. Your union keeps pretty tight reins on anyone with a wand. It's the rogue powers that we need to look out for. Sometimes we get a clue when it manifests in one of our clients' dreams."

Curiosity made his eyebrows rise.

"I'd enjoy talking to you later about being a Sandman," he said again. "I've never had much chance to talk with any."

To his surprise, Ayosha smiled at him.

"I'd consider that a blessing," she said. "Do you live on campus? We can take the El back together."

"I live at home," Ray said. "I know I miss a lot, but I couldn't afford the dorm fees."

Ayosha grimaced. "I have to live there. I'm from Georgia. I'm up to my ears in student loans. If it wasn't for the Sandmen Benevolent Fund, I'd be looking at debt until I'm a hundred years old."

"The Fairy Godmothers helped me out, too, but it didn't stretch to housing. That's okay. My parents need me."

"That sounds a lot more responsible than I heard about you fairy godparents," Ayosha said.

"What does that mean?" Ray was offended. He tried to control the impulse, but he knew it came out in his voice.

Ayosha wrinkled her nose, but he sensed it was more at her thoughts than at him. "Nothing. Maybe I'm just jealous. My parents sent me off, God go with you, don't let the doorknob hit you on the butt on the way out." She noticed the stricken expression on Ray's face. "Oh, it wasn't that bad. They want me to grow up and become independent. They've got my younger sisters to deal with. They're several years younger than I."

"Mine want me independent, too," Ray said. "I'm cool with that, but I get to run errands and chauffeur my brother and sister around so Mom doesn't have to."

"You have a car? Can I grab a ride?"

"Sorry," Ray said, deeply regretting having to refuse. "I use one of my folks'. I take the El, too." She looked disappointed. The gentleman in him urged him to offer. "I'll walk you to the station."

"I've got a boyfriend," Ayosha said hastily.

"I've got a girlfriend," Ray countered, maybe a little more emphatically than he needed to. "She's away at Howard.

Ayosha had the grace to look embarrassed.

"Sorry. I just hate to have men think I'm leading them on when all I'm doing is being nice to them."

"No offense, but men can be nice without expecting anything. My grandma would give me a hard talking to if I didn't offer."

Ayosha smiled. "Your grandma sounds tough."

"Not tough, exactly. Just wants us to behave like good folks. She's a fairy godmother, too." He set his face, waiting. They were getting along well enough, but if she said something sour about Grandma Eustatia, politeness would have to take a hike. Instead, she sighed again.

"Wish I had a grandmother like that."

Ray felt a glimmering impression of wistfulness from her. Could that be a need string? No, if she was a college junior, she had to be too old to need a fairy godmother. Their responsibilities ended when a child reached twenty-one. He opened his mouth to ask her, but the enforcers came around to steer them back into their places on the risers. He had just enough time to fit his earpiece before his console lit up in a virtual Christmas tree of lights.

CHAPTER 7

More acts came and went. Ray listened to them with half an ear while taking down the details from phone donors. In between, he heard Selane auctioning off a few more of her finds, and thank you messages from her fellow celebrities around the globe.

He had just finished the seventh in an unbroken chain of calls when the console went dark. He glanced up. A crowd of technicians and assistants bustled around the main stage. The lights focused down into a single spotlight in the center of the stage. Selane glided out into that pillar of light. It picked up the gems in her hair and made them twinkle. She looked like an angel straight from heaven. Beside him, Ayosha plunked her fingers down onto her keyboard and opened a fresh message on Twitter. With no calls to answer, Ray just sat and stared, wishing that his sister Chanel could be there. No doubt that she'd be glued to the television at home, like millions of people around the world.

The lady took her place at the front of the stage. The hundred or so people in the studio audience stared up at her as if they were in church. Selane was getting ready to sing her Gratitude Lullaby.

Rich music full of flutes and harps filled the air. Selane held the mike in both hands underneath her chin as though she was praying. She began to hum a gospel melody, her warm voice painting the air with honeyed sound. It wasn't magic, but it felt like a kind of enchantment. Ray felt his spirits lifting, wishing that he could have been more help then and every day.

"Thank you, Lord, for giving us this day. Thanks be to those who gave of themselves for your glory. Let not night upon our faces stay until I add their names to my story," she sang. Then she stopped to smile into the darkness. "Thank you, Steven, Tonesha, Mary and Peter, for sending your love across the distance. Thank you, Nadine, Carol, Letishia, Marcus, Don and Eli, for your generosity. Thank you to the fine people here at Public Television and the volunteers who gave of their time. And thank you to the children," as the spotlights went on over the knot of wheelchairs at the side of the stage, "who remind us to be grateful for what we have and to know we have enough to give of ourselves to them." She sang the chorus again, reeling off the names of people in the crew, and even a few of the volunteers, ending with the names of the children. One by one the little ones straightened themselves up in their seats and craned toward her. "And, Lord, rain down your blessings on Nona, Celeste, Robby, Deir, Rainbow and of course, Francisco."

The little boy broke into a beatific smile that made his thin face look like a Renaissance angel. Instantly, all the screens around the room were full of the image. Francisco noticed them, and his face went blank. Hastily, the picture changed back to a closeup of Selane. Francisco's caretaker rushed to kneel down beside the boy. Under the rolling music that boiled to a crescendo, Ray heard the boy keening a protest. His heart went out to Francisco.

Selane's voice soared upward with the recorded accompaniment, and her eyes lifted toward the racks of cannon-like lights on the ceiling.

"Send them all hope, and cure them of pain and anguish, Make for them a miracle, great Father of us all, For this is my dearest and warmest wish."

The audience broke into applause so loud it rang off the ceiling of the studio.

Ray noticed movement in the shadows near the side of the stage. At the word 'wish," the barefoot girl trotted out, making straight for Selane. He held his breath, wondering if he ought to run over and pull her back.

The diva noticed the movement. She stuck out an imperious palm to one side, just beneath the frame captured by the camera. Vickie halted in her tracks and put her hands up under her chin. A couple of the huge men in suits loomed up out of the shadows and shepherded the girl back.

"...Amen!" Selane sang, throwing that hand up toward heaven. She looked like a Christmas angel in her long white dress. "Thank you all! Keep those calls and messages coming in with your donations. Our appeal continues now until the day before Christmas. Every single donor will receive my undying gratitude and that of these precious children. Remember them in your prayers, as I remember you in mine. Sleep well, now. Until tomorrow. I love you all. God bless you."

Selane blew a kiss to the camera. The spotlight on her closed down to a single point, then switched off. It was like a birthday candle blown out. Ray shook himself, as though waking up from a dream.

"She's good," Rose said, poking him in the ribs from behind. That broke the trance completely, but he still watched Selane with an unshakable fascination.

The singer let her arms fall to her sides. Her entourage hurried to help her into her special chair and offer her cold drinks, a wrap, and a neck massage. One of the big bodyguards retrieved the microphone and handed it off to a stagehand before helping the lady to sit down. She had clearly thrown every last ounce of energy into her performance. Even when the caretakers pushed the children past her to say good night, she murmured back but hardly glanced their way.

Francisco tried desperately to catch her eye, but failed. The boy collapsed into his chair's cushions like a broken doll.

Ray felt sorry for him. He'd had his crushes as a child, and the thought of Mrs. Dance, his second grade teacher, still put a knot in his stomach.

"Unrequited love's a mean ol' woman," Fred Lincoln said, from the end of the second row.

"Sometimes it's a mean ol' man," Chris Popp said, a playful grin on his round face.

"To each his own," Rose said. "Or her. I'm not going to get involved in this discussion. I'm just sorry for that poor boy."

"Me, too," Ayosha murmured.

Ray relaxed. It was cool to be able to relax among friends. He glanced toward Ayosha. She didn't look quite as comfortable. He remembered that she didn't know the others yet. They were never ones to stand on ceremony, though.

"I saw you talking to Francisco," Rose said to her. "Did he open up to you at all?"

"A little," Ayosha said. "Poor little boy's unhappy."

"I'd be, too, if I was stuck in a wheelchair forever," George Aldeanueva said. "You make what you can out of your life."

"He's in love with her," Ayosha said, defending the child. Ray felt that need string again from her. Maybe she never had had her wish granted. A shame it was too late.

"I know." Rose sighed. "Poor kiddie."

At last, Selane rose to her feet. Her manager, Mr. Folger, approached with a huge, pale beige fur coat and wrapped it around her shoulders. He also handed her an item about the size of a small shoebox, an antique brass lamp. Ray and Ayosha exchanged glances.

"Come on, girl," Selane called.

From the edge of the stage, the girl in the green trousers trotted out. Selane looked dismayed.

"You're not still barefoot, are you? Put some shoes on! It's snowing outside!"

The girl glanced down.

"Oh, I'll just ride in the lamp. That's what I usually do." She crossed her arms at shoulder level.

Selane put her hand over the spout and glanced around.

"Not here, child," she said. "Someone get her a pair of shoes."

Selane's wardrobe mistress summed her up with a glance.

"What are you, size seven?" Minnie asked. She bustled away, and returned in two minutes with a pair of sneakers in her hand which she thrust at the girl. "Put these on. They might be a little big, but they'll fit."

Vickie sat on the floor at once and donned the worn shoes, tying the laces tight. One of the enforcers grabbed her arm and virtually hauled her to her feet. Before he thought about it, Ray sprang up and strode over to him.

"You treat her nicely," he said, fire in his voice. The big man turned to glare at him.

"You don't get in Miss Selane's business," he said. This time Ray stood his ground.

"Courtesy's everybody's business."

"He's right, Tommy," Selane said, with a smile for Ray. "There's no need to be rough. Thank you, young man."

"Yes, ma'am," Ray said. The bodyguard put up a forearm to push him aside, but Ray was already out of his way.

The entourage huddled around Miss Selane and Vickie, escorting them out of the studio. Ray watched until the big double doors in the cinder block wall shut behind them. A swirl of cold air mixed with snowflakes swept in and slapped him in the face. He found he was shaking with reaction.

Rose appeared at his side and put her arm through his.

"Sometimes people abuse their positions," she said. "Good for you for calling him on it."

"That girl doesn't stick up for herself," Ray said.

"No, she doesn't," Rose agreed. "What a change from the last genies we had here, isn't it? Pushing people around?"

"I guess." Ray felt himself relaxing.

"Oh, look!" Rose said, pointing across the room. "The chef's beckoning to us. You want to go pick up some goodies? Your young legs are less tired than my poor old ones."

Ray laughed. "No problem, grandma," he said. "Like you're too old for anything."

By the third day, the chef had taken to giving out all of the leftover food from Selane's table after the star went home. By contract, she couldn't serve any of it the next day, and she had made it clear she didn't want to carry it back to her restaurant.

It was top-drawer stuff, far better than the dry snacks that were laid out on their catering station.

Ray opened up his long stride and beat several of the volunteers racing across the wide concrete floor. The small, brown-haired woman welcomed him through the velvet rope with a throaty laugh. He grabbed a big platter of fancy sandwiches and hors d'oeuvres from the middle of the sumptuous array. The chef winked at him. Ray felt his cheeks burn.

"They're not all for me," he said, defending what must have looked like greed.

"I know," she said. "Go on. They'll love them. Fresh mustard cress, salmon, a little bit of cracked pepper, and butter. That little lady over there is a big salmon fan."

She nodded toward Rose. Ray frowned. The chef hadn't served salmon before. How could she know Rose's tastes? Maybe she was a Kitchen Witch, Ray mused. He hadn't met one yet, but rumor had it they existed. Over his objections, the chef helped him to a pile of cookies and small pastries at one end of his tray, along with a stack of napkins.

"Your girlfriend likes sesame seeds," she said. "I toast them and mix them with honey and maple syrup for these cookies."

"She's not my girlfriend," Ray said, automatically. But when he took the big plate back to the risers, Ayosha's eyes gleamed.

"Benne wafers?" she asked.

"The chef said those were for you," he said. "I don't know how she knew."

"That's so nice. It reminds me of home."

"Well, then, you ought to take them all," Alexandra said, kindly. "They'll make a nice snack for you."

"No!" But the young woman looked wistful.

"We insist," Alexandra said, with a smile. Ray and his friends nodded.

"Thank y'all!" Ayosha said, beaming. "I'd better wrap them up, or I'll eat them all now. I feel like such a pig!"

"You're not a pig," Rose said, reaching for a salmon sandwich. "We're all starved after a long day like that, and this is so delicious. It must be nice to be an international star like Miss

Selane." After a bite, she sighed with pleasure. "That just hits the spot."

Over her shoulder, Ray saw the people who had been pointed out to him as the officers of the Guild of Sandmen. The leader, Mr. Pinkwater, a white man who ranged six or more inches taller than Ray and had a shock of white hair and eyebrows to match, caught a glimpse of Ayosha sitting among the Fairy Godmothers, and frowned. Ayosha busied herself making a package of the chef's gift, but when she looked up, he caught her eye. The white eyebrows lowered over his long nose. Ayosha absolutely winced. Ray felt a surge of protectiveness toward her. That guy couldn't tell her who she could and couldn't associate with! He gave the man a glare, and got a cold stare in return.

"You're not eating," Rose said, putting a sandwich into his hand. "Eat. You'll waste away on those long bones of yours."

Ray hadn't realized until he started eating how hungry he was. Everything tasted so good he was certain then that magic was involved. He and George reached for the last canapé at the same time, and Ray withdrew his hand.

"It's all right, you take it," the older man said, laughing. "Estrellita will have dinner waiting for me. I shouldn't spoil my appetite like this. You can burn it all off, but me? I need to buy a bigger belt."

"I've got to go out this evening," Rose asked, after Ray had returned the tray. "You coming with me?"

"Maybe in a while," Ray said.

He glanced toward Ayosha, who was bundling up in a heavy coat, woolly watch cap and two scarves, one inside her coat and one over it. He only needed a light jacket. Women always seemed to feel the cold more. Rose nodded.

"You take care of business," Rose said, with an emphasis on the last word that said she understood he wasn't coming on to the girl. "Meet me at the bar in a while. See you there."

She went out with the others. Ray retrieved his jacket from the pile of coats behind one of the risers and shrugged it on. The rest of the Sandmen had gone. He and Ayosha were among the last ones left.

"Come on," Ayosha said. She headed out of the studio.

CHAPTER 8

On one of the shortest days in a Chicago winter, the sun had set long ago. Ray glanced up at the harsh orange glare of the sodium vapor lights. On the streets around the north side studio, they were all in working order. His own neighborhood suffered the occasional broken bulb that seemed to take the city a long time to fix. Sometimes the House Brownies repaired them to help keep the local families safe. The presence of such an important neighbor as a television station adjacent to a college campus was enough to make sure this area was maintained. The wind whistled around his ears and spattered his face with icy droplets of sleet. The cold wetness reminded him heavy snow was predicted for that evening. He loved wish-granting, but he hated trudging around in wet snow. The water seeped into his shoes and froze there. He thought about going home and skipping wish-granting for the night, but he couldn't. It wasn't just that Rose was going out in spite of the weather, and he'd be disgraced in his own mind if an old woman showed him up like that, but he got honest pleasure out of granting wishes, even to obnoxious kids like that Jacob the night before. He had his wand in his jacket pocket with his fingers resting on it in case he came across some kid who couldn't wait for the local fairy godparent to find him or her.

"I'm a little bit worried about that girl genie," Ayosha said, pitching her voice over the wind and the traffic.

"Me, too," Ray admitted. "She's just beyond clueless."

"You don't think she could go wrong, do you?"

"No," Ray said. "She isn't evil. Have you ever been around bad magic? It stinks, like burning tires. She didn't smell bad at all."

"No," Ayosha said, with a twinkle in those almond-shaped eyes. "She smelled like fruit."

Ray laughed. A man coming toward them walking a string of six dogs gave them a strange look over the scarf wrapped across his nose and mouth.

"How come you're not wearing a scarf yourself?" Ayosha asked Ray when he had passed. "It's freezing out here!"

"It's your thin southern blood," Ray countered. She was turning out to be a lot easier to talk to than he had feared. "We're tough up here in Chicago."

"Tough as mush! You wouldn't last a month in a Hotlanta summer!"

"You from Atlanta?" Ray asked.

"Yes. Well, not originally. I was born somewhere in south Georgia." Ayosha dipped her head a bit. "I'm adopted. My folks took me because they couldn't have children of their own. That was fine for about six years, then the other babies started coming. I have three younger sisters."

She looked blue. He didn't want to ask if her parents had started treating her differently once they started having babies who were their own flesh and blood. It wasn't uncommon. He had sat and listened to a lot of kids who had been pushed out of their parents' attention by the arrival of half-siblings.

"I'm that way, too," he said. "I mean, I'm not adopted, but my folks had me when they were pretty young. My brother and sister are several years younger than I am. Sometimes I feel like a third parent. I sure got to babysit a lot. Well, helping my grandmother babysit," he added. "Do you ever wonder? I mean, about your birth parents? Sorry. I shouldn't be nosy. It comes from hanging around with Rose. She asks everyone whatever comes into her head."

He half expected Ayosha to tell him to mind his own business, but she became thoughtful.

"All the time. When I turned eighteen, I applied to the state to open my birth records, but I got turned down. My birth parents blocked the application. I'll try again when I'm up to it. That's not now. I have too much to worry about with my school work."

"That's hard," Ray said. Her need string made him ache, so he stuffed the wand down further into his pocket and took his hand off it. "How'd you get into being a Sandman?"

"Facebook," Ayosha said. "I 'liked' a page about the influence of dreams, and got a message from the Outreach Officer of the guild. She and I chatted a bunch before I ever met any of them in person."

"Aren't they afraid of what kind of people they might get from social media?" Ray asked.

"You sure don't know about Sandmen," Ayosha said, but not harshly. "The Guildmaster said he had a dream about me. I thought at first that they were cyberstalking me, but he knew things that I had dreamed about, and I never post anything like that. I never even put those thoughts into a computer file."

"You must have a diary, like my sister and my mom," Ray guessed.

"I've been journaling all my life," Ayosha said. "I probably have sixty notebooks. They're private, so don't ask!"

"I won't!" Ray said, holding his hands up in surrender.

"...So I was kind of intrigued, and a little nervous. I brought my boyfriend along to meet with the Guildmaster and the Outreach Officer in a restaurant miles from the university. They gave me some sand to dream on. If I liked what I saw, then I was welcome to apply to join the guild. If I didn't, no harm, no foul, and they would never bother me again."

"What was it like?"

Ayosha put one gloved hand on her hip.

"You're gutsy, asking a girl what was in her dreams!"

Ray dropped his chin.

"Sorry."

"I'm putting you on," she said, patting him on the arm. "But we're almost there, and I don't talk about it to people who aren't like us."

Ray glanced up. Almost where? While they had been talking, she had steered them up St. Louis and around the corner onto Bryn Mawr. Ray blinked up at the sign for a little grocery store.

"You need to pick something up?"

"No. Dropping something off."

Instead of going into the store, Ayosha slipped behind the building. Ray reached deep into his pocket for his wand. He could try to defend them if somebody jumped out at them, but he wasn't cut out to be a fighter. Still, sometimes a brownie point was good for creating a nonphysical diversion.

There were four or five cars huddled up around the green dumpster behind the store. Snow piled on the roofs, but one, an ancient station wagon, was different than the others. The windows were fogged up. Ray took Ayosha's arm.

"There's someone in that one," he said. The wand in his hand tingled, and he took a moment to sort out the sensations. "At least three kids."

"The Newtons," she said. "They've been living back here for a while. Ernie lost his job, and they've got nowhere to go."

"What can you do for them?" he asked. "Do you give them money? Food?"

For answer, she reached into the collar of her coat and brought out the little bag.

"I can't feed them, but the Rahmans who own the store take care of that. I try to give them some peace of mind. It's hard to sleep when you're terribly troubled. I can give them good dreams. When they're lost in sleep, I want them to forget about where they're sleeping. At least I can help them wake up full of hope for a better day."

She pulled her other mitten off with her teeth and reached into the bag. From it, she pulled a handful of sparkling sand. In the shadows, it blazed and twinkled warm orangey-gold light like an ember. Ayosha tiptoed toward the car. The inhabitants, who must have been on the lookout for cops or intruders who would hassle them or try to steal what little the family had left, didn't seem to notice her. Ray could walk through walls while on the job, but he'd never been invisible.

She strewed the sand over the roof of the car with a sideways toss as if she was dusting a pastry board with flour. It hovered in the air for a moment, then settled down, passing through the metal roof. He caught a brief glimpse of orange light inside the cabin of the car, then darkness. Ray felt the magic take. The unseen children relaxed, and the painful strands of need thinned down to almost nothing. With their tension removed, he relaxed, too.

"There," she said, backing away. "That'll give them a good night's sleep."

"What will they dream about?" he asked.

"The kids like hip-hop music and skateboarding," Ayosha said. "Lots of color and noise and warm days. It makes them feel good. Deeana – that's the mother – dreams about being in her nice warm kitchen in the apartment they lost. Ernie gets comfort from remembering when he was a teenager hanging with his dad. I sort out the good memories and let them dream those overnight."

Ray cocked his head.

"Does that mean you can sort the bad thoughts instead?"

Ayosha made a face at him. "That's not my job."

"You did good," Ray said. It was a statement as well as a compliment.

"I like doing this," Ayosha said. "When everything else gets me down, taking care of people's dreams helps build me up again."

Ray felt the urge to do something to help that family. He rummaged around in his mental bank account. Another half point had added itself during the course of the day. He hadn't even noticed.

Can I help get the man a job? he asked silently. *What would that take?*

The brownie points seemed to droop dejectedly. Black voids loomed around the five little stars. There must have been some problems beyond mere homelessness troubling the family.

He didn't have to know the details. Sometimes the magic knew best. Ray slid the wand out of his pocket and aimed it at the car.

Do what you can, he thought, concentrating hard. The five bright lights blinked out in his mind. A veil of deep blue spread out from the silver star at the end of the wand and settled over the car like a blanket. Tiny filaments of light exploded outward, as if they were feeling out opportunity. Ray closed his eyes as they passed through him. They almost tickled. His bank account was empty, but he felt good.

"That's nice of you to want to help," Ayosha said. Ray jumped. "Sorry, didn't mean to startle you."

"I'm okay," he said. "It's nothing."

She eyed the wand curiously.

"I never saw a fairy godmother grant a wish before. That was pretty amazing."

"I wasn't granting a wish," he said. "None of those kids need me right now. That was extra magic I can use to do anything I want. We get some as a reward sometimes. I try to be responsible with it."

He felt his cheeks burn even saying something as goody-two-shoes as that, but she just nodded.

"That's a nice job perk."

"What's yours?" Ray asked, covering his embarrassment.

"Kind of job-related, too. I never have nightmares any more. I can direct myself to dream anything I can imagine. And I sleep really well. Which reminds me, I have got to get to the train. I want to drop off my stuff before I make my rounds tonight. This was only my first stop."

"I know. I have things to do, too," Ray said. He escorted her toward the street. "Come on."

CHAPTER 9

Selane waited until Tommy unlocked the door of her suite in the Four Seasons hotel and opened it wide. She bustled in past her staff, casually dropping the silver fur coat on the blond marble floor as she did. She heard Minnie sigh as she followed her employer into the room. Selane didn't have to look back to know that the wardrobe mistress had picked up the coat and brushed off the few drops of moisture from melted snowflakes. Selane didn't mind Chicago winters. She took them as a personal challenge. Stop her coming in to run her annual fundraiser? *Try it, Chicago. Just try*, Selane thought defiantly. *I've faced tougher situations than a little snow and ice.* She still clutched the brass lamp. At no time did she plan to surrender *that* to any of her employees.

Dennis had taken Vickie in hand. The girl was wide-eyed with astonishment at the thought of getting into the stretch limousine that awaited them outside the studio. The driver, a middle-aged white man with a round face and a mustache leaped out to open the door for her. The genie tried to climb in first, but Dennis held her back with a hand on her arm and a raised forefinger of admonishment. Selane shook her head. She had known some clueless people in her day, but this girl was almost sleepwalking through reality. Vickie had stared out the window at the city during the twenty minute ride from the studio, remarking happily about everything she saw. She seemed absolutely astonished at the miniature refrigerators in the arm rests, and accepted a can of soda with a smile of open

76

delight. In a way, her innocence was kind of refreshing – if it was for real. Selane wasn't taking anything for granted. The jury was still out on the wish, and though she had seen the girl turn into smoke several times already, that still could have been an optical illusion or special effects. What Hollywood could accomplish these days was downright scary.

Kiri, her makeup woman, appeared at her side. She had hung up her coat somewhere.

"Do you want your evening facial now? That cold is murder on your skin. You don't want any rough patches showing up on camera."

Selane gave her a one-armed hug.

"I want a glass of wine, first," she said. "Y'all come and sit down with me and have one, too. It's been a long day."

"Anybody there?" a brassy female voice called from the sitting room.

Selane stopped dead. Dennis moved in front of her. Tommy and Beatdown, her largest bodyguard, drew guns from inside pockets and glided forward. Selane retreated to the open door of the suite, ready to run if the voice belonged to a stalker. She'd had trouble with crazy people before. But how the hell did someone get up in the elevator? You needed a key card for these floors!

The men peered around the door frame, then withdrew.

"Well, hi, there, handsome men!"

By then, Selane recognized the boozy voice. So had Dennis. He let go of the genie's arm and strode into the sitting room, his hands spread wide.

"Rochelle, darling!" he exclaimed. "Selane, my love, look who's here!"

Rochelle Cox! How had the old bat flown here from the coast so quickly? Never mind. She had to make the best of the moment. Tired as she was, Selane arranged her face into the most welcoming expression she could muster. She glided into the chamber.

"Well, hello, sweetness," Selane gushed.

The sitting room had been arranged according to Dennis's very specific instructions for Selane's comfort. Around the insanely gorgeous gas-fed glass fireplace were arranged big, fluffy armchairs upholstered in her favorite pearl white. To the left of the gleaming hearth stood Selane's own special seat, which was kept in the Four Seasons' storeroom in between her visits. If it looked a little like a throne, well, who was to criticize? Its wide seat was covered in real silk velvet. Tucked all around it she had a half dozen fleecy cushions and soft, natural-hued cashmere blankets that she could arrange according to her mood. And that nasty cow, Rochelle Cox, was right in the middle of them, with her gray hair bleached to a shimmering silver-white and her skinny butt clad in powder blue Armani to match her cold, pouchy eyes. Maybe she thought that as a television personality as well as a producer and show runner, she was entitled to sit where she pleased. Well, she was wrong.

Selane moved in on the intruder, determined to claim back her throne.

Dennis got there first. He put an arm around Selane and held her tightly. She struggled for a moment, but in spite of his slender physique, he was as strong as iron.

"Rochelle, we weren't expecting you for hours," he said. He let go of Selane and took the old bat's hands in his. He bowed over them as though asking for a blessing. "How lovely to see you. Come, you must have a drink. The bar is over here. What would you like?" He moved a few paces away and beckoned to her, pointing toward the ebony wood dresser with its stainless-steel refrigerator and array of crystal glasses.

Rochelle smiled smugly. She wasn't going to take the bait. She always knew how to annoy Selane, and everybody else in Hollywood. She wasn't moving from that chair without a dynamite enema.

"Oh, anything, you English hunk, you. A pint of blood, a shot of bile, whatever you've got. Selane, baby, sit down! Nice suite. Must set you back thousands."

Selane realized to stand there any longer was to look like one of the many who came to worship at Rochelle's feet. She gave the older woman an air-kiss on each cheek, then settled into the armchair as far away from the other woman as possible. Rochelle was proud of her reputation in LA. She had a string of hit shows dating back five decades, and looked every year of her age. Too bad she couldn't have saved her face on video tape.

"I expected to see you at Cameron Clarke's bash last week," Rochelle said. "All of my friends were there. Except you, of course."

"Nonsense, Rochelle, love," Dennis said, returning with a glass containing three fingers of amber liquid. A raised eyebrow from him told Selane it was 40-year-old Macallan scotch from her private store and that she was not to make a fuss about it. "Everyone knows you have no friends." He paused, wickedly long. "Only those who want to bask in your radiance or beg favors."

Rochelle toasted them both with the glass and took a sip.

"You're still full of bull, Dennis. No kidding, Selane, the *Hollywood Reporter* and all the entertainment reporters were there. People kept asking where you were."

"I was here," Selane said, feeling a little hurt. "Getting ready for the telethon. No offense, Rochelle, but it's more important than a party."

"So, how are the kiddies?" Rochelle chirped. "Still dying?"

"Full of hope," Selane said. She kept her voice firm. "The charity is doing good work."

"Still trying to recoup your reputation from your visit to Colonel Whatsisname? Well, I have good news. It looks like the whole mess has been forgiven and forgotten. I got a call today from the head of the network. I sent in a proposal for the next season of *Celebrity Survivor*. He wanted to know why you weren't on it."

The wish was working out just fine, Selane thought, wriggling into the second-best armchair with pleasure. "So you're here to invite me onto your next program."

Rochelle let out a rusty laugh, as if her vocal cords had trouble remembering how.

"No. I'm not. I want to know why I shouldn't just call him back and tell him that you're a misguided little bitch who doesn't look beyond the end of her pert nose. Who knows if you're going to make another bad decision like that? And it'll end up costing me my job, which no way in hell I am going to jeopardize for your sake."

Selane felt her heart sink thirty stories to the dirty, snow-covered pavement.

"But you came out here," she said.

Rochelle waved a hand. "It was easier to tell you to your face. All my phones are bugged. I can't trust my own assistant, and you shouldn't trust yours. They all gossip. They've probably taken a thousand instant pictures of you in your scanties and posted them on the internet. Mortimer is wrong. You haven't changed. You're still the same as you were months ago. You're not sorry you did a private concert for a dictator. You're just sorry you got caught."

"Of course I'm sorry!" Selane said. If she could have shot flames out of her eyes, Rochelle would have been a heap of greasy ashes in the throne-like chair. "It was a mistake! I didn't read up on him until I got home."

The older woman made a dismissive gesture.

"Forget it. I don't believe you, and neither does *People* maga-zine. I'm not casting you. You've got nothing fresh or new to offer. Maybe you ought to talk to the producers of *Can They Still Dance?*"

"But, darling," Dennis said, oiling his way over to Rochelle with the gilded carafe of whisky in his hand. He sat down on the arm of the throne and poured another finger of the fragrant amber liquid into her glass. "Selane brings the kind of credibility to your show that no one else can offer. Her char-ity has raised millions. She has name recognition all over the world. In years to come, the trip to Africa will be a footnote."

Rochelle shook her head.

"But it's still a nuisance now. I don't want every press call about *Celebrity Survivor* to be all about her. She's too much trouble." She eyed the Englishman up and down. "What about you, Dennis? You're damned good at your job. I could get you offers for twelve new jobs by tomorrow morning. Fly back with me to the coast, and we'll talk about it. You won't even have to sleep with me. Well, more than once."

Selane saw her bright new future leaching away from her even before she had had a chance to enjoy it. If Rochelle bad-mouthed her to the studio, word would spread in minutes. The producers who had been burning up Dennis's phone line would shun her. If the gossip was too harsh, her record label might drop her. Even Dennis might leave! She'd be back to poverty and isolation in a week. Just the same way she started out. She'd have nothing.

Except… two more wishes.

Selane held the lamp to her like a teddy bear. An idea struck her like a twelve-foot wave, almost washing her off her feet with the obviousness of it all. She raised her chin high.

"You're so wrong, Rochelle. I have plenty new to offer you! You'll be calling me your best friend in the entire world."

Rochelle focused her fishy eyes in astonishment.

"What? You want to dedicate your next album to me?"

"No. I have something better." She held out the brass lamp. "I have a genie."

Rochelle threw back her head and let out a very unladylike guffaw.

"You must have caught something serious when you were overseas, honey."

Selane felt like snapping back, but she restrained herself. Very slowly and carefully, she sat back in her chair.

"I'm about to let you in on the greatest secret that anyone has ever seen, Rochelle. You want something special. I have it on tap. I can change your life. In exchange, you feature me on your little show, and you make sure I make it through to the winner's circle. I know those games are fixed. You'll fix them *my* way and make it worth my while."

The lines of the older woman's face arranged themselves into an expression of outrage.

"My *little* show? In exchange for a fantasy? You're out of your mind." She rose to her feet. "I'm out of here."

Selane rubbed the lamp hard with her palm. This had to work!

"Genie, appear to me!"

A billow of smoke exploded in the middle of the room. It cleared instantly and odorlessly, leaving Vickie standing erect with her folded arms out in front of her.

"Yes, Miss Selane?"

Rochelle Cox collapsed back into the throne, her jaw hanging open.

"What the everlasting hell was that? You're throwing smoke grenades at *me?* Who is this kid?"

Selane felt smug. Rochelle looked the way she must have that afternoon when Vickie poofed out of the lamp. But now she knew how to handle the situation. She flipped a palm grandly.

"This is my genie, Rochelle. She grants wishes. I'll let her grant wishes for you, three of them, and all you have to do is guarantee me that spot on your show."

"Uh, Selane, are you certain that is a good idea?" Dennis asked. He looked uneasy. Selane shot him a furious glance. He was not going to caution her out of a surefire star gig for a whole season on a major network!

"Of course it is!"

"This is crap," Rochelle said, standing up again and began to cast around her, poking in between the pillows. "Where's my purse? I'm going back to LA. You can't fool me with your special effects."

Selane smiled. She reveled in the moment that was coming.

"Genie, back in your lamp," she said, pointing to the spout.

"I hear and obey, Miss Selane," Vickie said obediently. She dissolved into a pillar of dun smoke and seeped into the small opening.

Rochelle stopped moving, her eyes watchful. She stepped forward and waved her hand through the space where Vickie had been standing. There was no doubt someone had been there. The girl's footprints were impressed upon the two-inch-thick carpet.

"That's impossible. This is some kind of setup!"

"How? We didn't know you were here yet," Selane pointed out. "Something that Dennis is going to mention to that so-called night manager downstairs."

"Where'd she go?"

Selane held out the lamp.

"In here. And she can grant you three wishes, just like in the fairy tale. But none of this happens if you don't sign me up for the season right now!"

"I want proof!"

"How much more proof do you need, darling?" Dennis asked reasonably, taking Rochelle's purse out of her unprotesting fingers. "The girl vanished right before your eyes. If you can believe one impossibility, is it so extraordinary to believe in the rest of the phenomenon?"

Rochelle tossed her head, throwing those famous silver locks back.

"If this is some kind of trick, I'll sue your ass back to the Stone Age, honey," she said. "Fine. I'll go along with your charade."

"Shall I prepare a letter of intent?" Dennis asked.

Rochelle made an impatient gesture.

"I'll keep my word. There isn't a star in Hollywood who has had to ask for more than that. Certainly not you. Three wishes? Go for it."

Selane knocked on the side of the lamp.

"Come on out, genie," she said.

The smoke issued from the spout. This time Rochelle had her eyes glued to the proceedings. She whistled and shook her head.

"Nice. If it's a trick, it's a good one."

Selane wanted to say that she had felt the same way, but she didn't want to display one iota of vulnerability. This was her ticket back to the front pages!

"What is your will, Miss Selane?" Vickie asked.

The diva pointed to Rochelle.

"She wants three wishes. I said you could do that for her."

Vickie glanced from one woman to the other.

"But you still have two wishes to go."

"You can't wait on those and grant some for her in the meantime?"

Vickie's dull face brightened.

"I don't know. I never tried. I ought to ask the Guildmaster."

"Where is he? Or she?"

Vickie shrugged. "I don't know. He was always kind of 'do your own thing.'" She held up her hands, palms facing one another, and stared down at the space. Colored smoke played between them, forming nebulous images that Selane couldn't read. "He's not answering me. I guess it would be okay."

"Fine. Do it."

Vickie shook her head. "She's got to rub the lamp. I can't break the rule."

Selane hated to let the brass object out of her hands, but Rochelle marched over and snatched it up. She buffed her palm vigorously on the side.

"Okay, genie. Oh, my God, I can't believe I'm doing this!"

Vickie looked pleased that the formalities were being observed. She put her hands up under her chin.

"What is your will, mistress?" she asked.

"God, I love this!" Rochelle crowed. "Okay, genie, I want to be young and beautiful forever!"

Vickie crossed her arms out in front of her.

"Watch it, love," Dennis cautioned her. He held up a hand to forestall the genie's motion. "I hear tell that the powers that grant wishes are literal. Do you really want to live forever?"

"Why not?" Rochelle asked, her scanty brows rising to the whitened hairline. "I work in Hollywood. An actress who hits thirty is over the hill. I'm invisible to the young squirts who run the studios these days. Even the old farts want agents and producers to be halfway out of diapers." She frowned. "But you're right. Let's phrase this correctly, so I don't end up unemployed in the year 6500. You've got the right kind of devious mind, honey. Walk with me." She beckoned to Dennis, who fell in beside her. They crossed the plush carpeting and disappeared into Selane's bedroom.

Selane felt hot resentment rising in her belly at the sheer nerve. She had to keep reminding herself that this was the way to get back to where she wanted to be. The wish had brought Rochelle clear across the country, with other producers to follow, and put the means to making them do what she wanted into her hand. She just wished she could keep hold of the lamp. She didn't trust Rochelle.

Magic, I hope you know what you're doing!

She glanced at Vickie, who was gazing at her with those big, pale eyes.

"What are you looking at?

"Just you. You're really beautiful."

"You don't have to butter me up, child," Selane said, sitting down and sighing. "You got the part. Are you sure you can go on granting wishes to her but still work for me? If I lose control of this situation, all my dreams will shatter. I couldn't take that."

"I think so," Vickie said. She squinted off into the distance. "I mean, I'll see what happens when I try. If it doesn't work, I'll know."

"Well, you tell me if it doesn't."

Rochelle strode back into the room, her lined face beaming.

"All right! Here's how it goes. I want to be young and beautiful again, just like I was when I was 27. Yes, that was after my first... doctor's visit. Everything else has been... improvements. And I want to live to be 120, looking just like that. And healthy. My mother always said that if you don't have your health, you don't have anything. My friends all have melanomas or diabetes or Alzheimer's. I don't want to end up that way."

"Is that your first wish, mistress?" Vickie asked.

"Yes," Rochelle said. "That's it. Hit me, baby!" She handed the lamp to Selane, screwed her eyes closed and balled her hands into fists. Vickie raised her arms again.

"Wait a second!" Dennis shouted. He reached into his pocket for his ever-present cell phone and set it to record video. "All right, love, go ahead."

The young genie nodded her head.

It didn't look like much of a gesture to set such a momentous event in motion. Selane was almost disappointed, until the blue smoke started to rise out of the carpet. She expected it to surround Rochelle, concealing her from view, but instead it seeped into the woman's body where it touched, as if the older woman's flesh was absorbing it. It was hard to tell at first, but the wrinkled flesh on the backs of her hands smoothened and plumped out, almost dimpling over the knuckles. The sharp, knobby bones of her wrists retreated into satin-smooth skin.

Her face underwent the most dramatic makeover. First the wrinkles erased themselves, then the ropy tendons sank backward, taking with them the small turkey wattle of flesh under her chin. The jawline didn't change markedly, although the skin along it changed shape. Selane had never really noticed the jowls until they were almost gone. Crow's feet and smile lines flooded with healthy, pinkish-white skin. The apples of Rochelle's cheeks plumped and pinked up. Beneath them, her cheeks hollowed slightly under fine bones. Selane eyed her critically. She hadn't known Rochelle when she had been that pretty. In fact, she was a beauty. Illogically, she was jealous. Maybe eternal youth would be *her* second wish.

The blue smoke stopped rising. Vickie lowered her arms.

"Well?" Rochelle asked, her eyes still closed. "When are you going to start?"

"I'm done," Vickie said. "You can look."

Rochelle opened her eyes and stared accusingly at the girl. "You didn't do anything! I don't feel any different."

"You're…" Selane swallowed hard. Her mouth was dry.

"I'm *what?*"

"Take a look, my love," Dennis said. He looked afraid to touch Rochelle for a moment, but he put his arm around her and guided her out of the room to the hall, where a full-length oval mirror hung on the wall. Selane waited, every nerve ablaze, until a whoop made her jump out of her seat like a stung cat.

"Oh, my God, I'm gorgeous!"

Rochelle came running into the room and threw her arms around Vickie.

"You're incredible, girl!" she shouted. "I don't believe it. I didn't think I was this amazing! I am going to knock eyes out. No one will ignore me now! Look out, world!" She turned to Dennis. "Show me the video."

They all crowded around the tiny screen. Rochelle chuckled all the way through it.

"If you ran it backward, it would be a horror movie. As it is, it's a fantasy! I cannot wait to take this girl to Hollywood!"

"Oh, no, you aren't." Selane wrapped both arms around the lamp. "Vickie doesn't go nowhere. She stays here with me."

Rochelle stuck out her lower lip. The pout looked cute now instead of petulant.

"So, how am I supposed to make my second and third wishes?"

"You come back to me," Selane said, holding her chin up. "Right along with that contract for *Celebrity Survivor*. And any other great projects you got coming along."

"Right, right!" Rochelle said, as if the reason for her visit had entirely escaped her memory. "Oh, baby, you and I are going places." She stopped and glanced summingly at Selane, and her expression grew sly. "You know I look younger than you, now. I'm going to look younger *forever!*"

"I earned my scars," Selane said, even though the words stung. "I'm happy in my skin."

"Well, I am going to enjoy my new skin!" Rochelle said. She rifled through the purse and came up with a square mirror. She admired her reflection, primping her hair and touching the smooth curves of her face.

"As long as you use your powers for good and not evil," Dennis said.

"I'm going to take over Hollywood," Rochelle said, striking a model's pose with one hand on her hip. "Which one is that?"

CHAPTER 10

A hand slammed down on the telephone console in front of Ray's nose. Ray snapped awake, jerking his head back with his eyes wide. One of Miss Selane's enforcers, the one with the round, bald head and piggy little black eyes set in an ebony-dark face.

"Your phone's hit eight rings. You're supposed to get it on no more than two! That's *two*." He held up his thick fingers in a V.

"Sorry, man," Ray said. He scrambled to hit the closest blinking button. "Hello, and thanks for helping Selane's Kids..." The woman on the other end was calling from Iowa and wanted to give a hundred dollars. Ray took her information, watching the enforcer move away in search of another victim.

"Long night?" Chris Popp, seated to his right, asked him. It was before the break so no one had been moved around yet.

"Yeah," Ray said "I had a pile of homework, but I couldn't get to it until Rose and I followed up all the need strings in the neighborhood. It took us a while to find the last kid. He had holed up in the boiler room of his apartment complex. I didn't know buildings had boiler rooms anymore."

"They still work," Chris said, nodding. "Built to last, unlike my furnace." He made a face. "It blew last night. I need twenty brownie points to fix it myself, and I only have seventeen. Still cheaper than calling a repairman. Not looking forward to sleeping in a cold house."

Ray checked his balance. He had five. The first three he had picked up overnight when he and Rose had made their rounds. The latter two were kind of an embarrassment. They had appeared in his mental piggy bank right after he gave up all his saved points to the homeless family in the alley that Ayosha had given good dreams. *I didn't need a reward. I didn't* ask *for a reward.* The brownie points just glowed.

"Take some of mine," Ray said. *Go on, go*, he told the three on the right. They blinked on and off like LEDs, then disappeared. Chris looked surprised.

"You?" he asked. Ray nodded. "Thanks, sweetheart! I could kiss you!"

"Well, don't," Ray replied, uneasily. Chris was the affectionate kind who hugged people just because. Ray liked him, but he wasn't as physical with others. "The cameras are on us."

"Hi, Mom!" Chris murmured, looking up at the black lenses and smiling. He touched his keypad and twisted his microphone toward his mouth with a theatrical flourish. "Hello! Thank you for helping Selane's Kids!"

"You look tired," said Rose on his other side, when Ray clicked off from his next call. "You were such a hero with that little boy yesterday. You wore yourself out searching the place until you found him."

"It wasn't that hard," Ray said. He stifled a yawn. "I mean, it was cold and dark, but that's no hassle. What's beating me up is I couldn't sleep. I couldn't focus on my anatomy homework, and every time I dozed off, I dreamed I was lost down there myself. Those tunnels seemed to be a thousand miles long. I'd fall into an endless hole, then I woke up in a panic. I think I saw every hour on the clock. I probably lost ten pounds sweating."

Rose nodded understandingly.

"Maybe you should ask your new friend for some advice," she said, nodding toward Ayosha, who was typing with both thumbs on a small tablet. "Professional courtesy, and all that."

"Maybe," Ray said. He didn't hold out any hopes for that. When he had met her at the coffee table during the first break, she had been more distant with him than she had been the previous evening. Still, anything that would drive off the occasional nightmare was a blessing.

He glanced over toward Miss Selane. She had a lot more people around her that afternoon. He thought he recognized a couple of them from interviews on the entertainment shows. Not actors or singers, though. They had none of her grace or charisma or style. In fact, the stocky woman wore flip-flops.

"Looks like the curse is off her," Chris Popp said.

"Why do you say that?" Ray asked.

"Don't you know who those people are? Neil and Nona Karburg are the two biggest producers in Hollywood! Didn't you go see *Superheroes in Action*?"

Ray peered at the brother and sister team.

"I guess I like their stuff, but the only people I remember are the actors."

"Those are the ones who are important," Chris confided. "Without them, there wouldn't be movies to watch. Oooh, I bet they're casting Selane in something! I wonder what?"

"Later, later," Rose said, poking Chris in the back with her forefinger. "The big bullies are coming back." She nodded toward two of the enforcers, circling around for another pass just ahead of the cameras.

Throughout the morning, Ray kept trying to catch Ayosha's eye. He hoped he was imagining that she was avoiding his eye. When the floor manager let them go for lunch, he sidled up to talk with her.

"Hey," he said, as she turned toward him, a cup of coffee and a plate of cheese and cut vegetables in her hands.

"How you doin'?" she asked, politely.

"Okay. Do you want me to walk with you this evening? I'd be happy to help out a little with the Newtons again if you want."

Ayosha started to speak, but a hand fell heavily on Ray's shoulder. His automatic impulse to grab the hand and twist it behind its owner's back was immediately checked by long practice. Instead, he turned a dangerous glare at the newcomer.

It was the Sandmen Guildmaster, Mr. Pinkwater. The white-haired man loomed down to stare into Ray's eyes.

"You need to let her go back about her business, young man," he said.

"I'm just being friendly, man," Ray said.

The guildmaster lowered his snowy eyebrows over ice blue eyes.

"Back off and let her do her job. Isn't one warning enough?"

"What warning?" Ray asked, searching his memory. "You've hardly said a word to me!"

Pinkwater shoved Ray away from him and nodded imperiously at Ayosha. She gave Ray an apologetic glance.

"Sorry."

"Where's he get off treating me like trash?" Ray demanded. "You Sandmen really think you're better than everybody else?"

"It's not like that," Ayosha said. "We work hard for our clients. He considers our work important to people's well-being."

"That doesn't excuse that kind of disrespect! What does he think we do? You're all the same as us."

"Sorry," Ayosha said again, her expression closed. She clutched her snack to her chest and sidestepped him. The guildmaster watched her until she returned to her station, and shot Ray another disapproving look. So did the other officers of the guild. Ray poured himself some of the terrible coffee and gulped down a mouthful of the hot brew too fast. He sucked air to cool off his scorched tongue.

"Let me, Ray." Alexandra, the chairwoman of the FGU, stepped up and laid a gentle finger on his lips. She must have used a brownie point of her own. The pain dulled, faded and disappeared. "Don't let Mr. Pinkwater get to you. His superiority complex is a running joke among the other helper guilds."

"He's got no business holding the Sandmen up as so superior," Ray said.

"When he says something like that, I just think, 'dream on, Wendell,'" she said, with a wicked little grin.

"Is that his first name? Wendell?" Ray couldn't help but grin back. "I rode his sister a few times, *Wendella*." That was the name of the water taxi that plied the Chicago River in the summer.

"I know," Alexandra said, her eyes twinkling at the shared joke. "Don't let him get to you. Ayosha likes you. She has her own mind and her own will. As long as she's an effective sandman, he can't give her demerits for making friends of her own age."

"Yeah, she's good," Ray said, not grudging the truth. "She has a good heart. Too bad too many people around here let themselves get pushed around a lot."

The other person who had aroused his inner 'white knight' was in the middle of the discussion at the other end of the studio.

Vickie seemed alternately to be pushed back and forth between the newcomers and being ignored. She looked pathetic, a little rag-bag of a girl in between all those well-dressed, toned fit and high-powered movers. She kept looking hopefully toward the chef lady and her freshly-laden tables, but every time she started to head in that direction, someone else took her by the arm. When they talked at her intently, her face went blank. If Ray hadn't spoken with her himself and known that she was pretty bright, he would have thought she couldn't understand what they were saying. Under pressure, she was withdrawing into herself. That just wasn't fair.

"No, she has to come with me," insisted the tall, bulky man that Chris Popp had identified as Neil Karburg, the producer. "Right now. I've got exactly what I want all thought out."

"Not a chance, Neil," said a beautiful woman in a light green power suit that must have cost in the tens of thousands, even fancier than anything that either Alexandra or the glamorous fairy godmother who did the local network news owned. "I still have business with her. You got here this morning. I have priority."

"Look at you, Rochelle! You already got one of your wishes. You're gorgeous. Now it's my turn. You can go again when I'm done."

"Don't you try to push me, Neil," Rochelle said, tossing her magnificent, shining tresses of hair. "I got you your start in the business, and don't you forget it!"

"This is different," Nona said. "You've had a chance. You said you want to think about your second, uh…" She looked around at the studio as if suddenly realizing that they weren't alone. "…Interview. Now we want our first interview with this girl."

"Selane decided to give me the next round," said the bald, round-bellied African-American man, pushing between the two women. He took Vickie by the arm and started to draw her to one side. Rochelle promptly rubbed the lamp in her hands. The girl vanished in a puff of smoke and reappeared behind her. The man looked shocked, then his eyes sparkled with rage. He moved to confront Rochelle, who turned up a defiant chin. He shoved his forefinger under her nose. "Don't you do that again! It's my turn. Selane decided!"

Selane couldn't be the one to decide between them because she was in front of the camera, crouched down among the kids in the wheelchairs. Poor Francisco kept trying to get her attention, but he couldn't compete with the lens. But Vickie was getting pulled back and forth like a tug-of-war rope.

Ray was afraid to intervene; the enforcers were looming. They might to toss him out into the street, but he couldn't stand to watch any longer. He put his plate down on the edge of the buffet table and strode over to the cluster of executives.

By the time he reached them, the bald executive had Vickie by one arm, and Nona Karburg had taken the other. The girl looked too terrified to move a muscle. Ray pushed the man's hand off and moved Vickie away. Rochelle let go.

"What are you doing? We're having a private conference!" she said.

"It's not so private, ma'am," Ray said, forcing a polite smile to his lips. "Everyone can hear you all over this studio."

"Oh," Rochelle said. She and her fellow high-powered types moved into a protective knot. Vickie was trembling in

Ray's grasp. He glanced down into her scared hazel eyes, and felt a wave of pity roll over him like a tide.

"Have you had anything to eat today?" he asked.

"Uh, no?"

He hated to see anyone afraid to defend herself. He put his arm around her. She was trembling.

"Come on," he said. With a look that dared any of the executives to stop him, he escorted her across the big room, skirting the area currently covered by the video cameras, around the wall to the catering table laid out for the volunteers.

Rose met him there.

"Bravo, Ray," she said. "You're my hero. Hi, Vickie. I'm Rose. What would you like to eat?"

"Anything," Vickie said, in a small voice. Rose took an empty plate and piled it high with sandwiches and bunches of grapes. She shoved it into the girl's hands and coaxed her to sit down on the platform at the rear of the risers. Vickie snatched up a sandwich and tore into it like a starving wolf.

A shadow fell over them. Ray glanced back. Minnie, the lady in charge of Selane's costumes, came bustling over and took the plate out of Vickie's hand.

"You don't want to eat that crap, honey," she said. "Come with me. Come on. She wants you to."

"She's hungry!" Ray said, fixing her with an accusatory glare. "And you folks don't seem to give a damn about her. Miss Selane is treating her like a toy!"

"Sorry. Selane's not evil, just too busy." The older woman sighed and looked over at the group of well-dressed men and women. They stared at Vickie like cats watching a mouse hole. "I'll look after her now, I promise."

Very reluctantly, Ray made way for her. As she promised, Minnie took Vickie to the roped enclosure and had the chef make up a tray full of fancy eats. Vickie shot an apologetic glance his way. Ray wasn't satisfied. He promised himself he wouldn't let the genie out of his sight.

"Is she okay?" Ayosha asked, softly. She appeared at his elbow.

"Are you even supposed to be talking to me?" he snapped.

"Don't be ugly," she said. Her brow wrinkled in concern. "Is Vickie gonna be all right?"

Ray sighed. "I'm sorry. I don't know. I wish I knew what was going on. I never got a chance to ask. You doing okay today?"

"I'm just fine. Y'all can come by with me when I visit the Newtons later," she said. "I'd appreciate it. If you can."

Ray consulted his inner piggy bank. A few stars twinkled there. Not enough for major magic, but maybe they could provide a little help.

"Yeah," he said. "That'd be good."

CHAPTER 11

"Now, now, now," Selane said, holding a hand in the air to forestall the rising arguments. The music accompanying a big dance troupe from the south side of Chicago drowned out their conversation so no one more than a few feet away could hear her discussion. Vickie stood close to her as if depending on her for defense against the avid eyes of the producers. "I know you want what you want. I am happy to give it to you, all of you! The good Lord knows how much I would like all of you to have your dreams fulfilled! Now, have you all talked to Dennis? He's got a bunch of paperwork for everybody. Is it all signed? Otherwise, I can't offer you the full and true Selane experience."

Dennis grinned at her over the heads of the visitors. She knew what he was thinking: she was auctioning again. Who knew she had such a talent for direct sales? When this year's appeal was over, she was going to have to look into her own show on QVC.

"Baby, we gotta have it," Nona Karburg said, with a smile that was supposed to be winning, but really made her look like a shark fiercely surveying its next meal. It had been known to make even A-list celebrities with egos from there to the Grand Canyon quail and cry for their mothers. "We want you, but this is like the best door prize in the universe! I mean, I saw Rochelle here this morning, and I didn't even recognize her. If it wasn't for her knowing... I mean, something we discussed once, I would have thought you brought in a ringer to sell us a load of BS."

Rochelle Cox primped her hair. She had sent the Four Seasons concierge out at two in the morning to buy her a new dress to fit her rejuvenated curves. Somehow, he had come back by six A.M. with that suit. It was businesslike and devastatingly sexy all at the same time, showing off the hot body she would have for another half century at least. Selane understood that Rochelle was her best selling point.

"You want what she's got?" Selane asked, with a shrewd glance at their faces. They would have promised getting her face on Mount Rushmore if she had asked. "It's possible. Just sign on the dotted line. And no take-backs."

Dennis moved into the midst of the group, armed with a sheaf of contracts and a pen.

"I don't like to be hurried," Neil Karburg said, his brows lowering over his broad nose. "I want my lawyer to go over these documents before I sign."

"The clock is ticking, my friends," Dennis said, with his winning smile. "The lass can wish for your empires to crumble in a twinkling, or build them up like the Himalayas. It would behoove you to secure your dreams while you can. Once Selane's schedule for the next few years is booked, well, we won't need any more contracts for a while. You know what opportunity is like. And if you don't want to sign Selane today, she might not have time to fit you in with her genie for a long while. Maybe never. You know magic. It's fleeting."

Selane smiled inwardly. They knew no such thing, of course. Their education in the metaphysical had been a private viewing in Selane's trailer of Vickie smoking in and out of her lamp. She held the brass shoe cradled in her arms. When Selane was on camera, it rested in a locked suitcase that no one was allowed to touch or move except for her. She had set Tommy to guard it. Vickie, bless her poor little addled head, didn't seem to care where it was, or where she was, for that matter.

Nona gave her brother an exasperated glance and snatched the pen from Dennis's hand.

"I'd have to be crazy to pass this up. We were going to use her anyhow." She scrawled her name in huge letters on the line Dennis indicated. "Neil, come on!"

"All right, but I think we're rushing." Karburg added his tiny, neat signature under his sister's. He pocketed the pen and held out a palm. "All right, hand over the lamp. I want to see something other than smoke."

"Are you sure you have the wording the way you want it?" Dennis asked. "One can't be too careful."

"He's careful," Nona assured him. "A lot more careful than I am."

"Now, wait a minute," said Corry N. The record producer passed his hand over his shaved head. "I need to start production on her album within a couple of weeks, you know? I get priority here. C'mon, Selane, show a brother some support."

"Corry, you have to sign first."

"We *got* a contract, Selane!"

"Which you tore up," Dennis said. "Audibly, over the phone, two weeks ago. This reinstates it, and, as of your first wish, cannot be reneged again."

"Oh, all right!" Corry took the paper and signed it on his open palm. "Okay. Me first. I got some big business to take care of."

"You second," Neil said. "Me first. I signed first."

Rochelle took the lamp out of Selane's arm and handed it to Nona Karburg.

"Nona signed first. Go on, honey. Stroke it."

The film producer's eyes gleamed as she touched the smooth metal. She squeezed her eyes shut and bobbed her head a few times. Then she opened her eyes and looked at the teenage girl in green.

"To hear is to obey," Vickie said, holding her crossed arms out.

"What did you ask for?" Neil asked.

"It's a secret," Nona said, brusquely. "And what do you care? Between us we get six wishes!"

98

A cell phone rang in her Lulu Guinness bag, eliciting an annoyed glance from the floor manager. Nona took the bejeweled device from the purse's depths and looked at the screen.

"She's the goods, all right," she said. "Hot damn! I got my black Lambo! Just like that."

"That's how it worked for me," Rochelle said, beaming.

"Pure chance," Neil said, with a dismissive wave. "One just turned up. It had nothing to do with magic. You wasted a wish, Nona!"

"No! I've had one of my assistants on this night and day," she said. "Lloyd just called to say a search popped up on his computer screen. The car is right here in Chicago. I can have it as soon as the money's transferred." She grimaced playfully. "I should have asked for it for free. How about it, genie? Can I rephrase the wish?"

"Sorry," Vickie said, ruefully. "You already said. Changing things after is against the rules."

"I told you to be careful of the wording, darling," Dennis said. Nona shrugged.

"Screw it, it's only six mil. I've wanted one of those since the factory announced them. Why they only decided make fifty of them I don't know."

Neil snorted. "I'll be more impressed if the registration shows that this car is number 51."

Selane felt a twinkle in her eyes. "I bet it is. You ought to check when you get it."

"I will." Nona held out the lamp. "Who's next?"

"I have to think about it," Neil said, holding his hands up.

"Me, too," Rochelle said. "But I'm not leaving this city until I get all three of my wishes granted."

Corry N. grabbed the metal shoe and gripped it in his big fist. "I'm gonna think about it and get it just right. You want to help me with the wording, genie girl?"

"Uh, sure," Vickie said uncertainly. "Um, you guys smell anything?"

Selane lifted her nose. She prided herself on its sensitivity. She sensed a faint whiff of burned metal. "They might have fried one of the Klieg lights. Nothing to worry about. The stage hands will fix it. Let's get to work. I have to go back to the children pretty soon. What's your wish, Corry?"

The music producer showed his brilliant white teeth. "Probably pretty close to what you wished for, pretty lady. Opportunity. I want the best talents around to flock to me. I need some new names in my stable. A whole bundle of them. They won't measure up to you, naturally. You're a genius. You got all that, genie-girl?"

"I sure do," Vickie said, smiling. Selane felt a momentary twinge of jealousy, but the way Corry had worded his wish, none of his new talents would be as good as she was. When the wave of energy passed through her, she added her own hope not to be outclassed. She smiled. Vickie was *her* genie, after all.

CHAPTER 12

Ray looked up from his console with a start. The desperate longing, like a gut-punch, hit him in the belly and made him double over with pain. Someone close by was hurting like they had never hurt before. In the two weeks since the beginning of the telethon, he hadn't felt anything this strong. It was bad. All he wanted to do was fix it. He glanced around. Every fairy godparent in the risers looked the same as he felt. He glanced toward the sandman contingent. They hadn't noticed anything. Ayosha, her long fingernails painted the same red as her knee-length wool dress, didn't even look up from her keyboard.

Alexandra, near the right end of the second row, raised her head as if scenting the air.

"We have a client. Whose is it?"

Ray concentrated, as Rose had instructed him and as he had read in the Fairy Godmothers' manual. The need string pulled hard at him, though it didn't feel precisely as if it was coming from his own heart. That meant he could help whatever child was hurting, but probably wasn't one of his own godchildren. He tried to follow the thread. In his mind's eye, the tight, red line started among the knot of kids in the spotlight and ended somewhere behind him. He looked back, but couldn't tell which of the five or six people above him it went to.

"It's me," Rose said. She reached down into the handbag on the floor next to her feet. From it, she drew her pink wand, more than two feet long and topped with a sparkling, silver-red star. "It's coming from Indigo Woodson. I wondered if she was going to need us today. Cover me, like they say in all those cop shows."

George Aldeanueva opened his hand, palm upward, and blew across it as if scattering powder on the air. Ray knew the tingling sensation of brownie points being put into operation.

As Ray watched, the floor director pulled his microphone down to his mouth and spoke into it. The mobile camera operators circling the children in their wheelchairs lowered their devices and retreated from the floor. The brilliant spotlights died away, and people began to look in every direction but toward their small group. Rose stood up and made her way down from the uppermost level of the risers. As she passed Ray, she poked him in the shoulder.

"Come with me," she said. "I could use your help."

"Sure," Ray said.

They probably didn't need the sprinkling of fairy dust, but making a wish was such a private thing, it'd be good to distract strangers' attention in another direction. Ray had noticed that Indigo, usually a bright, happy child in spite of her condition, had been looking apprehensive. Like a true grandmother, Rose went through the cluster of wheelchairs, touching one child on the shoulder, tidying up the mess on the tray of another, all without seeming to concentrate on one or another. Ray followed, feeling awkward. He was getting good at the wish stuff, but it'd be a long time before he had the same touch with people she did. He couldn't help but take their situation personally, and the last thing that a child in need wanted was someone who felt as bad as they did.

"Hi, Indigo," Rose said, kneeling down beside the little girl. Indigo Woodson had a narrow face with big, dark eyes, knife-sharp cheekbones and a thin, isosceles-triangle chin. Her hair fell in long, wavy ringlets down her thin little back. She could've worn a pair of dragonfly wings and looked completely normal in them. "Good morning, Berta." Indigo's mother gave her a brief smile that drooped back into a frown. "I was just remembering that I promised to read you chapter seven of that storybook you have. I can't wait to hear what happens next. Do you have time now?"

Indigo looked up at her with tears blurring her dark irises. She shook her head, and some of the tears overflowed onto her thin cheeks.

"My, my, what's the matter, sweetheart?" Rose asked. She glanced at Berta. "Do you want to talk about it? Trouble shared is trouble halved, you know."

"I can't," Indigo whispered. "Not here."

"Of course you can't," Rose said briskly. She smiled at Indigo. "Ray?"

Ray closed the gap in two strides and took the handles of the little girl's wheelchair. He pushed her toward the side of the stage, with Rose and Berta flanking her on either side. One of the production assistants, a mustached man in blue jeans, noticed the movement and headed them off.

"She can't leave," he said. "Where are you going?"

"To the ladies' room," Rose said. "This child needs to go right now! Shame on you for not giving them a break earlier. Little bladders can't hold out as long as yours can. Hurry up, Ray."

She prodded him in the belly. Surprised, he stepped aside. Ray needed no further urging. Indigo's need string was all but tearing him apart. He wheeled her out through the double glass doors and into the high, cinderblock corridor.

"I don't have to go," Indigo protested, as they stopped near the restrooms.

"Honey, we needed to get you out of there," Rose said. She crouched beside the girl and took her fragile hand in hers. "You have something you need to tell me, don't you?"

Berta startled. "How do you know?"

"Fairy godmother business," Rose said. "It seems like it's time Indigo had her wish. We're here to grant it."

The young mother's eyes went wide. "I thought you were just myths."

"Some of us are missuses, too," Rose replied, a twinkle in her round brown eyes. "And misters. Ray is my apprentice, but he's fast outgrowing anything I need to teach him."

Berta surveyed Ray with new respect in her eyes. Ray felt abashed under her scrutiny. He wriggled a little in his shoes.

"So, what's making you so unhappy?" Rose asked Indigo.

"My nana," the girl said. She glanced up the hall toward the studio doors. "She's very sick. I want to go see her!"

"Where does she live?"

"Near Tulsa." Indigo burst into sobs. She lowered her face to her chair tray. Her body shook with cries that tore out Ray's heart. Rose glanced at Berta. The younger woman lowered her head. She looked as though she wanted to cry, too.

"We said our goodbyes over the phone," Berta said. "It's too far away. Mama doesn't have very long."

"I want to see Nana!" Indigo wailed.

"I don't think there's time, little one," her mother said, kneeling and putting her arms around the child. "We'd have to make special arrangements. I just can't afford it. Be a strong girl. Nana would want to be proud of you. You'll see her one day in heaven."

"I want to go now!" Indigo looked even more forlorn and small when she cried. Ray dithered. He wanted to hug her, too, but he was afraid that he would break every one of her bones if he did. Rose patted him on the arm.

"Well, let's see what we can do, all right?" Rose asked. "But we want a little space to ourselves. Come on."

She pushed open the door of the ladies' room, and stopped still. A horrible smell rolled out of it. Ray gagged. His eyes and nose filled with tears. He dashed away the moisture on his face. That stench wasn't the usual unpleasant odor of a public toilet. Instead, it stank of burnt tires or acid fumes. He gulped in a breath and held it.

Inside the three-stall room, a pair of worn sneakers stuck out from the middle stall door. Someone was leaning over the toilet bowl. The deep retching sounds echoing in the room left no doubt as to what was going on.

"Vickie, are you all right?" Rose called. "Can we help you?"

The young genie pulled herself to her feet and tottered unsteadily toward them. Her face was so pale it looked green.

"Sorry," she said, with a weak smile. "I think I ate something bad. I feel so dizzy!"

Rose bustled over to take her arm.

"Come and sit down, honey."

Ray took the girl's other arm and helped her out into the hallway. Vickie slumped to the floor with her back against the wall. It had been a couple of days since he had seen her in the studio. She looked terrible. Rose reached into her purse for a tissue and wiped Vickie's mouth. Berta reached into a compartment at the rear of Indigo's wheelchair and brought out a bottle of pink indigestion medicine.

"Would this help?" she asked.

"I guess," Vickie said. She drank a tiny cupful of the thick liquid. She held her stomach for a moment and stared into space. "Yeah, I think that'll stay down."

"What have they been doing to you?" Ray demanded. "That's not food poisoning. That's bad magic. I've smelled that before. What's going on?"

"Oh, you know," the girl said, waving a hand. Ray frowned. She didn't like to speak out about the people who were mistreating her. Ayosha had warned him that Vickie thought if she ignored the situation, it would all go away. He knew it wouldn't.

"No, I don't. What are they doing to you?"

"Nothing," Vickie said, a little too quickly. "I have to do what Miss Selane says. She's my mistress. My first mistress," she corrected herself.

"Your first one?" Ray asked. "Didn't you ever grant wishes before?"

"Oh, sure," Vickie said. "For a long time. But, now there's...."

"There you are!"

The big enforcer, Tommy, burst through the double doors and bore down upon them like an approaching thunderstorm. He reached down and hauled Vickie to her feet.

"You come on back now. Miss Selane is looking for you."

"In a minute," Vickie said.

Tommy's hairless eyebrows drew down over his blunt nose. "Now." The word was full of menace.

Ray felt his temper boil over. He rose to confront the enforcer. Even though he was a little over six feet tall, he still had to crane his head back to face the massive man. He wasn't about to let pure physical size intimidate him. Not that time. He stared straight into the small, dark eyes.

"She isn't coming. She's sick. Do you want her to spread something to Miss Selane?"

For the first time, the big man looked uneasy. His cheek twitched. He glanced back over his shoulder toward the glass doors.

"She's got to come. Miss Selane needs her. She can stand a few feet away so the germs don't spread out."

Vickie clambered to her feet. She still looked shaky.

"I'll come. I've got to."

"You shouldn't," Rose said.

"I can't help it," Vickie said, unhappily. "I'm sworn to obey. I keep my vows."

Ray pulled her arm over his shoulder. "I'll help you."

"Miss Selane didn't say anyone else can be there," Tommy said, but he didn't sound as dogmatic as usual.

"Sucks to be you, bro," Ray said, not feeling a molecule of sympathy for him. "Rose, do you need me?"

Rose waved him away.

"No, thanks, honey. I've got it from here."

CHAPTER 13

Vickie's pale skin was green under the strong spotlights, but with Ray's assistance, she kept walking toward Selane's makeup station off to the side of the sound stage. The lady herself stood there in a pale green column dress like the stem of a lily. Her cloud of hair blossomed above it, framing a face more lovely than any of the Parthenon statues, but her expression was more like the illustration of the Furies Ray had seen in his mythology textbook. In one arm, she held the fluted brass lamp. She spotted Vickie and gestured with impatience, pointing at the ground beside her with one imperious finger. Tommy opened his stride to get there first. He leaned down and whispered in the star's ear. Selane nodded sharply. Ray halted the girl a good six feet away from the singer and her circle of friends and kept his arm around her. Her limp weight made Ray think she might fall down if he let go.

"Raymond, is it?" The star turned the big smile on him. Ray found it hard not to get lost in those creamy brown eyes. She had a kind of magic all her own. "You can go and sit down, honey. We're talking business."

Ray swallowed hard. He had to hold onto his resolve and face down his idol.

"I'm staying right here, ma'am," he said, resolute but polite. "Vickie needs me."

Selane stared hard at him, then appeared to make a decision.

"All right, young man," she said, waggling the finger at him. "But I am swearing you to secrecy. These people here are very important, and this is private business."

"Yes, ma'am," Ray said. He spotted a figure in red circling around behind the group of executives. Ayosha raised her eyebrows as if to ask a question. He gave a small shake of his head. No sense in both of them getting pitched out if Selane got angry. The young woman nodded and pointed back toward the risers. Ray understood. She would be there if he needed her help. A few more of Selane's security staff moved in between the little group and the rest of the studio like living walls.

"Number 51!" Nona Karburg said, triumphantly. She held her cell phone up so the others could see the pictures on the tiny screen. She flipped through them with a manicured fingernail "I told you! Right on the engine. This car doesn't exist! I told you it was magic! And it drives like a dream. Look at that baby! It can do 120 from a standing start."

"Beautiful," the young woman in the sexy dress beside them said. Ray hadn't recognized her at first, but Rose and the other older members of the FGU said she looked just like the old pictures of Rochelle Cox. The elderly producer had wished to be restored to youth. She looked amazing. Ms. Cox caught him looking her over and winked at him. He felt his cheeks burn.

"Well," Selane said to the others, "if you needed any *more* proof, there it is. I had no idea what Nona's wish was, so I couldn't set up that car if I wanted. And how about you, Corry?"

The producer grinned.

"It's working out beautiful, pretty lady. I've got singers and groups coming out of the woodwork, and they all think I am the best. 'Course, you know it's true. Can't wait to check the next one off my list. Of course, they're just the icing on the cake, after getting to work with you again."

Selane smiled, showing the dimples in her cheeks. "All right, then. Let's see who's next? Genie-girl, are you ready?"

"What is your command, my mistress?" Vickie asked, putting her hands together under her chin.

"My turn," Neil Karburg said. Selane handed him the lamp. "I know what I need for number two." He shot Ray a sharp look.

"Pretend I'm not here," Ray suggested. "What you say is none of my business."

"I appreciate your discretion," the producer said, with a nod. He didn't make threats or treat Ray like an underling. Ray felt respect for his approach. No wonder the man was a big success in Hollywood. The calm demeanor vanished, and his small brown eyes grew hard. "I wish that my ex-wife would disappear from the face of the earth, so my kids won't be affected by her drinking and drug habit, and that she'll never ask me for anything ever again, not personally, not from my business, or my life." He stared at Vickie.

"To hear is to obey, master," the genie said. She closed her eyes and bowed her head over her folded arms. Ray felt a wave of energy flow outward from the girl's body. It shook him like a mild earthquake. Almost from under their feet, the odor of burned tires rose. Selane fixed the nearest stage hand with an annoyed expression. He shrugged his shoulders in apology, then scurried toward the floor manager.

"How do I check that it worked?" Karburg asked Vickie. "That she'll leave me alone from now on?"

"I dunno," the girl said. She seemed listless, lacking in the friendly energy that Ray had been accustomed to seeing "It's hard to prove a negative. But you made the wish, so it came true."

"Huh? Well, good." Karburg seemed about to say something else, but handed the lamp back to Selane. Immediately, Corry N. reached out for it.

"Here we go. We're moving into awards season, and I want my piece. Lemme see, how should I word it, 'cause I don't want to win just this year. I want at least five Grammys every year until I stop making albums. Got that, genie-girl?"

Vickie nodded and closed her eyes. The magical force ran through them all again. Rochelle wiggled with pleasure at the sensation, such a sexy move that Ray felt even more uncomfortable being in the middle of a private conference. He knew magic felt good. He had just never seen someone enjoy it that much. Corry N. laughed and patted Rochelle on the rear end. She tossed her hair and grinned at him.

"Will someone make that stink stop?" Selane demanded, raising her voice so it could be heard over the music. Dennis touched her on the arm.

"I'll take care of it, love."

"Excuse me, Miss Selane," Vickie said humbly. "Is that it? I really need to sit down."

Selane flicked her fingers in a dismissive wave. Ray looked around for a place they could rest. Rose and Alexandra beckoned to them to join them in the risers. Rose patted the two empty seats beside her. Ayosha nodded at him from the other side. She would want to hear what was going on.

Ray helped Vickie toward the stands. The enforcers made way for them, then shepherded them all the way back. Vickie seemed even weaker than she had when he brought her back into the studio. Ray had to hold onto her to keep her from stumbling every other step. He couldn't say exactly how, but she looked diminished after making two wishes in a row. The bad smell was undeniable. He couldn't understand why. Genies were supposed to grant wishes. So what was wrong with the situation? The wishes the producers made were self-indulgent and a little spiteful, but magic could bring out the worst in people.

"Are you all right, honey?" Rose asked, helping Vickie into the chair. She wrenched the lid off a bottle of water and handed it to the girl.

Vickie nodded around the spout of the bottle. She emptied the entire pint in a few gulps and sat back with a sigh.

"I guess I'm just out of practice. It's been a while, you know?"

"What's going on over there?" Ayosha asked, nodding toward Selane's coterie.

"Chain-wishing," Ray said, in a low voice, putting on the earpiece attached to the console. "Those are some of the most demanding people I have ever seen! You wouldn't believe some of the stuff they asked for. I thought the kids I take care of can be greedy sometimes, but it's nothing compared with grownups with no limits."

Ayosha wrinkled her nose. The gesture made her pretty face look even more cute.

"I'm glad my clients are asleep!"

"Then how do you figure out what they need?" Ray asked. She hesitated. "I'm just curious. If it's classified or secret…"

"It's not classified," Ayosha said, with a little smile. "It's just that no one ever asks."

"If it's all right to know, I'd like to."

"Well, I can see their dreams over their heads. We all can. If I have a longtime customer, say more than a couple of weeks, I can see their dreams when I'm at home in bed. That gives me ideas to help them for the next night, or the next time they need me."

"That's pretty dope," Ray said, admiringly. "I wish we could do follow-ups with some of our kids, but it's one and done with fairy godparents."

"That's kind of why…" Ayosha shrugged and glanced over her shoulder toward the guildmaster.

"Yeah," Ray said, understanding exactly what she meant. "So, can you tell what I dream about?"

Ayosha put one hand on her hip and looked up at him through her lashes in playful challenge.

"Are you dreaming about me?"

"No!" Ray protested.

She laughed. "You're not one of my clients at the moment. I can tell you're not getting good sleep, though. How much caffeine do you drink?"

"Some coffee. A couple of Cokes. That's not too much. I sleep like a rock most of the time."

Ayosha shook her head. "Finals are coming. I know you took finals in high school, but it's different once you get to college. The outcome's more serious. This time in our life can make or break your career. Your subconscious knows that, and it has a harder time shutting off than it used to. The psychologist I work with might recommend sleep aids, but I don't. They always make me feel like I spent the night on a treadmill. I know a few vitamin supplements you can try."

"Ahem!" Wendell Pinkwater cleared his throat noisily. Ayosha bowed her head over her keyboard and went to work. The guildmaster glared at Ray.

Wendell, Ray thought defiantly.

The lights went on in Ray's console. He dashed the first button with his forefinger.

"Thank you for helping Selane's Kids. This is Ray."

He fell back into the easy routine that had been established over the last couple of weeks. Answering questions and entering information had become pretty automatic. His touch-typing had become faster. He was surprised at how quickly he could type a telephone number without looking down.

"How's Indigo?" Ray asked Rose, after the caller hung up. He scanned the group of children on the stage floor, but couldn't spot the girl or her mother. "Where is she?"

"They're on their way to see her Nana," Rose said. She sighed. "I don't know if either of them will last for long afterward, but she'll get there while her grandmother is alive. Poor little doll."

Vickie giggled suddenly. She slumped backward in her chair and stuck her legs out in front of her, waggling her sneaker-shod feet back and forth. Ray glanced down at her. He was glad to see that she looked better. Her pasty skin had regained some color. She nestled against him, putting her head on his shoulder. Ray shifted uncomfortably. He almost pushed her off, then noticed Tommy a few feet away. The big man glared at him. Ray straightened up, leaving Vickie draped against his side. The mobile camera operators were moving in, shoving the big round black lenses in everyone's faces. Ray pasted on a smile, and picked up the next call.

"Hi, this is Ray," he said. "How can I help you?"

In the background, he heard the avuncular voice of the on-air announcer telling viewers to call in and listing the rewards they would win. A brief glance at the big screens around the room informed Ray that no acts were performing just then. Instead, images of boxed sets of DVDs and CDs flashed through, interspersed with concert footage. Off on the side, Selane's makeup and wardrobe people were fussing around her, getting her ready for her next moment on camera.

"Miss Selane's got a new find," Ayosha confided, leaning in close. "I saw it a little while ago. It's a pair of bronze Chinese guardian dogs. Really pretty. Cloisonné enamel."

"Guardian dogs?"

"You know, with big curly manes and their mouths open? The male has a world orb under his foot, and the female has a puppy. You'll see when she auctions them off." She bent over the keyboard to type in a tweet about the upcoming item.

A faint phone signal burbled, capturing his attention. Ray glanced down at his console for a light, then realized the sound was coming from his own cell phone, deep in his left-hand pants pocket. He'd forgotten to silence it! He reached into his pocket for his headphones and drew one up to his free ear. Surreptitiously, he pushed the answer button on the phone, and pretended to take a donation call.

"Hello, this is Ray," he said.

"*Who is that girl?*"

Ray stopped himself just in time from asking who it was. He recognized the voice of his girlfriend, away at Howard University. She sounded completely honked off.

"Hi, Antoinette!" he said. "I was going to call you tonight at the normal time."

"I tuned in on line to see if Selane was singing, and the cameras were on all of you! Now, who is that girl?"

"I, uh," he glanced guiltily at Ayosha. "She's a sandman, Antoinette. Her name's Ayosha. Wave hi," he pleaded with the young woman. "My girlfriend's on the line."

"Oh," Ayosha said. She gave a bright smile and fluttered her fingers at the camera. "Hi, girlfriend."

"No, not her!" Antoinette barked in Ray's ear. "The one who's hanging on you! *That one!*"

Ray glanced down at Vickie. She was leaning on his chest, tapping at his shirt button with her forefinger and playing with his collar with the other. He hadn't even really noticed. He glanced up in embarrassment. The cameraman grinned at him over the eyepiece of his device.

"Antoinette, that's Selane's genie. I'm kind of… babysitting her."

Astonished silence fell on the end of the line.

"She's working for Selane?" Antoinette said at last. "But there aren't any genies left in Chicago!"

"That's right," Ray said. "She's from California. She came out of a lamp among Selane's special finds."

"You're kidding! God must really love Miss Selane. Well, if anyone deserves three wishes, it's her. Look at all the good she's doing for those kids."

"I guess," Ray said. He knew it sounded lame. He could hardly tell her in the middle of the star's own charity telethon how Selane really treated the kids. "Look, Antoinette, I got to go. I have to answer more calls."

"That's fine," she said. She sounded mollified. Ray was relieved. He hated it when his girlfriend was out of sorts. He never knew what to say. "Call me later, okay?"

"Okay. Love you."

"You, too."

Ray clicked the phone off. He reached for the console, but it went dark. He looked up. The camera operators scurried away. Tommy left, too. Ray breathed a big sigh of relief. The production assistants were shushing the crowd. Selane rose from her personal chair, and a couple of grips pushed the dolly with the big pillow forward into the spolights. Ray leaned forward to see what Chinese guardian dogs looked like.

CHAPTER 14

"Now, you know my little friend Francisco," Selane said, crouching beside the boy's wheelchair and smiling for the cameras. "He's the bravest soldier here. He is my hero, and he ought to be your hero, too. He's here to represent all the other children with Spaulding's syndrome. Tell them what a donation can do for you, Francisco."

"Well, they're working on gene therapy," the boy said, his big black eyes fixed on her. "Something that keeps our systems from leaking minerals out of our bones."

"You mean leaching, don't you?" Selane asked. Francisco nodded, falling silent.

She was going to have to get a new spokesman for the charity. Instead of looking into the camera lens, Francisco persisted in staring at her. That adoring look would have been worth a couple million dollars extra for the telethon if he'd only turned it so the people back home could see it. And why did he always have to whine at her? He knew how she hated that. Wasn't she spending special time with him?

Selane rose and turned to Celeste. That girl had star instincts. She perked herself up and beamed at the camera. Behind her, Selane heard an anguished wail. She glanced back. Francisco beat on his tray with his thin little hands. His caregiver moved in and put her arms around him. He stared at Selane as though she had betrayed him. Selane smiled thinly at him and turned away. She couldn't stay with one child the whole time. The audience needed to see everyone they were helping, not just the one boy.

She went from child to child, spotlighting them for the cameras. It was difficult, when all she could think about was what wish she ought to make next. She found it so hard to choose. Her producers – yes, that thought brought a warm glow to her heart – were already two wishes in each. Should she ask for eternal youth, too? Rochelle was absolutely loving her transformation. Ideas kept bouncing through Selane's head. She *could* have it all, if she phrased it right. Her career was about to get several of the biggest boosts ever. Those were assured. Wishes ought to be saved for the impossible. What ought to be her next request?

Somehow, she got through the rest of the day. Selane had heard her own voice extolling the virtues of the bronze dogs and congratulating the winner on his generosity. She reached way down into her soul to croon the Gratitude Lullaby. A glance at Dennis, smiling at her from off to the side of the stage, told her that she hadn't forgotten any of the people she needed to thank.

When it was over, she tottered to her chair and fell into it. Minnie knelt at her feet and eased off the sky-high Christian Louboutin heels Selane had been wearing for oh, how many hours?

"Thank God," Selane said with a sigh.

"I do, honey," the wardrobe mistress said. "You want your slippers?"

"Flats, of course," Selane said. She aimed a playful kick at Minnie. "You want me to go out of here looking like a housewife?"

The older woman went about her business, unperturbed. Selane let her head drop back on the headrest. Beatdown stood there.

"It's time to go," she said. "Is my trailer locked up?"

"Yes, Miss Selane. Everything's ready."

"Go get the genie-girl, and let's go back."

"Yes, Miss Selane."

The petite chef came bustling over with a little tray for her. The chef had gotten the hang of Selane's likes and dislikes over the previous weeks. This time, she placed two pristine white napkins on the star's bosom and lap, covering the priceless couture gown. There would be no possibility of a spill. On the white plate were three green rolls about the length of Selane's thumb.

"Those look good," Selane admitted.

"Spicy lettuce wraps," the chef said, her dimples deepening with pride. "Tilapia, ginger, pine nuts and a few shreds of Thai chili. They'll give you a little pick-me-up. Thank you for mentioning me in your song tonight."

Selane smiled. "Well, you've taken good care of me this month. I hope these won't give me such a pick-me-up that they'll put me through the ceiling." The woman looked worried. "Oh, I'm just teasing you! I'm sure they're perfect."

And they were. Selane enjoyed the crunch of the lettuce, the firm bite of the fish and the refined tang of spice that warmed her down to her belly. Despite her fears, and that ridiculous stench that seemed to have permeated the studio for the last few days, everything was going swimmingly.

"Miss Selane?" Beatdown was back. His craggy face wore a tentative look.

"What's the matter?" she asked.

"That girl won't come with me."

"What do you mean she won't?" Selane sat up. The chef lifted the tray away. "She has to do what I say!"

"That boy over there," the enforcer said, indicating the tall young man with the cross-hatch razor cuts in his hair. Raymond, Selane remembered. He was usually so respectful of her wishes. "He said he's taking her home with him. He said she needs to be away from people for a while."

How dare he? Selane thought at first, then dismissed the feeling of outrage. Everything had been going well. The fact was that she was still in control of the situation.

"Never mind," Selane said, flicking a hand. "I've got the lamp. She's got to come when I call her. Minnie, give Raymond Vickie's coat."

"Yes, honey." The wardrobe mistress bustled off. She brought the flat shoes and tucked Selane's feet into them. Then she delivered the padded down anorak to Raymond.

Selane watched as his expression went from wary to surprised. Tension eased out of his broad shoulders. He was a good man. It'd be nice for Vickie to have a boyfriend like that: considerate, not to mention handsome. One day, when her three wishes were fulfilled, Selane wouldn't need her any more, so the girl had better have someplace friendly to go. Raymond helped Vickie into the heavy jacket and waited while she zipped it up.

Corry N. came and crouched down at Selane's feet. He ran one hand up her shin, stroking her satin-smooth skin.

"You leaving now, baby? I'm coming back with you. Buy you dinner and talk about our future? I'll make a reservation with the concierge. The studio time is booked for the New Year. I'll be conducting the backup orchestra myself. It'll be like old times."

Selane squealed with delight.

"I'd just love that," she said. She held out a hand to have him help her up. "Come on. I am so ready to get out of here!"

CHAPTER 15

Selane's departure was the cue for everyone else to leave. Production assistants guided the studio audience to the exit doors, heading off any who tried to get back to ask Selane for an autograph. The big spotlights winked out, and overhead fluorescents went on, bathing the huge cinderblock room in harsh white light.

The volunteers in the stands took off their headsets and gathered their belongings. Ray peered across the stage toward Selane's catering tables. The woman chef caught his eye and beckoned to him.

"She's ready," Ray announced to the others. They bustled toward her, but Ray beat everyone else to the velvet rope.

That day, the small woman had brought a bunch of six-inch cakes with that smooth coating of icing and beautiful decorations, just like the ones on the cooking shows. On top of all the other goodies that she piled onto a disposable tray for him, she handed Ray the largest and prettiest of the cakes. Decorated with orange flowers, it had an "E" on top.

"Carrot cake," she explained. "For your grandmother."

Ray had stopped asking how she knew things about people without asking. She had to be a kitchen witch, that was for sure.

"Thank you so much, ma'am," Ayosha said, accepting a covered dish that smelled warmly of cinnamon.

"Enjoy it," the chef said, beaming.

"Do you want to come to dinner?" Ray asked. "My grand-mother said to invite you."

"Well, that's so nice!" Ayosha said, beaming. "I just can't to-night. I'm really busy. Tell her thank you and another time?"

"Sure. You're busy? Do you need me to help out?" Ray asked.

Ayosha beamed up at him.

"Not this time," she said. "Ernie Newton got a job! I'm sure what you did helped him out a bunch. I can just start him on a round of encouraging dreams so he won't fall back. See you tomorrow?"

"Yes," Ray said. "Later on. I'll be in after two. I've got chem-istry class in the morning. I can't miss any more, or I won't be prepared for the final."

"I am sure you'll do fine. Night, everyone," Ayosha said, with a smile for the other fairy godparents. She offered a more restrained farewell to the Sandman Guild officers, and flitted out. Ray carefully avoided meeting Wendell Pinkwater's eyes.

"Come on," Ray said to Vickie. "I called my grandmother. You're invited to dinner."

"Thanks," Vickie said. She frowned uneasily. "I don't know. I should probably go back to Miss Selane's hotel. I can get something to eat there."

"I insist. My grandma wants to meet you. It'll be okay. I already told Miss Selane you're coming."

"Oh, okay! If you're sure she thinks it's all right."

"It's all right." Ray gripped her arm and marched her to-ward the street door. He hoped the limousine would have left by then so he wouldn't have to deal with the enforcers again. Icy air hit him in the face when they stepped outside. As usual, Vickie seemed completely nonplussed by her surroundings. She didn't even blink at the tiny ice crystals pelting against her cheeks.

"Is she really taking care of you?" he asked. "Where have you been sleeping?"

"In Miss Selane's suite at the Four Seasons. It's pretty nice. She gave me a room. I have never slept in a bed like that before! It's huge! I mean, six people could lie in it. But after one night I went back to my lamp. I like small places better."

Ray surveyed the sidewalk ahead of them. It had been scraped clear, the snow piled on either side, leaving the pavement wet but not slushy. Vickie wouldn't have to wade through icy water in her sneakers.

"I've never been to the Four Seasons," he said. "It must be pretty nice."

"I guess," Vickie said. "The lobby is pretty. We just go right to the elevator when we go in. Sometimes they bring me food. I meditate most of the time. She plays a lot of music. It takes me to different places in my head."

Everything seemed to be a new experience for the young genie. She was interested in everything about the Chicago El, commenting on the ironwork, the screech of the train wheels, and even the rows of colorful, vinyl padded seats that faced each other over the muddy rubber aisle.

By the time they reached Ray's street, Vickie's hair was plastered down and her nose was bright pink. Ray kicked clods of gray snow off the wooden stairs at the front of his house and steered Vickie up to the door. Before he could get the key out of his pocket, the door swung open.

"Welcome!" said Grandma Eustatia. She enveloped the girl in a hug. Eustatia Green was a short, stout woman with golden-bronze eyes that were the same color as her skin. She wore her wavy silver hair combed back from an unwrinkled brow. Her advancing diabetes was making it more difficult for her to walk, but she held herself as straight as a queen. She took good care of herself, and copious numbers of brownie points from her fellow fairy godmothers helped keep the symptoms at bay, but her hard early life had set her back. Ray vowed that when he was a famous doctor/scientist, he would make breakthroughs that would reverse the symptoms as if she never even had it. She always laughed at his pronouncements. She laughed, then, her warm chuckle as welcoming as her open arms. "Come in, honey. Welcome. So, you're Vickie.

Well, come on this way. You can dry off in the powder room. Dinner's ready."

Ray's younger brother and sister were already at the table, staring intently at the ham casserole. Chanel, twelve and precocious, immediately seized on Vickie as a potentially better source of information about the telethon than Ray had proved to be.

"You have to tell me everything that Selane did today!" she pleaded, clutching Vickie's thin sleeve. "Did she sing? How many dresses did she wear?"

Grandma Eustatia smiled and scooped potatoes and greens onto Vickie's plate.

"You have to let the girl eat, Chanel. Be hospitable."

"It's okay," Vickie said, with a shy grin. "She wore two dresses today. One was a goldeny color, and the other was moss green. Her shoes were exactly the same color as the dresses."

"She must have a thousand pairs of shoes," Chanel crowed. "Oh, my God! Did she wear her pearls? She has a green pearl necklace that's like five feet long!"

Detail by detail, his little sister divined all the gossip of the day. Ray watched the girls in silence. He glanced up to see his grandmother watching him with humor brimming in her eyes. She never missed a thing.

"My daughter and son-in-law are at a play downtown for friends, Vickie," she explained to their guest. "They send their apologies for not getting to have dinner with you."

"No problem," Vickie said, scraping the last of the ham casserole onto her fork. Getting a square meal had restored her usual cheerfulness. "Maybe I can meet them later."

"You'd be welcome any time," Grandma assured her. "We're so happy you can stay with us tonight."

"My band's coming over at seven to practice," Bobby said. He wriggled, impatient to be up and gone. "Can I take snacks out to the garage?"

"Yes, you may," Grandma said. "You can do the washing up tomorrow."

He eyed the carrot cake on the side table and sent a speculative eye toward his grandmother. Skinny as he was, he could put away an astonishing amount of food.

"Can we have some of that?"

"That's for Grandma!" Ray protested. "The chef sent it specially for her."

"I think there's enough for the *seven* of us," Grandma said. "It's only fair that we save some for your parents."

"Yes, ma'am," Bobby said, crestfallen. He cut a huge chunk for himself and shot off into the kitchen as soon as he got permission to go. Ray could tell his mind was on the Face Dancers and their music, not anything his older brother was up to, especially if it had anything to do with magic. Chanel had had a brush with it, and was eager to learn more, even if she was too young to join any of the service guilds.

"Did you grant any wishes for Miss Selane?" Chanel asked, gazing in awe at Vickie as they ate their share of the cake.

"Uh, yeah, but I can't talk about that," Vickie said, with an apologetic grimace. "I have to keep her confidence."

"Oh." Chanel made a face. Having interrogated the guest to the point that there was nothing left to ask about her idol, Chanel pushed back from the table. "May I be excused, please?"

"Of course, honey," Grandma said. Chanel ran upstairs. In a moment, Ray heard Selane's music begin to drift down the stairs. Chanel had all the singer's albums.

"We can't seem to get away from her voice no matter what we do," Ray said, with a wry grin. Vickie laughed.

"So, do you like being a genie?" Grandma said. She stood up and began to stack dishes. Vickie sprang to her feet to help.

"Yes, I do," Vickie said.

"Didn't you ever think of becoming a fairy godmother instead?" Grandma handed her a towel and turned on the taps over the big stainless steel sink. She tipped the casserole dish and watched it fill up with soapsuds. "You must have a natural aptitude for listening, to be a genie."

Vickie squirmed. "Uh, well, I'm not so good with kids."

"Really? You seem to be a patient and caring girl. Why not?"

"I'm okay as a genie," Vickie insisted.

"Well, you know Ray is in the Fairy Godmothers Union. I put him up for membership." Grandma Eustatia went on in that gentle but firm way she had. "My favorite grandson, even though, you know, you're not supposed to have favorites. How old are you, child?"

Vickie shrugged. She twisted the yellow-striped towel in her hands.

"Oh, I don't know. I was fifteen a while back. Maybe sixteen by now? Seventeen? I don't keep track. Calendars are unnatural. Only the seasons of the year are real. We sow, we reap, we sing songs and wait for the sun to come again."

That sounded like old hippie stuff to Ray, but he recalled that she had been raised on a commune. Must be her parents' influence.

"No, child, I asked, how old are you? What year were you born?"

"Uh," Vickie had to think hard. "No one ever asks me that. I think it was, uh, 1953. Yeah. That's right."

"Say what?" Ray asked. That would make her...? No, his brain refused to do the addition. "How long have you been in that lamp since the last time you came out?"

"I don't know," Vickie said, squirming in her chair uneasily. "A while, I guess. Everything looks new and different every time. It's interesting, but it's scary, too.

"I can just imagine," Grandma said, passing her the clean dish to dry. "Now, you know that you can tell me anything you want to. I'd love to hear about your life before you became a genie. Ray tells me you have a sister. When was the last time you talked with her?"

"Oh, a long time ago," Vickie said. "I went away."

"Were you in school?"

The girl shook her head.

"No, school was too harsh a scene for me. So much was happening outside that I thought was more important."

"I can imagine," Grandma said. Ray could, too. She had to have been a teenager during the 1960s. From what he had seen on line, it was a weird time.

"What have you been doing since then?"

"Playing the guitar. I worked in a coffee shop. I really liked it there. The people were nice. The cook made great vegetarian food. I don't eat a lot of meat. When I do, I thank the soul of the animal for its sacrifice."

"So do I," Grandma said. "How nice that we have something so spiritual in common. Do you ever go to church?"

Vickie's eyes widened until Ray could see the whites all around the irises. "Uh, no."

"You should. Come with me some time. It would give you some helpful perspective on what life is like. Sounds like you could use some bearings so you can branch out and see what else is going on out there."

"Uh, I dunno. I don't think I can now." Vickie looked as though she was about to say something, then stopped. She concentrated hard on the dishes she was drying.

Grandma met Ray's eyes and nodded significantly. Ray backed out of the kitchen.

"I got to make a call," he said. "I'll be right back."

"Good boy," Grandma Eustatia said.

Ray let the kitchen door swing closed behind him. He heard his grandmother's soft voice rising in a questioning tone, and Vickie's brief replies. He couldn't understand what they were saying.

He walked slowly into the living room, thinking hard. It was hard to process what he had just heard. She must have been hiding in her lamp for decades! And she sure wasn't ready for the reality around her.

Ray settled into his dad's man-chair, and turned on the television so he could be certain he wasn't overheard. He fished his cell phone out of his pocket and hit the first key on the speed-dial. After three rings, his best friend's deep baritone answered.

"Hey, man! How's it all going?" Loud hip-hop music blared in the background.

"Hey, Hakeem, you where you can talk?"

"Yeah, I can talk. Gimme a sec." Ray watched the dining room to make sure Vickie wasn't coming out looking for him. After a few seconds, the noise in his ear lessened, and a door slammed close to the receiver. "Ok, that's better. What's up? I got to get back to Dannie pretty soon."

"Look, you were a genie...?" Ray began. Hakeem interrupted him, sounding pained.

"For about five minutes, Ray! Okay, it was longer than that. But, yeah."

"Did your guildmaster, that Froister dude, ever make you grant wishes for more than one person at a time?"

"Like, *no*," Hakeem said, scornfully. "You think those guys ever loosened the leashes on us? If I ever wanted to know what it was like to be a dog, I never have to wonder again. Sometimes I wake up and check my wrists to make sure the bracelets are gone for good. I'll leave the magicking to you and your Miss Rose and those other guys."

Ray shot a guilty look at the heap of textbooks sitting on the bench of his mother's upright piano.

"They give you a manual or anything?" he asked. "A rule-book? Anything to tell you what you're supposed to do or not do?"

"Are you yanking on my chain, bro? They told us what they wanted us to know. It was bad enough. How come you asking? You sound like you got a reason."

"This little girl who came around the studio...."

"Oh, yeah! You and Miss Selane! How's that cooking? She notice what a fine specimen of a man you are yet? You can tell her you have a friend who's just as good looking."

"Shut up, *Darrell*," Ray said. That was Hakeem's real name, and invoking it made his friend realize that Ray wasn't horsing around.

"What's the story, man?"

"This little girl I met is a genie. She is at the far end of clueless." Ray hesitated and glanced up the stairs. That was something he did not want Chanel to overhear. The banging and twanging coming from the back yard meant there was no danger of Bobby hearing it, either. "Look, you can't tell anyone else what I'm telling you."

"No problem, Ray," Hakeem said. "Cross my heart. Ex-genie's honor."

"Miss Selane owns the lamp, but she's been kind of lending it out to other people before she's finished with her three wishes. And they aren't finishing up with their wishes, either. I think maybe there's six or eight of them. I'm smelling bad magic, even though the wishes sound ordinary to me. It feels bad, too, like something's mounting up, like a volcano getting ready to explode. The girl doesn't seem to know if it's allowed or not. Did they ever pile up wishers on you? Is that normal?"

"Huh! Well, I can tell you that those guys didn't give a sack of crap for our welfare, man. If they didn't wish on us like that, there had to be a reason. Your genie doesn't know?"

"She doesn't seem to know anything," Ray said. "She doesn't want to know anything, and I don't know how to find out."

"Can't help you there," Hakeem said, with genuine regret. "Froister and all the other real genies disappeared after that one night, you know. The other guys, the gangbangers, they don't talk to me no more. They don't hassle me, which is just fine, let me tell you. They all want to pretend it never happened. But none of the real genies tried that on us. It was kind of sequential. When Froister used up my three wishes, he handed my lamp over to one of his subordinates, the red-headed guy. And they really didn't care what they did to us. So, yeah, if they didn't pass us around, they knew something would probably happen. Wish I could tell you what, but I'm not going back in there again ever to find out. One thing I did learn is that what you don't know can still kill you. Good luck with that little girl."

"Thanks, man," Ray said.

"No charge. Gotta go. Watch out for that volcano, brother. I don't want anything to happen to you."

"Me, either," Ray said. He pushed the END CALL button and stared at the phone.

He stood up, filled with resolve. If Vickie couldn't look after herself, he would have to help her until she could.

When he returned to the kitchen, he found Grandma sitting at the small round table near the window, her arm around Vickie. Maybe the girl no longer qualified for the full fairy godmother routine, but Grandma was surely doing her some good. No one could break down barriers like his grandmother.

"Now, you can come and talk to me any time," Eustatia Green was saying. "I won't mind. I don't sleep a lot any more, heaven knows, so if it's the middle of the night, that's all right."

Vickie gazed at her with worship in her eyes. "I will. Thanks a bunch."

"It's my pleasure," Grandma said. "Now, I think Chanel's made up a bed for you in her room. You've had quite a day. I am sure you'd like to rest. Ray, would you like to take her up there?"

"Yes, ma'am," Ray said. He offered a hand to Vickie. She stood up.

"Thanks," she said, "but I'm not sure."

"Of what?" Ray asked.

Vickie opened her mouth to reply, but she vanished suddenly in a puff of dun-colored smoke. Ray reached out and waved his hand through the thin air.

"That wasn't her, was it?" Grandma Eustatia asked. "She didn't just run away on us?"

"No, ma'am, it wasn't," Ray said. He felt resentment rise up in him like high tide. "Miss Selane must want to wish on her again."

"Poor thing," Grandma said. She patted the vacant chair beside her. He sat down. She set a plump hand on his knee. "Ray, what do you know about her life?"

"Not a lot. You got more out of her tonight than she's said in the whole time I've known her."

"She's unhappy. It doesn't take much to see that."

"It's from being a genie," Ray said.

"That's just a symptom of the disease, honey." Grandma's kindly eyes were wreathed in sorrow. "She's let others do the ordering of her life, and she doesn't know what to do."

"She never says no, even when she knows what people are doing is wrong," Ray said in frustration. "Why doesn't she stick up for herself?"

The hand patted his knee.

"She had her soul taken away from her, dearest."

"How? Is that some genie thing?"

"No, Ray, she got raped."

Ray was aghast.

"She did? How come she couldn't magic herself away?"

"One of her masters did it." Eustatia Green shook her head. "Her sister's man. A long time ago. A long, long time ago. That's why I don't like guilds that don't have a proper apprenticeship program. You don't learn how to extricate yourself from a bad situation. You don't feel like you have anyone at your back."

Ray knew that there had to be some important reason Vickie shied away from talking about herself. Ayosha had been right about how deep it went. A hole opened in the pit of his stomach. Once again, he was grateful for the way that the Fairy Godmothers Union looked after him. It protected him from the mistakes that he could have made, and the advantage others could have taken of him while he was vulnerable. In fact, it gave him strength to spare.

"Well, I'm at her back," Ray said. He stood up. "Will you excuse me, please? I've got to go."

Grandma smiled up at him.

"Of course you do, honey. Call me if you need me."

"I hope I won't."

Ray grabbed his coat and ran out into the night. It was snowing again, big heavy flakes that landed on his shoulders like lead weights. From his pocket, he drew the midnight blue wand. The silver star twinkled at him as though listening.

"All right, magic," he said. "I need a lift to the Four Seasons. It's, uh, it's fairy godparent business." He swung the wand wide, trying to body-English himself into the sky. A thin veil of blue exuded from the star, then twinkled to Earth in sparkles that extinguished themselves before they hit the gray snow. Ray shook the wand. "Oh, come on, magic! I got to get there! Vickie needs me!"

The magic wasn't buying the excuse. Vickie was decades out of date to get a wish. He summoned up the four brownie points he had been holding onto. They jumped up and down, eager to serve, but couldn't provide him with enough oomph to fly. Fairy godparents often got a boost of luck when they needed it, but there was no useful lift into the air, no sudden taxi with a broken meter slowing down in front of him on the darkened street. Hakeem had a car. Ray tried his number, but it went straight to voice mail.

Time was running away from him. He was afraid that Vickie was being forced to add to the bad magic that was amassing. Maybe he could persuade Miss Selane not to make any more wishes.

Ray ran back into the house and looked up the Four Seasons on his computer and tapped that in, too. He phoned the number, then hit the END CALL button in frustration.

"What's the trouble, baby?" Grandma Eustatia stumped into the living room.

"That had to be Miss Selane pulling her back," Ray said. "I called the hotel switchboard, but they won't put me through. They won't even admit she's staying there!"

"Well, would you?" Grandma asked, reasonably.

"I've got to get down there!" Ray said, frustrated enough to want to kick something. "They treat her like a toy. She's no more to them than a slave. That's why I hate the whole idea of genies."

Grandma took his arm.

"I understand. The vast and almighty power looks good to you, until you realize that none of it's yours. But that girl seems happy being a genie and having people tell her what to do. She needs family, but the good Lord only knows where they are after all this time. She got away from them on purpose, Ray."

"I thought so. So did Ayosha, the sandman I met? She's a psychology major. She said Vickie had undergone a major trauma. Now, I know what."

Grandma nodded.

"I saw you two on the television. Ayosha is lovely as well as smart."

Ray hardly heard it.

"Look, I have to get down there and get Vickie back here. God knows what they'll do to her. I can tell that it's killing her having to grant too many wishes out of sequence."

"It's all wrong, surely. Wait until Sharon gets home, and you can take the car."

Now Ray did kick the sofa. Grandma clicked her tongue in disapproval.

"I can't wait that long!" he said. "Mom and Dad will be so late. If I hammer on Miss Selane's door in the middle of the night, they'll probably call the cops. And I have class tomorrow morning." Ray felt dismay. "I'd better take the El." He calculated. The Howard El red line would dump him off at Chicago Avenue. It would be a cold, icy slog north to the hotel. It would take *forever*.

"We can do better than that." Grandma reached for the phone on the end table next to the maligned sofa. She hit one of the speed-dial buttons. "George? Eustatia Green. I am so sorry to disturb you at this hour, but we've got a little bit of a crisis."

"No, Grandma!" Ray said, alarmed.

"But what is the union for, except to help its members?" Grandma said, reasonably. "He'll pick you up in a little while. You just sit here with me and let's work out what you can do, all right?"

CHAPTER 16

The puff of smoke containing Vickie appeared in the middle of the biggest argument that Selane had ever had with anyone. Selane huddled into her favorite chair, clutching the lamp to her like a talisman. For once, even Rochelle hadn't had the heart to steal the throne from her. She sat on one of the other wing chairs, pulled close to Selane's with one hand protectively on the star's knee.

Neil Karburg paced back and forth across the white carpet, as he had been for over an hour. When Vickie arrived, he wheeled and grabbed the girl by the arms. He shook her, making her untidy brown hair toss like straw.

"Where's my wife?" he demanded.

The thin little teen looked bewildered.

"I don't know. Why do you think I know?"

"Louanne's disappeared!" Neil exclaimed. He flung her away from him and went back to pacing. Vickie tripped backward and sat down on the carpet. Dennis strode over and helped her up. "The kids have been calling me, frantic. My daughter and her husband went to her condo, but Lou's gone. Her phone's on the table. Her car's in the garage. The police think *I* had something to do with it."

"Well, you did," Vickie said. "You wished her off the face of the Earth."

"Don't you say that!" Neil bellowed. "Don't you dare say that!"

"But it's true," the genie said in a tiny voice.

"Just like that?" Nona asked. She was across from Selane on an ottoman with her hands clasped together so hard the knuckles were white. Her face was as pale as Neil's was red. "Did you murder her?"

"No," Vickie murmured. She wrapped her arms around herself. "I just granted the wish. I told you the powers are pretty literal."

Dennis bolted down another tumbler of scotch in one gulp.

"This is terrible. Neil, you should have been thinking more clearly."

Karburg threw his head back.

"I can't! Where she's concerned, my brain goes right out of the window. She makes me crazy. She always did. She can't be gone forever!" He loomed over Vickie. "Take the wish back!"

The genie took a step backward, looking for someplace to hide.

"I can't do that." Her small face brightened as a thought struck her. "You have one wish left. You can use it to undo the wish you made."

Neil goggled like a fish. He stopped dead and clenched his fists.

"I... no! I had plans for the third wish. Big plans!"

"Don't be ridiculous, Neil," Dennis said, in irritation. He flipped a hand over. "If that's the only way to bring her back, you have to do it!"

Neil turned and aimed an angry forefinger at Selane's assistant.

"Don't you tell me what to do, Dennis! Are you going to get me a make-up wish?"

"I'm not the one who wanted his ex-wife out of existence!"

Neil went back to pacing. "Oh, that woman! She always ruined my life! I don't know why I ever married her!"

"You used to love her, Neil," Rochelle said. "You and Louanne were a great couple for a long time."

"Wish her back, Neil," Nona said, wringing her hands. "I feel something terrible will happen unless you do."

Selane couldn't bring herself to say anything. She felt as guilty as if she had done the murder herself.

"Maybe she's not dead," Neil said. "Maybe she just went into hiding to make my life miserable." He shot a nervous glance at Vickie. "Are they going to find a body? Will they think I did it?"

Vickie shook her head.

"You wished her off the face of the Earth, so I don't think so."

"The police want you back in L.A., Neil," Dennis said. "You'll have to go. It'll be no problem. You have an airtight alibi. All of us were with you all day, except when Selane and Corry went to dinner. We have dozens of witnesses."

"I'm not going to tell the cops about the wishes," Neil said. "Nobody had better mention a genie." His eyes flashed. Dennis shook his head to reassure him.

"No, of course not. What we talked about is none of their business. Even that."

"But my kids! They love her! My daughter Callista was crying when she called me. The boys have been calling everybody we ever knew to find out if they heard from her. Maybe she was kidnapped!"

"Who would kidnap her?" Rochelle said, reasonably. "She's your *ex*-wife. If I know you, you didn't give her that much maintenance in the divorce decree. She's not worth a ransom demand."

Neil's mouth worked, and he met no one's eyes. Selane knew perfectly well Rochelle was right. He couldn't deny it. Dennis waved his scotch glass.

"Go home, Neil. It could be just as you say it is. She took off, leaving behind anything that would lead you back to her. Hire a fleet of private detectives. If she…" Dennis swallowed heavily. "…If she still exists, then they'll find her. She's just not that imaginative. She's probably at a spa out in the desert. She's lying in a procedure room with her hair in a towel and cucumber slices on her eyes." He didn't look as though he believed it any more than Selane did. "Find her. Then you won't have to waste a wish. Go."

The big producer dithered, looking from one face to another. Selane gave him her most sympathetic expression. She really felt for him. She'd been her own worst enemy enough times to know when someone had painted themselves into a corner they couldn't escape from. She thought of those children who had lost their mother, and felt tears come to her eyes. Neil shrugged.

"Well, maybe."

The door of the suite slammed open, and shrieking voices erupted in the hallway. Selane started up in alarm. Dennis waved a hand at her to stay where she was. Tommy and Beatdown slipped out of the room, reaching into their jackets for their guns.

Nona looked past Selane at Vickie.

"Did it hurt? When she disappeared?"

"Probably not," Vickie said. "I don't know. But when I disappear, it doesn't hurt."

Nona nodded. The reassurance seemed to calm her a little, but not Neil. He just couldn't stay still.

Selane heard frantic female voices in the private foyer. Tommy only had to raise his voice a little. The others quieted down. The door clicked shut on silence. Beatdown came into the room with Corry N. in tow.

Selane stared at him in horror. When they had parted a couple of hours ago after dinner, he had looked as dapper and cool as he always did. His clothes were disheveled. One shoulder of his almost priceless gray Armani cashmere coat was torn, and the left side of his face was scratched from the bottom of his sunglasses to his chin. The worst part was the haunted look in his eyes. Dennis helped him off with the coat and handed him a handkerchief to stem the bleeding.

"What happened to you?" Selane asked.

Corry patted at his cheek. "I went down to listen to a singer at Howl at the Moon piano bar. She was spectacular! Voice like a 1940s lounge singer, and a body like the Venus de Milo.

We were talking plans for the future, getting a little cozy, when another lady I had scouted out last night came in. She jumped Miss Lounge Singer like she was a cage wrestler! Attacked her right in front of everyone in the bar. Then the sister act I talked to yesterday turned up, and they all got into it. They were fighting over me!"

"I can't see you objecting to that," Rochelle said dryly, her eyes half-lidded. "In fact, I would have bet on you taking them all home."

The whites of Corry's eyes showed around his dark irises.

"No, man, it was scary! They wanted to kill each other. It was like something out of *Highlander*, where only one can survive. I tried to get out of there. I got into a taxi, and they piled in on top of me. I just barely made it out of the elevator to your door. If it wasn't for your dudes here, they might have torn me into little pieces. Why were they acting like that? Is everyone in this town high on meth?"

"It's probably your wish," Neil said, with a bitter laugh. "The magic doesn't seem to be working out for any of us."

"It's terrifying," Nona agreed.

"I warned you," Vickie said.

"Shut up," Neil growled at her.

"Don't talk to her that way," Rochelle said. "She *did* warn you. You had to word your wishes exactly the way you wanted them to work. She said the magic is absolutely literal. I can't remember exactly what you said, Corry, but I bet you wished that you had singers crawling all over you."

Corry looked astonished and horrified.

"You telling me I made my own stalkers?" he demanded. "Damn!"

"I have to go and be with my daughter and sons," Neil said. He pounded a fist against the wall. "This can't be happening. I bet Lou just flitted off to the Caribbean with one of her toy boys."

Dennis took his tiny phone out of his jacket pocket. "I'll make arrangements for you straight away, Neil. I will call a charter company I use. They fly out of Chicago Executive Airport about forty minutes north of here." He made a face. "I can't get you a helicopter, but I can call you a limousine. You can be on your way in less than an hour."

"Forget that," Nona said, standing up. "I'll get us to the airport in twenty-five minutes. I have the fastest car in the state. Number 51, remember? Tommy, call the valet and have them bring it down."

"Yes, Ms. Karburg," the enforcer said. He picked up the house phone.

"I'm coming with you," Rochelle said. She squeezed Selane's knee and let go. "I can help. I have five dozen private detectives in my files. If Louanne is anywhere at all, we'll find her."

"Is there room on that plane for me, too?" Corry asked, plaintively. "I got to get out of this town."

"Corry!" Selane exclaimed, seeing the promised recording session vanishing. He must have understood exactly what she was thinking. He came over to take her hand and wrap an arm around her.

"It's okay, baby. I just made Chicago a little too hot for me."

She searched his face for reassurance. "Well, all right, as long as you come back."

"Count on it, Selane," Corry said. He ran a knuckle down her cheek. "I've got a bunch of thinking to do. I'll come on out when the appeal is over, and we'll make beautiful music together. It'll be a crystal-clear joy to hear you sing again."

"All right," Dennis said, clicking his phone off. "The pilots will have a jet fueled up and waiting for you in forty minutes. Come on, I'll walk you downstairs."

Selane followed them into the foyer, clutching the lamp in her arms. Tommy helped them all into their coats and scarves. Feeling sick to her heart, she kissed each of them goodbye. The door closed behind them, leaving the huge suite deserted, except for Selane.

And Vickie. The girl stood in the middle of the sitting room, looking as clueless and lost as ever. Compared with the luxury of the furnishings, she was still a pathetic little rag-bag. Her bare ankles showed in between her harem pants and those ill-fitting sneakers. Selane realized immediately that something was missing.

"Where's your coat, genie-girl? Did you lose it?"

"It's back at Ray's house," Vickie said, apologetically. "We were having dinner."

Selane felt more remorse added to the bellyful she was already carrying. "I'm sorry, Vickie. I can call for something from room service for you. I didn't want to add to anyone's troubles. I thought you could just undo the wish for Neil."

Vickie dipped her head.

"No. I'm really sorry. It doesn't work that way. I never had so many masters at the same time, but I know you can't take back a wish."

"Clueless little thing," Selane said, torn between affection and annoyance. She sat down in her throne chair. The day had been so successful up until then. She had the world at her feet. She felt sorry for Neil, but she was sorry for herself, too. All that magic, and it still didn't help undo what she had done to her career. All her dreams were dashed again.

Tears welled up in her eyes and spilled onto her cheeks. She dashed them away, but more came. Vickie reached into the air and came out with a big white handkerchief. She handed it to Selane, who buried her face in it. She sobbed, the cries coming from the very bottom of her soul.

"I… I don't want anyone to see me this way!" she said.

"Should I go?" Vickie asked. "Back in my lamp?"

"Yes! No!" Selane couldn't make up her mind. She felt a weight settle on the arm of her chair. Vickie put her arm around her and stroked her hair with the gentlest touch. Selane froze. Normally, she would go off like a rocket if anyone touched her hair, but it was so incredibly soothing. She needed that comfort. The tears came again, bursting out of her in huge, racking sobs. Selane cried until she was exhausted and the white cloth was sodden with tears and mascara. Vickie sat beside her, humming a soft tune and running her hand gently over Selane's neck and shoulders.

"You know I never want to hurt anyone," Selane said at last.

"I know."

"I want things because I didn't have them, but I don't want to take them away from other people. I'd never wish anybody dead!"

"You didn't," Vickie said. Selane felt herself calming down a little.

"Can I get Louanne back with one of my wishes?"

"No," Vickie said. "Mr. Karburg has to do it himself. He's lucky he didn't make the third wish yet. It can still work out okay. He just has to think about it some more."

The gentle stroking was beginning to ease Selane's heartache. She relaxed against her cushions, staring at the orange and blue flames dancing in the fireplace.

"You're half my age and you're acting like my mama," Selane said. The irony wasn't lost on her.

Vickie smiled. "I had a baby. My little boy." Her face went blank. Selane stared at her.

"You? You had to be awful young, just a baby yourself. Something happen to him?"

"My sister took him away from me. I guess it was the best. Having a genie for a mom….? Maybe not so good."

"Is that what they told you?" Selane asked.

The girl shrugged. She was never eloquent at the best of times. Her body language spoke more than her tongue. She went back to gently running her hand over Selane's hair. The unconditional affection let Selane relax for once. The girl didn't want anything from her. She wasn't asking for favors. She wasn't being kind for the headlines or the blogs. She was just showing human decency.

A baby. Thoughts of a long-lost warmth in Selane's arms made her squeeze her eyes shut tightly over sudden tears.

"I had a baby, too," Selane said. Her voice broke. "I lost her."

"I'm so sorry," Vickie said. She hugged Selane.

"That's water under the bridge," Selane said, struggling to regain her composure. Vickie tightened her arm around the older woman's shoulders. The two of them sat together for a while. Maybe they were kindred spirits after all.

All too soon, she heard noise at the suite door. Dennis burst back in, followed by Beatdown. Selane stood up suddenly, unwilling to look vulnerable to anyone else. Vickie didn't seem to mind. She never did.

"Neil's on his way. What the hell happened, Vickie? What went wrong?"

"The wish," Vickie said simply. "He was too angry when he made it."

"Well, why didn't you stop him?"

"I'm a genie. I can't tell him not to, if he says that what he wants. I have to do what the master of the lamp wants. He has the power to decide, not me."

"Too much power," Selane said suddenly. She felt as she was sitting on a powder keg, ready to blow. "Dennis, I feel so guilty!"

Dennis ran his hands through his floppy blond hair.

"You gave him what he wanted, Selane. It's not your fault."

"But it is! I made it possible for him to get that wish."

"He can unwish it when he gets his mind back," Dennis said. "Unless she just went off like he thinks she did."

Another knock sounded at the door. A calm voice called from the hallway.

"Miss Selane, I'm the night manager. May I speak to you a moment?"

"I'll get it," Dennis said.

He returned in a moment, not with a man in a suit, but the youth from the television station. Selane peered at him.

"Oh, it's you. Raymond, isn't it?"

"Yes, Miss Selane," he said. "I had to ask the manager to bring me up here. I had to see you."

"In the middle of the night? Well, what can I do for you?" she asked.

"Vickie was going to stay at my house," Raymond said. "I came to get her back. I've got a friend waiting downstairs to drive us home. My grandma is waiting. They were talking when she… disappeared." He held up a shopping bag. "I brought her coat."

Selane almost smiled. God bless him, he wasn't afraid of her at all! He saw her as a dragon to slay on behalf of the damsel in distress. Well, thank the good Lord that he didn't freak on out over magic.

"What are you, then? You're not a genie, are you?"

"No, ma'am. I'm a fairy godfather." From his coat pocket, the young man drew a long blue wand that could not possibly have fit in there in a normal way. "So's Grandma Eustatia. She's a fairy godmother, I mean. She got me into the union."

"Wish I had a fairy godfather," Selane said thoughtfully. "I could use one about now."

"I'm sorry, Miss Selane," he said, as kindly as he could. "We can only grant wishes to kids who are under twenty-one."

"Too bad," Selane said, with a sigh. "I'm sorry, Raymond, but I don't want her to leave. I've had a bad night."

Raymond crossed his arms.

"Then, I'm staying, too."

Dennis peered at him.

"Just who the hell do you think you are?"

Raymond's eyes grew wary, but he held his ground.

"Nobody special. I'm just looking after Vickie because she's not too good at looking after herself."

"She's my genie! She has to grant wishes for me when I ask her to!" Selane said. "I don't have to explain myself to you."

"No, ma'am," Raymond said. He had good manners. She could tell he was holding back an outburst. "You can ask her for wishes, but you don't have to run her ragged. She won't say no. She hasn't yet. But you have to treat her like a person."

"I always treat her like a person! Don't I, Vickie?"

"Yes, Miss Selane," Vickie said. Raymond groaned and shook his head.

Dennis's phone rang. He snatched it out of his pocket and turned his back on them.

"Hello? Yes, captain, Mr. Karburg has departed. He ought to be landing at LAX in about four hours. No, I'm sorry, I don't know anything about Mrs. Karburg's whereabouts. I haven't seen her myself in, oh, three years. No, nor has Miss Selane.

You have to understand how *busy* she...." He drifted away into one of the other rooms.

Selane eyed the young man. She couldn't throw him out without looking like a monster. What harm would it do to have him sitting with Vickie? She assumed he probably meant to sleep with her, but Selane had ruined his plans. At least, that's what she would have done in his place.

"Well, you're my guest now. May I offer you a drink or something?" Selane asked.

"Not at the moment, ma'am. Thank you.... May I sit down?"

"Surely you may. Where are my manners?" She plumped herself into the cushions on her throne and gestured grandly at the deep white chairs opposite. Raymond waited until Vickie was sitting down, then took a seat himself.

"Excuse me," Raymond said, taking an elderly cell phone out of his pocket. "I have to tell my ride I'm not coming down. Is that all right?"

"Of course," Selane said. The boy tapped a couple of keys.

Dennis returned, tucking his own phone into his pocket. "I have talked to the police detective in charge of the case, Lieutenant Grant. They're acting on the suspicion that Neil had something to do with Lou's disappearance. I pointed out that the alimony he is paying is so small a proportion of his wealth that it's less than he contributes to charity every year, including, I might add, the Spaulding's Syndrome Appeal. I made it clear that he had parted company with Louanne permanently because of her infidelity, and did not go out of his way to interact with her. I left it at that. I hope Neil can calm down on his way to L.A. He won't be very convincing if all he can do is bellow. I believe that the lieutenant found me credible. I shouldn't have to make a formal statement."

"He doesn't want to talk with me, does he?" Selane asked.

"Not as a suspect or a witness," Dennis said. A hint of a smile curled the corner of his mouth and crinkled his eyes. "More of a fan."

"I can handle that," Selane said, sitting back with a sigh. "I hope Lou turns up safe and sound."

CHAPTER 17

Ray perched in the white upholstered chair. He couldn't help but feel intimidated by the mere surroundings. Miss Selane's suite must be worth more than his parents' whole house. It was like a pretty slipcover, though. The fancy carpet and expensive furnishings just barely concealed a quivering mass of power like an atomic pile. He had felt it the moment he had come into the room. Magic had been done here, plenty of it, including in the very chair in which he sat. Magic in and of itself wasn't bad. He knew that from the manual, as well as his own experience. It was how it was handled and what was done with it that caused the problems.

The bad smell that had overpowered them all in the studio was present here, too, although air freshener and perfume had been sprayed to try and bring it down to a manageable level. Ray felt as though it was choking him and stinging his eyes. He put his hand into his coat pocket and touched the star of his wand. The cool presence of the good magic that it had done helped him feel as if he had a protector. The sparks in his mental bank account were on the subdued side. He couldn't blame them. It wasn't that the overwhelming magic felt evil, exactly. It was more… warped and twisted, and there was far too much of it.

He wondered if Selane and Mr. Dennis were aware of the mass of power. He couldn't think of how he could bring up the subject without making it sound too weird. They accepted that fairy godparents and genies existed. How could he explain to them that magic had to be handled responsibly? They had to finish wishing on Vickie's lamp, or who knew what would happen?

"Is there some way to check whether Louanne was made to disappear by dint of Neil's wish, or if it just put an idea in her mind to go away?" Dennis asked. He nibbled on a fingernail.

"I don't know," Selane said. The star looked worried. She kept glancing at Ray and Vickie, maybe hoping for some reassurance. She held the lamp tightly to her chest and squeezed her eyes shut. "I wish…" Vickie came to crouch at her feet. Ray sat forward, waiting. Selane opened her eyes again. "… No." She put the lamp in her lap.

Ray coughed. The magic was still building. It filled the air like smoke. Everyone in the whole hotel could probably smell it by then. It could blow up all of Michigan Avenue! He reached for his wand and held onto it. He could do something, but what? He dealt with little wishes for children. He was never trained to deal with a mass of energy like that. He felt as though he wanted to grab Vickie by the hand and run away

Suddenly, the power was gone.

Ray fell back in the big white chair as if someone had removed his bones. What a relief!

Selane must have felt it, too. She turned on the megawatt power smile and aimed it at Ray.

"Well, maybe I was wrong, Raymond. If you want to take Vickie back with you tonight, it shouldn't be a problem. I'll treat you to a taxi. You'll make sure to get her there in the morning? I could always rub the lamp, but you are right. I need to treat her like a person."

Ray glanced at his watch. It was almost two A.M. He could still get a few hours' sleep before dropping Vickie at the studio and head up to Northwestern in time for class.

"Yes, Miss Selane."

The star turned to her assistant.

"Dennis, will you see to it?"

"Of course, my darling," the Englishman said. He went to pick up the house phone. Dennis's cell phone rang. He took it out of his pocket.

"Police? I just finished speaking with you. No." His face screwed up into a grimace. "Illinois State Police? What does that have to do with…? No. Um. I see." He listened for a long time without speaking.

The skin of his face drew in, outlining the bones. Dennis suddenly seemed old. Selane stared at him.

"What happened?" she asked.

"That was a state trooper. There's been a car accident. Nona dodged a lorry on the motorway, and rammed into a concrete barrier. None of them were wearing seat belts."

Selane bounded to her feet, setting the lamp on a marble end table. "How bad is it? What hospital are they going to?"

Dennis strode over and held both her hands in his.

"Neil is going to the hospital, darling. We can see him there. Nona and Rochelle are dead."

"Dead?" Selane wailed. "What about Corry?"

"Not in the car," Dennis said. "The trooper didn't mention him. I don't know where he is. They're searching the roadway for him." He didn't say, 'for his body,' but Ray could hear it implied in his voice.

The star's eyes were wide with horror.

"I did this. It's because of the magic. I'm responsible! Oh, my God!"

Ray stood up.

"I should leave, Miss Selane."

She turned desperate eyes on him.

"No, please!" she said. "Don't go. For God's own mercy, please don't leave me."

"Yes, ma'am." He thought hard. "Should I call Pastor Barnes? He leads my grandmother's congregation. He's a good man."

"No! I don't want anyone else who doesn't know already," Selane said quickly. "There's going to be questions. Lots of questions." Her fingers ground together as if they were trying to destroy one another. Vickie came over to hug her. The two women clung together.

Ray woke up the brownie points. They seemed to have recovered a little from their stupor. *Can you do anything for her?* he asked silently. A couple of them seemed to shrug, and vanished from his mental piggy bank.

The police arrived shortly, two burly men and an equally burly woman. Selane received them like a queen condemned to the gallows. She answered their questions patiently, and signed a few autographs along with the police report. Dennis departed with them to make the identifications at the morgue.

Ray called home to let his folks know he wasn't coming back that night. His mother picked up the phone. While she wasn't a fairy godparent herself, she had lived among them all her life.

"You do what you have to do," Sharon Crandall said. "I'm glad you're there."

Ray hung up. He might be there, but there was little he could do. As the dark hours wound on, he grew more and more sluggish for lack of sleep. Selane tried to make small talk, but little of what she said made sense. She couldn't alight anywhere for long. She fretted out loud. She was always crying. It was the first time Ray had ever seen her with her makeup in such a mess. He felt terribly sorry for her, but he also worried about his chemistry class. He was bound to miss it now. He couldn't flunk out of college, not when so many people had made sacrifices to get him there! Ray didn't know what to do.

Dennis returned, shepherding Minnie and Selane's makeup technicians into the suite.

"We heard," the wardrobe mistress said. "Such a tragedy!"

"I'm sorry to wake you up," Selane said. Her face was streaked with tears and the remains of her cosmetics. One of the makeup women dabbed at her face with a tissue.

"You need to sleep, sweetheart. Let's put you to bed."

They surrounded Selane and led her through the white and gold doors into the master suite.

Ray and Vickie waited in the sitting room.

"I never knew anyone who died before," Vickie said. She looked morose.

"I have," Ray said. At least the genie was safe and not doing any magic for the time being. He sighed and settled back.

He drowsed now and again in the chair, but he wasn't able to sleep soundly. He had nightmares, as he had for the last several days. Selane's cries became part of them.

Sounds coming from the bedroom told him that the ladies were having a tough time getting Selane to settle down. Just when it sounded like they had gotten her tucked in, she got up and walked around some more.

Minnie emerged and made a beeline for Dennis.

"Call the hotel doctor. Maybe he can give her something."

An avuncular man in his fifties with a bushy mustache appeared shortly. He went in to see the patient. Ray listened to his calm voice as he administered a sleep medication. He might have been able to relax, if it wasn't for Selane's desperate whimpering. The doctor emerged from the bedroom.

"Give her a few minutes," he said to Dennis. "Don't disturb her. The medicine I gave her should help."

He left. They waited. The soft sobbing didn't stop. It built up into shrieks of dismay. Instead of falling asleep, Selane was having hysterics.

"Dennis! Dennis, help me!"

The assistant didn't look that much better himself, but he went in and closed the door behind him. From the sounds of it, the lady was in the midst of a full blown temper tantrum.

Dennis came out, his phone to his ear.

"Well, I don't care! It's not working. Give her something else! What do you mean there's nothing stronger? Do you hear how bad she is? She needs to sleep. She is the heart and soul of the charity appeal. Tomorrow morning – in five hours, she has to be on her way to the television station and be on that stage. She can't appear in the state she is in now!"

Ray roused as an idea struck him.

"I think I know someone who can help her, Mr. Folger." Ray got his own cell phone out.

The blond Englishman came over. His eyes were red and his skin was slack from exhaustion and worry.

"What do you need?"

"You might need to arrange a ride," Ray said. The call connected, and a sleepy voice answered. "Hey, Ayosha? I'm really sorry to bug you. Look, can you come here? There's a client for you.... I know it's Monday night. I've got class tomorrow, too. Thanks. I really appreciate it."

Within the hour, the night manager escorted Ayosha into the suite. In spite of having been hauled out of bed in the middle of the night, she was as pulled together as though she had had all morning to get ready, in a midnight-blue wool dress and neat black leather boots. She looked as awed as Ray had been, but she was all business, too.

"Who needs me?" she asked him.

"It's Miss Selane," Ray said. "She's had a fright."

Dennis swooped in.

"Miss Gilbert," he said. "Thank you for coming. Are you a fairy godmother, too?" He looked horrified at himself. "Oh, God, I never thought those words would come out of my mouth without me being sarcastic!"

"No, sir," Ayosha said. "I'm a sandman. I can help her sleep."

Dennis's shoulders relaxed.

"You can? I'd be grateful. I'll pay you... what kind of fee do you charge?"

"I don't," Ayosha said shortly. "Just let me help her. I'd be glad to."

Ray followed her into the master bedroom, decorated in soft tans and grays. Selane lay on the big bed in a shimmering gold nightgown. She eyed them distrustfully.

"Why can't everyone just leave me alone? I should suffer!"

Ayosha shook her head.

"I won't hurt you, Miss Selane," she said. "Nobody needs to suffer for anything."

She brought the gleaming bag out from the collar of her dress and dug into it for a bigger handful of sand than Ray had ever seen her use before, and tossed it. Selane gawked at the sparkling cloud as it shot toward her. She squirmed out of the sheets, scrambling to get away from it, but when the twinkling particles rained down and touched her skin, she relaxed. One of her arms fell over the side of the bed. Her eyes closed, and she breathed softly. Just like that, she was asleep.

Ayosha pulled the sleeping woman up so her head was on the pillows and tucked the silver-colored quilt around her. She sat down on the edge of the bed and glanced up at Ray.

"I'll take over from here," she said.

Ray was grateful to escape to the sitting room. Dennis sprang up from the settee. Vickie stared at him from her chair. Her eyes looked out from sockets that looked like a pair of bruises.

"Is she all right?" Dennis asked.

"Yes," Ray said. He sat down in his chair again. "She's asleep."

"Thank God," Dennis said. "Will she stay that way?" Ray nodded. "I have to get a few hours' shut-eye. Do you mind?"

"No."

"Well, er, make yourselves comfortable. There are a couple more rooms." He gestured vaguely toward the other inner doors.

Ray looked at the bedrooms, which were just as grand as Vickie had said, but he didn't feel comfortable using any of them. He returned to his chair and tried to get a little sleep.

It was no use. Even a brownie point didn't dispel the sewer monsters and aliens that haunted his slumbers. He just sat. Vickie drew up her legs and went to sleep with her head on her knees. Ray waited.

In a while, Ayosha came out and sat beside him. Vickie stirred and woke up.

"Is she okay?" she asked.

"She's dreaming of her baby girl," Ayosha said. "A little girl with dark brown skin and a tuft of curls on top of her head tied in a pink ribbon. I didn't know she had ever had a baby. It's not in any of her bios."

"She told me tonight," Vickie said. "She said she lost her."

"My goodness. That's so sad." Ayosha sighed. Ray felt that trace of a need string from her again. She must never have gotten her wish when she was growing up. Too bad it was too late.

"What's wrong?" Ray asked. When she looked up, her eyes were bright.

"Oh, it just makes me miss my mother."

"Your mom in Georgia?" Ray asked.

"Both of them," Ayosha said. She roused herself and shook her head. The longing vanished. "But you're not sleeping, either. I can feel sleep toxins just radiating out of you."

"Nightmares," Ray said, apologetically. "It's nothing."

Ayosha raised an eyebrow.

"Nothing? When you have a fine and experienced sandman right here? Settle in." Ayosha waved to him to lie back in the chair. She produced the small bag again and sprinkled a pinch of dust over his head. Ray felt it land like soft rain on his skin. He closed his eyes.

The next time he opened them, daylight was streaming in through the sheer curtains at the far end of the room. Ayosha and Vickie sat together in a corner by the fireplace, chatting quietly. When he sat up, Ayosha glanced his way.

"Feel better?"

Ray stretched, and realized that he felt rested, even energetic. He grinned. The sandman girl had on a long-sleeved stretchy green dress that looked like it cost ten thousand dollars. It was probably a loan from Selane. Vickie's clothes were the same as they always were, but they were clean again.

"Lots better. Thanks! Did you two get any rest?"

"Uh-huh. Just fine. I told you I always sleep well." Ayosha frowned at him. "I saw what you meant about your dreams. Pretty bad. In fact, I wouldn't have said they were normal for someone like you."

"What's that mean?" Ray asked. Ayosha hesitated, then waved a hand.

"Nothing. I chased them away for you."

"Thanks."

"No problem. Vickie and I have been talking about what happened last night before we got here. We thought you ought to know, too."

Ray reached for his phone and glanced at the time. Ten A.M.! He groaned. His Tuesday Chem class had started half an hour ago. No point in trying to go, and nothing he could do about it. Maybe the professor would let him make up the hours later on. The two girls studied him in concern.

"Go ahead," Ray sighed. Ayosha beckoned Vickie close.

"Tell him what you told me."

Gradually, they coaxed the whole story out of her. Ray was horrified.

"What happens now to the wishes that they never got around to making?" Ray asked.

"I don't know," Vickie said, her small face creased with worry. "That's never happened to me before. I can feel them still out there, but I can't do anything about them."

Ray staggered into the shower of one of the spare bedrooms. Shaving gear had been laid out for him, along with a clean shirt and clean shorts. By the sharp creases and chemical-laden odor, the garments were probably brand new out of the hotel store or one of the other shops in the building. He let the water run over his head for a long time, trying to sort out the mess the magic had caused.

Selane had recovered from the trauma of the night before, but she was quiet. She breakfasted alone in her room. Her staff arrived to dress her and apply her makeup for the day.

Dennis made sure all of them got room service, too. Ray feasted on a chorizo-tomato omelet, bacon, pastries, fruit, juice, and some really excellent coffee, plus whatever the girls didn't eat. When they had finished, the enforcers herded them all down to the long stretch limo and into the compartment near the driver. The singer emerged from the passenger elevator, dressed in a glamorous peach gown that rather unfortunately echoed the yellow tinge of her face. She didn't look at any of them. Dennis Folger slipped into the seat nearest the door and clicked the button that signaled the driver. Tommy sat down close to Ray.

"Don't talk to Miss Selane," Tommy warned them. "She needs to prepare. You don't talk to the press. You don't tweet or post anything about what happened. Everything goes through her publicity. Got that?"

"Yes, sir," Ray said. Ayosha and Vickie nodded solemnly. Not a word of thanks for their help overnight, or for the sacrifice Ray had made in missing school. Business as usual.

CHAPTER 18

"Ray!" The Blue Fairy descended on him in all her morning glory as he came into the studio and hung up his coat. She had on a trim two-piece suit in her favorite color. "Eustatia called me about last night, but I didn't expect to see you here today." She glanced over his shoulder. "Did you come here with Selane?"

Ray took her aside, glancing at the stagehands who eyed them curiously.

"Alexandra, do you have a few minutes?"

She nodded. "Of course, Ray."

He told her everything that had happened, from what his grandmother had learned from Vickie, all the way through to the middle of the night call to Ayosha. By the end, Ray felt as if he was babbling. The guild president listened without interruption, although she did nod and click her tongue sympathetically now and again.

"She couldn't sleep, Alexandra. She feels responsible for it all. And I guess she is," Ray concluded.

The guild president shook her head sadly. "Two people were killed, another injured and two more missing? That is a catastrophe! I feel terrible for her. This is why we don't let untrained personnel out with live wands, Ray. I wish we could help her, but we don't have that kind of magic."

"I know. The trouble is that Mr. Karburg is the only one who could wish his wife back home, but he won't. Mr. Folger talked to him today. All he can think about is his sister."

"Let's hope that they can work it out between them," Alexandra said. "As long as she has a genie, however she is misusing her, it's possible that there is a solution."

"Vickie said she can't wish anyone back to life," Ray said. "Maybe if Miss Selane gives one of her two wishes to Mr. Karburg, he can use his last one to get his wife back."

"You can suggest it," Alexandra said. She sighed. "It's not perfect. I wish there was something more we could do."

He hesitated. "Um, I'm not supposed to talk to anyone about what happened."

"Of course not, Ray." The union president smiled at him. "You are a union member. You came to me for advice on a matter associated with our function. Naturally we will keep her confidence. If the police ask you for a statement, you give a full and truthful account, but otherwise, I think it's appropriate to do what she asks. You don't want to draw attention to yourself, do you?"

"No!"

Alexandra chuckled. "Then, let's get to work."

Ray helped her up into the front row of the risers. He was glad to let her sit between him and Mr. Pinkwater. Ray caught the sandman guildmaster giving him a dirty look.

What did I ever do to you? he thought, *Wendell.* From the other side of the tall, white-haired man, Ayosha offered a contrite expression. Ray shook his head. The fact that her guildmaster was a jerk wasn't her fault. She had been a star.

Ray looked out for a moment he could talk privately to Selane to offer his idea. It wasn't easy to find a time to suggest the trade to Miss Selane. In between appearances in front of the camera and talking to reporters there to cover the accident, she kept rushing outside to her luxurious trailer to cry. She kept Vickie close by her all day long, except when Minnie took her over to the catering table for meals. Vickie kept shooting helpless looks toward Ray and Ayosha, but didn't dare leave her mistress's side.

The volcano of bad feeling that had erupted the night before had gone away, but a new one was building in its place.

It put everyone in the studio on edge. The enforcers snapped more often at the volunteers than usual. Both Alexandra and Wendell Pinkwater cautioned their members to keep their cool.

Selane seemed to be sleepwalking through her day. The kids had noticed it. Practically all of them were sending off need strings that drove the fairy godparents frantic. In fact, everyone had noticed it. The floor manager was beside himself trying to guess which of the cameras she was going to look at next. The diva's instinct for drawing every eye to her was back-firing big time. She sang one of her best known ballads, pouring her heart into the microphone. Normally the blues made Ray feel happy and sad at the same time, but this performance just made his heart feel heavier than before.

The people in the studio audience had the same reaction. When the recorded music ended and Selane went to talk with them, they shifted uncomfortably in their seats, replying to her in a few terse words for the camera. Normally, they'd be looking at her with worship as if she was one of the saints. Not that day. Raw emotion like hers would have been more understandable at a funeral, not at a celebration of hope like the Appeal was supposed to be. Even the frail kids in their wheelchairs looked sorry for her.

"Hello, I'm Selane," said a voice from the enormous speakers on the walls. Ray jumped. "You may know my music, but I want to tell you what's in my heart…"

He glanced up. The huge screens cut from the live studio to a recording that the singer had made before the telethon began. Then, she wore the pearl-colored evening gown, with the lights in her hair, and her face looked like one of the archangels, ethereal and glowing. She smiled at the camera as though taking the unseen viewers into her confidence. The recording could not have been a greater contrast to the diminished woman standing on the side of the stage with the microphone dangling from her hand. One of her attendants swooped forward to take the black baton from her. Minnie led her toward the special chair, already set up and waiting.

The director emerged from the glass booth and made for Selane. Tommy and the other enforcers surrounded her protectively, but he pushed them aside with both hands like Samson shoving the pillars of the temple.

"Miss Selane," he began, smiling gently.

She held up a hand.

"I know what you're going to say!" she said. "I know I'm off my game. I've had some very bad news. I lost a couple of dear friends last night."

"I know, ma'am, but everyone's so sorry for you they're not thinking about the charity." The director gestured toward the risers. "Look at the phone banks. We haven't had more than a few calls all morning."

Her brows drew down.

"Well, what am I supposed to do about that?" she asked.

"Ooh," Chris Popp murmured from the seat behind Ray. "I see a temper storm brewing!" Ray found himself holding his breath.

Before the diva could produce the expected outburst, Dennis Folger stepped in. He put an arm around her and smiled at the director.

"Perhaps you're right, sir. Why not let Miss Selane have a little while to process her loss? Run the recordings and some footage from previous days. I also see some very talented people waiting for their turn to perform. Why not let them have the spotlight for a while, eh? There's a good fellow."

"Right," the director said. Ray could tell that he didn't like it, but he had to make the best of a bad situation. "Could you pull it together for four PM? We get a lot of viewers tuning in to bid on your newest find. I can't run that from the archives."

Dennis turned Selane so she wasn't facing the director.

"We'll do our best. Come on, my darling. Let's go sit down. I'm sure that the chef has something delicious for you."

He herded her toward the far side of the sound stage. Her people crowded around her, placing her personal chair and footrest for her, taking off her shoes and massaging her feet, fluffing up her hair. The white-clad kitchen witch bustled out from behind her velvet rope with a snack-sized tray. Vickie sat cross-legged on the floor beside Selane and spoke to her. The singer looked down at the girl, smiled sadly and shook her head.

With the phone banks dead, there was no reason for any of them to sit there, wasting their time. The fairy godparents got up and stretched, then went over to chat with the children. Everyone's nerves had to be twanging from all the need flying around. Ray saw his chance. He took off his earpiece and went over toward Selane.

As he expected, Beatdown headed him off, standing in his path like a silk-suited brick wall.

"What do you want?"

"I need to talk to Miss Selane," Ray said, doing his best not to be intimidated. "Magic business."

The big man shook his head as if trying to dislodge a fly that had landed on it. Even if his employer was waist deep in magical matters, he didn't handle it as naturally as she did.

"All right, but make it fast. She needs to rest."

Selane's gaze was on Ray as he approached. She stretched a long, frail hand toward him. He closed the rest of the distance between them, but he didn't dare touch her. She took the initiative, and grasped his wrist in a vise grip. Her eyes, for all they were beautifully made up, still looked tired and haunted. He noticed that she clutched the Aladdin's lamp to her in her other arm.

"Raymond, I never got a chance to thank you for being so kind to me last night." She smiled. The expression was more tragic than anything else.

A couple of her ladies tittered. Ray felt his cheeks burn.

"I was happy to help, Miss Selane," he said. "Um, may I talk to you for a minute? In private?"

"Why, certainly! Beatdown, get this nice young man a chair." She waited until the big man had brought over one of the metal folding chairs. He set it up beside her. He didn't point at his eyes, but Ray got the idea. Her staff backed away to a respectful distance. "Please sit down, Raymond. What may I do for you?"

Ray took a deep breath.

"I had an idea to run by you. It might not fix everything, but it might help."

"What is it?"

Carefully and respectfully, he outlined his idea. He knew she would be resistant to the concept at first, but he was surprised at how vehemently she refused to consider it.

"Not a chance," she said. "Impossible! How dare you ask me?"

Tommy heard the tone of her voice and took a couple of steps toward them. She waved him away.

"Why not, Miss Selane?" Ray asked, reasonably. "You have two wishes left. You'd still have one. Can't you feel the magic building up here? Something else bad could happen if you don't let it all go."

She shook her head.

"If I give up one of my wishes, I could make a horrible mistake like Neil did. I don't want that to happen. I need one as a backup."

"A backup?"

"In case I make a mistake, I could take it all back."

Ray gawked at her. A new idea crystallized as clear as glass in his mind. This one really *would* solve everything.

"You can fix it all, Miss Selane. Everything."

"I can? How?"

"Baby!"

A deep, baritone voice interrupted them. With cheeks ashen under her makeup, Selane sprang to her feet. Corry N. came toward her with his hands out. Selane pushed past Ray as if he wasn't there. She gazed at the music producer. He was freshly shaven and dressed in all black, and he wore darker glasses than usual. Ray stood up, though his legs were shaky with relief. The man was alive.

"Oh, Corry!" Selane threw her arms around him. "We thought you were dead! No one knew where you were! I thought you were in the car with Nona and Rochelle."

"No, baby," he said, stroking her shoulder with a thumb. "I changed my mind. I had them drop me off at a different hotel for the night to throw off my stalker squad. I didn't answer my phone because the first six hundred were from all of them. I didn't know about the accident until this morning when I turned on the television this morning. This is a terrible tragedy! Are you all right?"

Selane nodded.

"I'm fine, but poor Neil is destroyed. First his wife, and now his sister. They won't let us in to see him until this afternoon, but I don't know what to say to him, Corry. I don't know what to *do*."

He held her tightly. "We'll get through this, baby. Don't worry about it. You can do a tribute to them in your album. I've got my lyricist working on a couple of numbers right now. I made the call right after I saw the newscast. It'll be the biggest hit either of us have ever had." He glanced up to see Ray. His tender expression hardened into all business. "Something I can do for you, young man?"

"I'm sorry, sir. I was talking to Miss Selane about an idea."

Selane reached out to touch his sleeve.

"Yes, I promised I'd hear you out, Raymond. Come and sit with us, Corry. Now, tell me, Raymond. You said I could fix everything that has happened."

"You can, Miss Selane," Ray said. He sat down on the metal chair and fixed his eyes on hers, willing her to understand. "Here's what you have to do. Use your second wish to take back the first wish. That will undo everything. You'll go back to the way you were when it all started. There'd be no accident, or anything else."

Selane stared at him.

"Take back my wish?"

"Yes, ma'am," Ray said. "If Mr. Karburg didn't want his ex-wife off the face of the Earth, he wouldn't have had to fly back to L.A. If Ms. Karburg never had that car, they wouldn't have gotten into a car accident." He didn't add, *and get killed.* It was all so clear in his mind, he was shocked when she turned her eyes away.

"No, I can't do it."

"But, Miss Selane!"

"No!" she almost screamed the word. "They're gone! Neil can bring Louanne back. It's his choice! If I do that, Corry will… he'll go back to the way he was when I…."

The music producer seized her hand and kissed her fingers. "Never, baby," he vowed.

"But they don't have to be gone," Ray said. "This would be the best thing you could do."

"They are gone." Selane tossed her hair and held her head high in defiance. "Corry is going to start my career off again. I made enemies. I ruined my own life by being foolish and greedy. Everyone *hated* me. Corry will guide me forward. He has powerful connections. I can't let that go. If I do what you say, I'll have nothing at all. Nothing to look forward to."

"The kids here worship you, Miss Selane," Ray said. "That hasn't changed."

Selane glanced at the cluster of wheelchairs. Each of the little faces was turned her way. Francisco regarded her with the same unrequited passion he always did. Selane dropped her gaze.

"I'm sorry," she said. "It isn't enough." But he could tell she wasn't really thinking about her records. Or the kids. Or the fame.

"What are you doing it all for?" Ray asked softly. "What's really important to you now?"

"I don't know," she said, then added abruptly, "I had a dream last night."

"The daughter you lost?" Ray asked. She looked startled, and her eyes grew wary. "I'm sorry. Ayosha could see your dreams. She told me. I wouldn't tell anyone else."

She patted his hand. "I know. I had to give up my child. I regret that every day."

Corry beamed at her.

"Well, sweetheart, if you do what this young man suggests, you can use your third wish to get her back. And you don't have to worry about me. I'm here for the duration. I won't walk away from you again." For the first time, Selane's face brightened. "You'd do it for that, wouldn't you?"

"Yes! Yes, I would!" She turned to Vickie, her soul in her eyes. "What about it? If I turn back the clock, that would be my third wish. To get my daughter back so she can love me forever, the way it ought to have been. How's that sound?"

Vickie shook her head.

"I can't do that."

"What do you mean? She's your boss! So am I! You do what she says!" Corry boomed. Vickie shrank away from him. Ray glared at him.

"Don't you yell at her that way! I don't care who you are!" He looked down at Vickie. "Why can't you?"

The genie was too terrified to speak above a murmur.

"I can't make anyone love anyone else. It wouldn't be an honest emotion. I could make it so you two meet, but she could walk away the next minute. If she is still alive, she's a human being with free will. I can't guarantee *forever*."

Selane folded her arms.

"Then I'm not changing my mind," she said. "That's that. I'm desperately sorry for Neil, and for the others, but I can't sacrifice the rest of my life for theirs. No."

"But, Miss Selane," Ray began.

"Shouldn't you be over there answering phones?" she asked. "Tommy, Raymond here needs to get back to work."

Ray felt a huge hand clomp down on his shoulder and haul him to his feet.

"Go on back, boy," Tommy said. "Go now, and I won't count this one against you."

CHAPTER 19

"So that's it," Ray told Rose, over a cup of the terrible coffee. He drank it anyhow, hoping the caffeine would drive away the frustration he felt. He glanced toward the middle of the stage, where Selane was talking to the camera about a silver candlestick. "I feel like we're sitting on a nuclear pile, and there's no way off it."

"Except for that poor, stubborn woman," Rose said. "Well, you can see her point, can't you? She's holding onto what she knows she has. I might be as afraid to walk outside in the unknown as she is."

"Like you ever have been," Ray said, with a dry tone in his voice. The little Jewish grandmother was the toughest person he had ever met.

"Well, I can put myself into her shoes." Rose sighed. "You know, it's bad, but I'm getting used to the smell. That's how people justify letting evil be in their lives. They let it become part of the background and don't look at it." She glanced toward Selane. The star was surrounded by her entourage, getting her ready to present her latest 'find' to the camera. Everyone treated her like she might break into pieces at any moment. Ray was afraid that she might. One more wrong wish, and she might blow them all up. "You can't let it go, Ray. She does listen to you, even if she doesn't like what you say."

"I can't keep going over there," Ray said. "Her bouncers are going to take me outside into the street and stomp on me!"

162

A little smile played on Rose's face. Her brown eyes twinkled.

"They're terrified of you, honey."

"Oh, come on! They're ten times my size!"

"But they don't know anything about magic. You take wishes and genies and all that in your stride. It's everyday stuff for you. They left all that behind in bedtime stories. To discover that it's real… pffft!" Rose flicked her fingers. "These big, strong men become little boys all over again. You're the adult here."

"B.S."

Rose smiled at him and tweaked his cheek painfully between thumb and forefinger. He winced. He hated it when she did that.

"Try again, Ray. This is like granting a different kind of wish. People have died. More bad things could happen. You need to push her into making the right decision."

"How? She doesn't have to listen to me!"

Ayosha came over and poured herself some coffee.

"How y'all doing?"

"How do you think?" Ray asked, a little bitterly. "It feels like this place is going to explode. I could fix it, but she won't listen to me!"

The girl made a rueful face.

"I suppose this isn't the best time to ask you to come to my birthday party," she said. "Tomorrow night. Nothing big, just some pizzas. Everyone's gonna watch me take my first legal drink. My roommate thinks I ought to have a mint julep 'cause I'm from the south, but I think I'd rather have some white wine." She wrinkled her nose.

"I'd really like that," Ray said. "Thanks. And thanks again for the sand last night. This is the first afternoon in a week when I'm not falling over from not sleeping."

"My pleasure," Ayosha said. "I never saw anything like what was going on in your head. I should talk to the officers about having a sandman assigned to you for a while until you work through whatever stuff's going on."

"I don't know," Ray said. He was uneasy about making himself vulnerable to the disapproving Mr. Pinkwater. Ayosha touched his hand.

"Trust me, okay?"

"Yeah, I do," Ray said.

"I've been seeing that need string from her for weeks," Rose said, thoughtfully. "I had no idea she was still eligible. I'll catch up with her and try to figure out what it is that she wants so badly." Rose put her cup down and went after Ayosha.

Ray gulped down the last of the nearly-cold coffee. He wished he could go out for a cigarette. The sensation of bad magic felt squishy and horrible underfoot, like rotting mud. He had to talk Selane into some kind of compromise. He hoped Rose was right about her bodyguards being afraid of him.

Selane let the last few notes of her Gratitude Lullaby fade away. Her voice had been shaky. She was ashamed of her performance. The uneasy faces in the audience told her she had sounded bad. If it wasn't for Corry and Dennis being there for her, she would have run away and hid.

The caretakers went to get the kids ready to take home. Little Celeste looked up hopefully as her mother wrapped her in her winter coat. Selane felt bad. She hadn't spent much time with them at all. The reporters had been absolutely relentless, questioning her about her last moments with poor Nona and Rochelle. Couldn't they see she just wanted to be by herself to grieve?

But that wasn't the kiddies' fault. Selane surrendered her microphone to a stage hand, and went to say goodbye to each of the children. The fairy godparents, as she now knew them to be, made way for her.

"Good night, Celeste," she said.

"Good night, Miss Selane," the girl said. She gave a bright smile, but Selane could tell she was weaker than she had been before. Selane felt tears in her eyes. Life was precious. Who knew how long it would be before the terrible scourge of

Spaulding's took this sweet girl away? She knelt down and enfolded the girl in as gentle a hug as she could.

"God bless you, child."

Celeste's mother looked surprised and gratified. Selane went around to each child, saving Francisco for last, so she could spend the most time with him.

"Good night, Francisco," she said, kneeling beside him.

His eyes brimmed with anger.

"You don't care about me," he said.

"I do care," she insisted. She tried to take his hand. The bone-thin arm jerked out of her grasp. He turned his thin body away from her as far as he could. Selane felt rage rising in her. The ungrateful little brat! She rose. She thought of a dozen things she could say, and swallowed all of them. There were too many cameras there. Later, she would have to talk with Dennis about making another child the spokesperson for the charity.

"He's suffering," Raymond said. Selane jumped.

"You! I told you not to talk to me anymore."

The boy grimaced.

"I'm sorry, ma'am, but I have to. Have you thought any more about making that wish?"

"No!" People turned around to look. She lowered her voice. "I don't know what to do! It's hard."

"The right thing isn't always easy," Ray said, "but it's the best thing. I say that to myself all the time."

"Well, isn't it easy for you? You do it all the time."

He shook his head.

"It's *not* easy, ma'am. It's my responsibility to help kids make the best wishes they can. You have a chance that not many people do. The children we meet get to make only one wish. 'Every child deserves one miracle.' That's our motto. You get *three*. Why not do it right this time? I'm begging you. There's something bad building up here, just like last night. It's from all of the unfulfilled wishes, and the ones left behind by your two friends."

"How dare you talk about them?" Selane hissed. "How dare you?"

Raymond went on without apologizing. "Someone has to. If you can't feel it, you must be the only one here who can't."

"I can feel it!" She could, too. It was like being in a sauna with a dozen angry skunks and fourteen alligators.

"Look! There's a magical explosion building. It's doing harm to everyone who has to wade through it, like radioactive waste." He swept an arm toward the children. "It's affecting them, too. That much wrong magic is probably shortening their lives even more than they already would be. You don't want that. You're doing this telethon to save them."

Selane was torn. Her heart said to give in, but her mind kept playing dozens of scenarios, all of them ending in disaster."

"I can't decide now," she insisted. "Let me sleep on it. All right?" Her mind rolled up a memory of the night before, and it haunted her. "But what if I don't sleep? I have to sleep, Raymond!"

"I'll talk to the Sandmen," Raymond promised. He left her and went over to speak with the tall man with white hair. Soon, a little Asian woman with a broad face and permed curls came to join her.

"Hi, Miss Selane, I'm Brenda. I'm a big fan."

"How nice," Selane said.

Raymond didn't come back, but she could feel his eyes on him anyhow. Minnie wrapped Selane in her fabulous fur coat, and Dennis restored the lamp to her arms. She looked around.

"Vickie!"

The girl hurried toward her, the big padded coat in her arms. Clicking her tongue, Minnie helped her put it on.

Corry came over, shrugging his camel-hair coat on.

"Ready, baby?"

She nodded. The enforcers marched ahead of her, opening doors and making anyone in the way stand aside. The driver had the door of the limousine open and waiting. Vapor drifted out into the night air.

Corry N. pulled the collar of his beautiful coat up around his ears. "Brr! I hate this weather."

Selane eyed him.

"Didn't you have a hat?

I did," Corry said, with a grin. "One of them pulled it off. Miss 1940s." He glanced up, and his expression changed to one of horror. "Oh, my God, there she is!"

A dark-haired woman with a figure Selane would have called Junoesque sprang out from behind Selane's trailer. She dived onto Corry and wrapped her arms around him. He fell backwards against the car. Her eyes were wild.

"You're mine! I don't want you thinking about anybody but me!"

Corry tried to push her off. He felt for the open door and slid along the enameled metal. Another woman, this one with long blonde dreadlocks, grabbed Miss 1940s by the hair and hauled her head back.

"You don't dare! He wants me and me alone!" They fell into the car, grappling and scratching at one another. Tommy grabbed each of them by the ankle and started to pull them out.

"Corry, baby! We're here!" Two women who had to be twins hurtled toward him. "We've been waiting for you! Come home with us!"

"Oh, no, no, not again!" Corry backed away from them. Any other time she might have laughed at him running away from four beautiful women, but they seemed to have gone insane. The twins dived at him. One of them caught his arm. Corry spun out of her grasp, and fell over onto the tarmac, just as a pair of headlights came around the corner.

"No!" Selane screamed.

The taxi stopped, but not in time. Corry lay flat on the street. The women scrambled to surround him. Beatdown threw them off one by one as if they were as light as teddy bears, and knelt beside the record producer's body. The driver got out. He looked shocked.

"I didn't even see him. I'm sorry!"

Selane felt misery rise up and envelop her like the cold wind. She wrapped her arms around herself and began to sob.

In no time, she was surrounded by flashing lights. She opened her eyes. A thousand cell phone cameras were aimed at her, blinding her. Through her tears, it was all one yellow-white blur.

Oh, God, it was going to be on the internet in a second. This couldn't be happening again!

"No, no pictures. Stop it, there's a good fellow. I'll make a statement for you in just a few minutes. Clear the way. We need to get an ambulance for this man. Back off, please."

Selane could have collapsed with relief. Dennis had come to the rescue. He and Tommy took her by the arms. The flashing went on, but it was all at her back.

"Come on, darling, let's get you back inside. Chop chop! She'll freeze. Hurry, Vickie, come with me. Get those doors open!"

"Corry!" she wailed.

"Come on, Miss Selane," Brenda said. "I'll make sure you can get some rest."

Selane stared, not seeing the woman's face. Her heart beat so hard her ribs felt like they would shatter. "I don't want a stranger. Where are those kids?"

"Ray and Ayosha," Vickie supplied, helpfully. "They're inside."

CHAPTER 20

"It's my fault! Why didn't I listen to you?" Selane wailed again and again, holding onto Ray's hand like a life preserver. "Make it stop! Help me!"

"I'll try, Miss Selane," Ray said. "Take it easy."

"Thank God the studio audience is gone," Dennis said, walking up and down beside them. His cell phone rang, and he snatched it out of his pocket. "Yes? Oh, God bless you." He looked down at Selane. "He's conscious, darling. He came to in the ambulance. He'll make it. Some broken bones, that's all."

The kitchen witch came over with tray. On it were two steaming cups, one of warm golden-green liquid, and the other of deep, golden red.

"Chamomile and valerian with honey for Miss Selane," she told Ray. "It will help to calm her."

"Thanks," he said. He yawned widely. "Sorry."

Minnie took the cup from him. She sat down and put an arm around Selane's shoulders.

"Drink it, sweetie. It'll do you good."

"I don't want it!" Selane sounded like a petulant child. Minnie must have heard it a million times, because she paid no attention to it at all. She held the cup to the singer's lips and waited until she swallowed.

He was tired. One night of good sleep wasn't enough to make up for all the nightmares of the last several days. He yawned again. The chef handed him the other cup.

"This one's for you. Black tea, gingko and GABA, and lots of sugar. Bottoms up."

"Thanks," Ray said. Within a few sips of the sweet, astringent liquid, he felt his mind clearing.

Word had spread rapidly among the fairy godparents and the sandmen about the second accident. All of them had stayed in the studio in case Miss Selane needed them. Luckily, all the children were already gone. Most of the stagehands had left for the day. Only a couple of janitors in boiler suits were there, emptying waste baskets and sweeping up the floors.

When both teacups were empty, Ray crouched down beside Vickie at Selane's side.

"You have to make the wish now, Miss Selane."

He felt pity for the haunted look in the star's eyes.

"I will, but I need Corry. He was going to bring me back again. He was going to help me. I can't wish him away."

"And maybe he will still be able to afterwards," Ray said. "I am so sorry, Miss Selane. I'm as tired as you are. Look, if you word the wish right, and take it all back, it should work out just the way it ought to be. Corry wouldn't want to stop working with you. He's crazy about you. Everyone can see that. It will work out all right."

Selane wavered. She searched his face for reassurance.

"And if it doesn't?"

"It will," Ray said, projecting confidence he didn't feel. "I swear."

Selane studied his face.

"All right, what should I say?"

"What did you say the first time?"

"This is what you said to me when you made the wish," Vickie said. "You said, 'I wish the producers were pounding down my door for the Selane experience. I wish they needed me the way they used to.'"

Selane narrowed her eyes at the genie. "You remember every word I said that day?"

"Just the wish," Vickie said. "It's important, so I memorized it. I always do that, because I forget things a lot."

"So, you have to reverse that," Ray said. "You have to take it all back." Selane took a deep breath. Ray flung up his hands. "No, not yet! I need to remember things as they are now. I want you to put into the wish that all the members of the Sandmen and the Fairy Godmothers Union who were here can remember, too."

"Why?"

"In case you still need help later," Ray said. "Do you want to keep the memory, too?"

Selane shook her head. "No. I never want to think about what happened to Rochelle and Nona ever again." She clutched his hand. "But you have to promise me, Raymond. I'll only do it if you swear you will help me to find my daughter. All right? Do internet searches, send out some magic power, hire private detectives, or whatever you have to. Otherwise, I've got nothing. Once I make this wish, I go back to where everyone's mad at me."

"Not me, my love," Dennis said. Selane smiled up at her assistant.

"Everyone except Dennis."

"I promise," Ray said. "Let me get a piece of paper from my book bag, and we'll write it down so you can't make a mistake."

Selane settled back in her big chair. Ray strode to the wall where his coat hung. He rummaged through the bag and came out with an assignment notebook and a pencil stub, and headed back.

"Ray!"

He stopped in the middle of the soundstage. Ayosha was headed his way, with Mr. Pinkwater in tow. Instead of the tall, white-haired man looking imperious and arrogant, he seemed embarrassed. When he caught Ray's eyes, he halted. Ayosha, with uncharacteristic fury on her face, grabbed him by the arm and hauled him forward. They met in the middle of the felt-covered floor.

"The guildmaster has something to say to you, Mr. Crandall," she said formally. She let go of the man's wrist and folded her arms.

"Ayosha…" Pinkwater said, his pale blue eyes pleading.

"Don't tell me another single thing!" she snapped. "Tell him!" She stalked away. The guildmaster looked at Ray. The awkward silence continued.

"What is it?" Ray asked at last.

"I… owe you an apology, young man," Pinkwater said. Ray felt his eyebrows climb his forehead. Whatever he expected the man to say, that wasn't in the top fifty possibilities.

"For what?"

The man's mouth worked back and forth. Eventually, it opened.

"Your bad dreams," he said. "Miss Gilbert asked for a panacea for the nightmares you have been suffering. I… had to admit that I have been responsible for them."

"You what?" Ray asked. His limbs suddenly felt as achy as though he had a fever. "You mean you're the reason I have been having nightmares? It's not my schoolwork?"

"Well, no. From all accounts, you're an excellent student. Hardworking. Your English 101 professor is my sister-in-law." For the first time, the man's pale complexion took on some color. It flushed red. Ray felt his temper soar.

"Why? Why would you do that to me? I never did anything to hurt you!"

"You were wasting Miss Gilbert's time," Pinkwater said, fussily. "She is here to work for a noteworthy cause, and you kept on distracting her from her duties."

"I never interrupted a thing she was doing while she was at the keyboard," Ray retorted. "I was just trying to be friendly with her. You don't have any right to interfere with her making friends! She's a stranger in town! Do you think she's going to hang with you *old people?*"

"Now, that's uncalled for," Pinkwater said, but his protest sounded weak. "She has her friends on campus."

"And a boyfriend!" Ray had a sudden flash of intuition. "Is he one of you, too? A sandman?"

Pinkwater squirmed. "Well, er, yes."

"And you thought I was going to break her up with him? Like that's any of your business even if I was?"

"I can see I misjudged you, young man. I am sorry that there's been a misunderstanding."

"You bet there has," Ray said. He paced back and forth, clenching and unclenching his fists. If he had stood still, he would probably have punched the man in the belly. "I know what you sandmen think of fairy godparents. Well, you're wrong. We do good! We're dealing with kids who are hurting, face to face, every day. I'd like to see you do that! But, no, you sneak around and attack people while they're sleeping! Maybe *your* club is the one that ought to be dissolved as useless."

At a distance behind the guildmaster, a cluster of Ray's friends had gathered together on the empty risers. Fred Lincoln made a gesture in the man's direction and cocked his head. Ray waved a hand, but he kept his face impassive.

"I am deeply sorry," Pinkwater said. His face stayed red. "I believe that I have underestimated the capacity of your union and the passion of its members. I won't interfere again. You have my word."

"Well, all right," Ray said. The man had capitulated. Ray didn't know what else to say. He wanted a while to get over being mad. He stared at Pinkwater. "I'm busy now."

"We had our reasons for wanting to protect Miss Gilbert from outside influences at this event," Pinkwater said, slowly. The icy eyes bored into Ray's. "Important ones."

Ray matched him, glare for glare.

"Oh, yeah? How important?"

CHAPTER 21

"S he is?" Rose asked. Ray sat on the edge of the risers staring into space. The rest of the fairy godparents sat with him. 'Showing solidarity' was what Alexandra called it. His head was spinning. "Does she know?"

"No," Ray said.

"Well, should you tell her? Should you tell Miss Selane?"

Ray rubbed his forehead. "I don't know. It would solve everything, wouldn't it? 'Here, Miss Selane, this is the daughter you gave away. Grew up beautiful, didn't she?' 'Here, Ayosha, this is the mother you've been missing all these years. She's rich and famous. I don't know why she didn't try to find you after she made it big.' How would that sound?"

Rose shrugged. "All right with me. You're right; it could be a little abrupt. But, doesn't it make your job easier?"

"No, not really," Chris Popp said. He turned a palm up. "If you told her you already know where her daughter is, you'd have no leverage to get her to make that wish. She has to. Poor Corry N. is in the hospital. He was lucky not to be killed. Next time, it could be Miss Selane herself, and that would be a tragedy!"

"I think it is wrong," Mrs. Durja argued, her dark eyes intense. "She ought to know. It is dishonest to keep this information to yourself."

"What do you think, Ray?" Alexandra asked, gently.

Ray sighed, trying to shake the confusion out of his head. "I hate to say it, but one problem at a time. I will tell her later,

honest. At least now I know I can keep my promise to Selane."
He looked up at Rose. "Did Ayosha tell you what her wish
would be?"

Rose shook her head. "I'm not her godmother. I felt that
while I was talking with her."

"Go on, Ray," Alexandra said. "I can feel the bad magic
building again."

That mucky, marshy feeling was growing stronger. Ray
could almost sense the oozing mud around his feet. He wanted to wash it off.

"You're right," Ray said. "She has to make that wish."

He got up and steeled himself. It wouldn't be easy. He
headed toward Selane's side of the studio. He concentrated,
trying out the right phrasing for the wish over and over in his
mind.

"Did he say sorry?" Ayosha asked. Ray almost jumped out
of his skin.

"Uh, yeah," Ray said. All the words he wasn't going to say
rushed to his lips. He pressed them together to keep the truth
from escaping. It wasn't time for it yet. "Look, this is going to
be very hard for everyone. Can you stick around for a while?"

She looked at the big clock over the director's booth. It was
almost ten.

"I guess so. I have an early lab." She gave him an uneasy grin.
"And tomorrow's my birthday, remember?"

Ray took both her hands in his.

"I remember. Please don't leave. Just wait for me, okay?"

"Well, all right, boyfriend," Ayosha said. "Can you tell me
why?"

"Not yet. I don't want any distractions right now. For
anyone."

"Sure," she said, a puzzled frown wrinkling her smooth
forehead. "I'll wait."

"I wish that the producers did not have the full Selane experience," Selane suggested. She shook her head. "No, that
doesn't sound right. I wish they didn't need the… Oh, that
sounds awful!" Ray scratched out that phrase. That made about

sixty different iterations of the wish. None of them sounded right yet. He shifted on the metal seat.

Vickie perched beside him on the arm of the chair. Her untidy hair looked more flyaway than ever. She pointed at the page next to Ray's pencil point.

"What if you put here, that she wishes they didn't pound down her door?"

"But I do, child," Selane said. "I don't want to ruin my chances for the future, just take back the mistake I made the first time."

Ray had erased phrase after phrase until he had worn through that sheet of paper. He tore the page out of the notebook.

"Let's start over," he said. "I wish…?" he prompted her.

"This is too hard!" Selane said, throwing up her hands. "I wish I had never found that lamp in the first place!"

"That's it!" Ray said.

"Yes," Selane said, looking relieved. "That's what I want. You got that, genie-girl?"

Vickie raised her elbows and squared them off.

"To hear is to obey!" she said.

"No!" Ray said. "Stop! That's perfect, but you have to put in the part about us remembering. All right?"

Selane nodded. Ray printed the sentence in his book as neatly as he could and handed it to her. She took a deep breath.

"This is it, then. Vickie, I wish that I had never found the lamp in the first place, but that the fairy godparents and the sandmen who have been here in the studio…"

"…And me," Vickie added.

"…And the genie of the lamp will remember all the events that took place but will no longer be true, but I won't. Because I don't want to," Selane added. "That's my wish."

Vickie closed her eyes and nodded her head sharply.

Instead of the seeping of energy like oil flowing like the previous wishes Vickie had granted, a blast of power went through Ray's body. It made him gasp in a breath of air and sit up straight. It woke him up better than the kitchen witch's tea.

The chair rocked violently to the right. Ray clapped his feet to the floor before it overbalanced. He realized that it had been weighted down on the left for the last hour, but it no longer was.

Vickie was gone. So was her lamp.

Ray sat alone beside Selane, who reclined in her big, comfy chair with her feet up.

She smiled at him with an expression that said *diva indulging devoted fan.*

"Did you need something? Raymond, isn't it?"

She didn't remember! He rose to his feet.

"No, ma'am. You asked me for a favor. I'm going to go do it."

"Well, isn't that nice of you?" Selane said. She looked around. "Where's Dennis?"

"Right here, my darling." The blond Englishman hurried to her side. "What do you need?"

"Did anyone call today?"

Dennis took his phone out of his pocket, and slipped it back again.

"I'm sorry, my darling. I put in several calls today. Perhaps they'll return them tomorrow."

Ray walked away.

The sandmen sat in a group of chairs pulled around the volunteers' catering table, drinking coffee and sharing a plate of cakes and cookies that had to have come from Selane's chef. They watched him approach without the same hostility that they had shown over the last several days. He was glad.

"It's over?" Mr. Pinkwater asked.

"Yes," Ray said. "You can feel it. All that swamp ooze is gone. Everything is back pretty much the way it should have been."

"Well, thank God for that," Pinkwater said, sincerely. "And thank you."

"No problem." Ray turned to Ayosha. "Can I talk with you a minute?" he asked. "It's really important."

"Now?"

"Yes." He looked up at the big clock. There wasn't a minute to lose. He held out his hand. "Now."

She followed him around the corner into the area where the props were stored. It was a little dark, but private. Ray glanced around to make sure that no one else was close enough to listen.

"So, what's on your mind?" she asked. "What did you have to tell me that's so urgent?"

"It's me," he said. He took the blue wand out of his shirt pocket. The silver star gleamed softly in the dimness. "I'm your fairy godfather."

"You're kidding me, Ray. You're younger than me!"

"That doesn't matter. Your birthday's tomorrow. Soon. At midnight. In a few minutes, it will be too late to make your wish."

"I don't *need* a wish," Ayosha said.

"Please," Ray said, putting all the urgency he felt into his voice. He took her hands. "Listen to me. I can feel it in you. The same as you can read my dreams. All of us have felt it. You give off what we call a need string. The string connects to the fairy godparent who is supposed to grant it for you. It's not always clear, but eventually we figure it out. You need something really bad, and I can help. Wish for it. I'll grant it, I promise."

Tears filled her eyes. "You can't know. It's none of your business."

"I do know," Ray insisted, "and I swear no one will hear it from my lips if you don't want me to tell anyone. It'd have to be all you."

"All right," Ayosha whispered. She looked down at her hands. Long, slender hands. A musician's hands. He always thought so, and now he knew why. She looked up at him and poured her soul into her voice. "Find my mother for me."

Okay, magic, do your stuff, Ray thought. He waved the wand.

A veil of blue light spread out from the star. It enveloped Ayosha, then spread out to the walls and up to the ceiling. The power welled up like no other wish Ray had ever granted in his life. A rush of wind rose around the two of them, making the girl's hair dance.

A piece of paper swirled down from the ceiling like an oversized snowflake. Ray caught it and handed it to her.

"What's this?" she asked, clutching it in her hands. It had an ornamental header, blocks of small print, an official seal in one bottom corner, and a tiny footprint inked in the other.

"It's your birth certificate," Ray said.

Her eyes shone with joy.

"I tried everything to get this!" she said, clutching it in both hands. She peered down at the print. "Baby Girl Dell. Six pounds, two ounces. December 21." Her expression changed to shock. "Mother, Selane Dell. Father, blank. *She's* my mother? Her? Miss Selane?"

"Yes. She is," Ray said. The clock on the far wall clicked over to midnight. "Uh, happy birthday?"

Ayosha glared at him.

"You knew?" she demanded.

"For about two hours," he said, with an apologetic shrug. "Mr. Pinkwater told me."

Ayosha goggled in horror.

"They knew? Everybody in this room knew *who my mother was except ME?*" Her voice rose to an angry crescendo. One thing Ray could tell Ayosha had inherited from her mother was her temper. "I'm gonna open up a can of *whoop ass* on somebody!" She wheeled and focused on Selane, who lay on her big chair with a cup in both hands. Ayosha marched toward her.

Ray opened up his long stride and ran to Selane's side. She looked up at him curiously, but at peace.

That peace wasn't going to last more than a couple more seconds, Ray thought.

"I kept my promise," he said. Then he ducked out of the way as two angry women lit into each other. Ayosha brandished the birth certificate at Selane, flapping it in her face.

"What do you want, girl?" Selane asked, sitting up. "How dare you come flying over here like a harpy and hit me with a piece of paper?"

"You?" Ayosha breathed. "You gave me up! You never went looking for me? Why? How come you denied my request to meet you? Was it because you thought I'd be after your *money* or something?"

Ray retreated to the risers and the rest of the FGU. They were at a safe distance, but they could hear every word.

"Be careful what you ask for," Rose said. Her eyes danced. "I think Selane deserved what she got."

Instead of the beautiful reunion that Selane probably always pictured, she had to face an angry young woman, not a squalling infant; a young woman who was perfectly capable of expressing how disappointed and hurt she was to be denied knowledge of her birth mother. Ray watched, glad he wasn't in the middle of it all.

To give her credit, once she got over the shock, Selane humbled herself to apologize.

"You don't know what I was like then, before all this, Ayosha. You had a good upbringing. They promised me you were given to a kind and decent family."

"But I was ashamed of myself!" Ayosha cried. "I didn't know who I belonged to!"

"You belong to yourself, child," Selane said. "Like I belong to me."

"That's not what I mean!"

They glared at each other, through almond-shaped eyes that were so alike that Ray couldn't understand why he had never seen the resemblance before. Their voices rose up to the beamed ceilings and echoed like shrill rolls of thunder, each trying to outshout the other. Ray could tell they were going to go on for a long time.

A half dozen new brownie points jumped up and down in his mental piggy bank.

Stop that, he thought at them. *I didn't do anything special!*

He got his chemistry text out of his bag and began to read over his neglected homework. Out of one ear, he half-listened to the argument under way until the voices faded into a distant cacophony.

Something shook his shoulder, waking him out of a peaceful dream of meadows and chemical formulae that gamboled over the grass like sheep. He raised his head from the smooth white page and looked up into Rose's eyes. She smiled.

"Go home, honey. They don't need you anymore."

CHAPTER 22

On Christmas Eve, the stagehands pushed the latest skid of 'finds' into the prop area. Ray had been waiting there for its arrival. He waited until the men parked it, then went through the boxes one by one. There, in the fourth box from the top, he moved a folded lace mantilla, and spotted the brass Aladdin's lamp.

"Yes!" He picked it up and cradled it.

One of the men in overalls returned. He pointed at Ray.

"Hey, kid, hands off! That don't belong to you."

"Yes, it does," he said. He pointed to the ornate carving on the side. "See, right there, it says Ray Crandall."

The stagehand waved a dismissive hand. "Just get away from there now, all right?"

"Yes, sir," Ray said, retreating. He ran back around the rear side of the risers so Selane's enforcers wouldn't see he was away from his post. He made for the catering table. In honor of Christmas, she had ordered a cappuccino machine and fancy cookies for the volunteers. The star herself, in a slinky red dress and tiny red lights in her hair, was making the rounds among the children, spotlighting each one of them for the cameras. She made a special plea for donations because it was Christmas. He knocked on the side of the lamp, careful not to rub it. He didn't want to have to deal with three wishes.

"Vickie?" he said. "Are you in there?"

A stream of dun-colored smoke issued from the spout. It coalesced into the shape of the teenaged girl, however old she really was, in her cropped t-shirt, green harem pants and bare feet. Minnie had now never given her sneakers. Vickie grinned at him.

"Hi, Ray," she said. "It's so cool when you knock. How'd you find me?"

"I've been keeping an eye out for your lamp," he said. He handed it to her. "Take it. You're free of Selane now. Try to be more careful who gets you next time. As long as you still want to be a genie, that is."

"But I'm not free," Vickie said.

"What?" Ray asked. "But she never found the lamp. She's never seen it."

"But I know, and the magic knows. She wished on me. I'm still in thrall for her third wish. It's in the rules. Three wishes, whether she knows about them or not, or whether I do." She gazed at him, her hazel eyes full of hope. "You can ask her for me."

Ray shook his head. "She's not talking to any of us. Since it never happened, we're all beneath her notice. I don't know how I can get her to make that third wish."

Vickie sat down on the floor and crossed her legs. "You'll figure something out. You're smart."

Ayosha came around the risers.

"Ray, you found her! Hi, Vickie! Merry Christmas."

Vickie smiled up at her. "Is it Christmas? What year?"

"Haven't seen much of you since Tuesday. How's … your mother?" Ray asked. "Both your mothers?"

"I called my mama in Georgia. She was as surprised as I was, but she's all right. I'll be flying down in the New Year before schools starts again. As for Miss Selane…" Ayosha sighed. "She's sort of nicer now, though not much. We're going to work it out. Right now, she wants a double-shot mocha skim latte."

"I'll make it," Ray said. He picked up a cup and put it under the spigot. "I need to ask a favor."

"What do you need? I owe you plenty."

"It's nothing," Ray said. "It was your wish."

Ayosha shook her head.

"But you made me take it. You could have let the clock run out, and you didn't. What do you need?"

"It's not me," Ray said. "It's for Vickie. Selane never made her third wish. Vickie's going to have to hold onto that forever if she doesn't make it, and you know what that could do." Ayosha raised an eyebrow.

"I sure do," she said. "Come on back with me. Vickie, you're my old friend from school, and Ray, you want an autograph for your little sister, don't you?"

They skirted the sound stage. With Ayosha escorting them, the enforcers didn't even try to stop them from entering Selane's domain. They were waiting beside the star's fancy chair when the spotlights dimmed. The diva herself strode away from the children in the wheelchairs and plumped herself down among her minions. Minnie changed Selane's shoes from sky-high stilettos to enameled flats.

"Mama," Ayosha said, sitting down in an almost equally luxurious chair beside her. Selane winced for a moment, then relaxed into the reality, beaming at the girl. She really was happy having her daughter back. Ray was glad. "These are my friends from college. This is Vickie and Ray."

The glorious visage turned toward them, acknowledging each for a moment.

"Oh, yes, I think I've seen Raymond."

"Here's your coffee, Miss Selane," he said, handing her the cup. He searched her eyes for recognition, but didn't find any. The magic had truly done its work. Selane examined the latte for fault and found none. She took a sip, and licked the foam delicately from her lip.

"You're with the Fairy Godmothers Union, aren't you?" she asked Ray. "You're all such wonderful volunteers. I don't know what we'd do without your help!"

"Yes, ma'am," Ray said. "My sister's a big fan of yours. She would love an autograph from you, if you wouldn't mind."

"For a big fan, I would be *delighted*." Selane clicked her fingers. One of the makeup women came over with a folder of photographs and a pen. Selane flipped through the pictures until she found one she liked. "What's her name?"

"Chanel."

Selane laughed, throwing back her head theatrically.

"Isn't that a coincidence? I'm wearing Chanel today." She signed it in big, flamboyant strokes and handed it to him. Ray clutched it. Chanel would be thrilled out of her mind. He couldn't wait to get it home to her. Maybe he would wrap it for her Christmas gift. "Do you like being a fairy godparent?"

"Yes, I do," Ray said. "It's really rewarding. Um. I get to grant one wish to each child who needs me. If, uh, if *you* could have any wish in the world, Miss Selane, what would it be?"

Selane patted Ayosha's hand. "To tell you the truth, I have what I want most in the world. Her gaze wandered across the sound stage, toward the children in the wheelchairs, and lit on little Francisco, her poster boy. "He's such a fighter," she said. "I wish I could make him well."

"I hear and obey," Vickie said. A rush of power flowed through them, bringing with it a sensation of completeness and peace. Selane shivered. Ray and Ayosha exchanged glances. The room fell cool, but it smelled sweet.

"Did someone open up that door?" Selane asked fretfully. Minnie rushed over to her with a cashmere wrap tinted to match her dress. "The weather is cold enough to freeze the air solid!"

"No!" Francisco exclaimed.

Ray looked over at the boy. His patient caretaker had put a container of juice on his tray. The boy put out his thin hand in protest.

Instead of weakly pushing his juice off the tray as usual, he shoved it. It went flying, breaking open and spilling on the floor. Francisco stared at it. Slowly but deliberately, he pulled himself up in his chair. To his astonishment, and everyone else's, he was able to sit straight. He worked his arms back and forth. He was still thin, and his muscles had been atrophied from his long illness, but he could move on his own.

"Mama!" he shouted. His mother came running from the side of the stage. He held his arms up to her. She burst into tears and threw her arms around him.

Selane watched the boy, her eyes wide.

"It's a miracle," she whispered. "A Christmas miracle."

"Spontaneous remission," Ray said. "It happens once in a while."

Another brownie point popped up in his mind.

Stop that! he thought.

Selane rose to her feet and bustled out onto the sound stage. She signaled to the director in his booth. The lights came on. A stagehand hurried over with a microphone. She seized it and addressed the cameras that clustered around her.

"Beloved supporters, ladies and gentlemen, I wanted to show you a marvel! You know my young friend Francisco. Through the generosity of viewers like you, I wanted you to know that one child has recovered from the horrors of Spaulding's Syndrome! So, please, get on the phone and make your pledge! Come on and make more Christmas miracles like this one!" She knelt beside the boy and smiled into the lens.

Francisco ignored her. He was too busy enjoying his newfound mobility.

The other children looked at Francisco with expressions of mild envy. Ray felt the air, but he sensed no desperate need from any of them. Still, no reason he shouldn't give them what he could. He took all the brownie points in his mental piggy bank, including the newcomer, and threw them toward the children. Two immediately ricocheted back, rewarding him for his generosity. Ray shook his head.

He went back to the risers and climbed into his seat beside Rose. Vickie followed him, sharing half his seat. The phones were ringing like crazy, and the volunteers were punching buttons and typing in donations. In the row behind him, Chris Popp had taken over Ayosha's job of entering tweets and posts. He clucked his tongue over a rash of replies and retweets that appeared on his screen. Ray was satisfied. It was the best wish that Selane could have made.

From the internet, he knew that the people who had come out to see her were alive and safely back in L.A. They had never even been there in Chicago. Maybe one day they'd seek out the 'Selane experience' again. Maybe not. And Antoinette had come home from Howard for Christmas. She'd be waiting for him as soon as the telethon was over.

"We did it," he said.

"*You* did it," Rose assured him. "Now, we need to find Vickie a place to live where she can straighten herself out and be happy. You deserve it, honey," she told the girl.

"I'll ask around," Ray said.

"No, I already have," Mrs. Durja said, leaning over from the second row. She smiled at Vickie. "While all of you have been arguing, I have been asking. We have djinni in the family. My cousin in Milwaukee said that the chapter in Santa Fe has a place for you. You still have some growing up to do. And you just go to school, Ray. You try to do too much."

"There's always more to do!" Ray protested. But he looked over at Ayosha, sitting on the side of the studio, watching her mother get ready to sing. The girl looked so happy. He'd done all right. Three seats down, Wendell Pinkwater leaned forward and gave Ray a thumb's up. Ray grinned. The vendetta was over.

At the end of the day, Selane stood alone in the spotlight to sing her Gratitude Lullaby. The first verse was all about Francisco, but she went on from there to name every single fairy godparent and sandman among the volunteers. Ray sat up proudly as she sang his name. He felt grateful himself. Vickie nudged him in the ribs.

"Pretty neat, huh?" she asked.

"Good," Ray said. "I'll sleep well tonight."

Introducing Angelina Adams

When Shahid Mahmud approached me about this series, like many of the other senior writers, I had a moment of trepidation. Writing a novella for a small press sounded like something I'd enjoy doing, but I had current book contracts to fulfill. Then, he explained that it was an opportunity to work with a less-experienced writer, who would write a companion novella to my piece. That element made the project irresistible. To give a junior writer a chance to publish a professional piece under the aegis of a better known writer, as Anne McCaffrey had done for me all those years ago, was the right thing to do. I was in.

I thank Anne McCaffrey and her son, Todd, for introducing me to Angelina Adams. I met Angel in the Worlds of Anne McCaffrey track room at a DragonCon many years ago, and liked her on sight. You can't help it; she sparkles. Not in a terrible vampire way, but in a bright, enthusiastic fashion that makes you want to be part of whatever makes her so happy. She has a generous soul, she is hard-working, she has worked at her own writing for years, and she is fun to be around. All of these traits made her an obvious choice to approach for the Stellar Guild project.

Mike Resnick, our editor, asked me to base my novella on one of my previous books, *The Magic Touch* (recently re-released by WordFire Press). I had always meant to return to the series one day. Working with Angel made it enjoyable to relearn the world I had created. She approached the project with intelligence and insight, and accepted changes with grace. "Homecoming" is a touching story, flavored with humor and pathos. I am sure that you will enjoy it, as well as Angel's own future work, when she starts to publish it.

WISHING ON A STAR

Book Two
HOMECOMING

ANGELINA ADAMS

CHAPTER 1

Traces of light pushed against the darkness as Vickie waited for the right moment to open her eyes. The slim, brown-haired girl slowed each breath until she could feel her heartbeat vibrating through her chest. The air felt so chilled and crisp she could almost believe it was possible to take a bite of it and consume the fresh mountain energies like a perfectly ripe apple. The promise of warmth brushed against her skin and she trusted that now was the perfect moment! She opened her eyes and gasped in delight at the vibrant intensity of a New Mexico sunrise. Colors appeared like magic out of a dusky sky that only minutes before had blended perfectly with the shadowed ridge of the Sangre de Cristo Mountains.

The young genie drank in the breathtaking sight as she floated a hand span above her favorite spot in the Pecos Wilderness. It had been more years than she honestly knew since she had last made the effort to venture outside of her lamp to meditate. She was enjoying her reawakened appreciation for the marvels of nature. For decades Vickie had been content to spend most of her time in a semi-amorphous state, out of touch with the world as she turned her thoughts inward and embraced deep-theta meditation. There had been plenty of time to explore creative daydreaming. The few instances where someone had rubbed her lamp had been pretty typical: she would respond to a summons, grant three wishes, and return to her lamp. But events this past Christmas hadn't kept to the usual pattern.

Her last master had made magical requests that had seemed harmless at the time, but the memory of how wrong the magic could have gone gave Vickie the heebie-jeebies. She wrinkled her nose and gave a testing sniff to reassure herself the stench of burning ozone was long gone. She never wanted to smell like that again. There wasn't enough soap in the world to cleanse the taint of bad magic. Fortunately, now all she could smell was the tang of the nearby fir trees. Thank goodness members of the Fairy Godmothers Union had come to her rescue and straightened out the magic. Well, Raymond and Rose in particular, but with the full support of the Chicago chapter of the FGU.

Raymond had been the first fairy godmother, or rather godfather, she had ever met. He was amazing; so nice and smart—practically the poster boy for tall, dark, and handsome. It was such a shame he had a girlfriend. When Vickie was with him, she had felt safe for the first time in ages. It was nice having someone help her out of a bad spot. Vickie had quickly come to appreciate how wonderful it was to have friends. Raymond's mentor, Rose, was as motherly as he was heroic. She was the epitome of Vickie's previously uneducated idea of what a fairy godmother should be: kindly eyes, wide smile, and dark hair sprinkled with silver. The older woman also tended to treat everyone like a favorite grandchild. Thinking of Rose now made Vickie feel warm, happy … and hungry.

Her stomach rumbled. She reached forward and pulled an oversized wicker basket out of thin air. Vickie hummed happily as she flipped open the top to reveal the red and white checked cloth covered insides that held the dwindling remains of a feast. When it came time for Vickie to leave Chicago, Rose had insisted on sending the young girl off with what the fairy godmother considered to be a "small care package."

It had taken days for Vickie to run out of chicken paprikash. The plum crumb cake had gone quickly as well. Fortunately there had been enough of the delicious apple latkes that there were still one or two left. She was hoarding the cinnamon raisin walnut challah that tasted as if Rose had used magic when making it. Vickie had learned her lesson after devouring the blueberry scones. While it had been pure heaven when she was eating them, she had regretted it when she had a terrible craving for them the next day and there were none left. She poured herself a cup of the homemade mulled apple cider and allowed herself one large piece of challah.

Vickie was happily consuming her breakfast when an insistent vibrating pulse reminded her of Rose's other parting gift. Not sure if this gift was a blessing or a curse, she licked a few delicious crumbs from her fingers and drew a palm-sized black mirror from her pocket.

As friendly as the members of FGU 3-26 had been, due to some recent unpleasantness with a now defunct chapter of the Djinni, Demons, and Efreets Guild, they hadn't been thrilled to have a genie in the neighborhood. Since each of them responded to Vickie as if she were the fifteen-year-old she appeared to be, rather than the somewhat older genie she technically was, they were reluctant to allow her to drift back into her usual solitary existence. When Mrs. Ganya Durja, a member in good standing with the FGU, suggested her nephew, who was a respectable member of the DDEG, had a place for Vickie with the Santa Fe chapter, the young genie had decided to just go with the flow. She had never seen New Mexico, and Jai Chanda had seemed nice when he popped into Rose's living room to offer Vickie a personal escort to his home. Regardless of how pleasant the distinguished looking man in the white duster had seemed, Rose was unwilling to send Vickie off without a means of staying in touch.

The star on top of Rose's rose-colored wand had shimmered with a rainbow of silver, gold and pink as Rose cast a special wish. Suddenly, the black mirror had appeared in her hand. She had seemed quite pleased with herself when she handed the mysterious object to Vickie.

"Um, thank you." Vickie stammered hesitantly. "What is it?"

"It's a phone," Rose said.

Vickie glanced from it to her, her expression making it clear she was trying to decide if she was making a joke. Vickie knew what a phone was after all. Just because she had lived in a commune before she became a genie didn't mean they had lived in a cave. They'd had electricity. They even had a big black and white TV. Their phone had been slightly smaller than the bread box. It was black and had a clear plastic circle that would spin around when you dialed the phone. She had enjoyed sneaking into the main house and listening to people from nearby farms talking on the party line.

"I can make calls on this?" she asked.

"More than calls," Rose said proudly. "It is one of those smart thingies that all the kids are always going on about. You can listen to music, watch videos, and do all the stuff my grandkids do with theirs. I made sure it runs on magic so it should always work."

Vicki had no clue what Rose was talking about, but she was grateful for the gift.

"Thank you so much, Rose," she said warmly, giving the fairy godmother a hug.

Ray took the 'phone' from Vickie and turned it in his long fingers.

"Nice job, Rose!" he exclaimed. "Instead of a land line, you gave her a ley line. Sweet!"

Now, a ley line was something Vickie did know about, being well versed in spiritual and mystical alignments.

"How do I use it?" she had asked, looking at it with more interest. If this was somehow attuned to ley lines, it could be an impressive work of magic that Rose was quite right to be proud of.

Just then, Ray had found the right spot to tap. The dark screen suddenly showed a picture of the circular dial she remembered. Amazing!

"Watch," Ray told her before he held the glass with the picture of a dial close to his mouth, "Call Raymond."

A musical trill came from Ray's jacket. He grinned and pulled out a silver and white device that went silent at the touch of a button. He handed Vickie her black glass. She noticed that instead of the dial there was now an image of his handsome face smiling at her from the mirror. He motioned for her to hold it up to her ear like he was doing with the thing in his hands.

"See?" his voice echoed from the black glass into her ear. "It's a phone."

She couldn't deny the amazing evidence before her, and tried to pay careful attention as he taught her how to call Rose.

"I'm afraid it is time for us to leave," Mr. Chanda said kindly as soon as she had gotten a basic understanding of how to work the black mirror.

Vickie found herself reluctant to leave her new friends. She placed her lamp in the velvet lined satchel Jai had brought with him to protect it from accidental rubbing in transit. Vickie looked at Ray and Rose in silent appeal.

Rose gave her a motherly hug, "Now you remember to stay in touch and enjoy getting to know your new family."

Vickie had clutched her care package to her chest. "I will," she promised.

Then she and Jai had vanished into a puff of dun-colored smoke that swirled and waved in their wake. When she opened her eyes again, they were in his home in Santa Fe.

During the past couple of months, Vickie had tried to keep her promise to stay in touch with Ray and Rose with mixed results. She couldn't seem to get the hang of controlling the ley line. One time she had told it to 'Call Rose' and had ended up talking to a young woman with a thick accent who was visiting Stonehenge with a friend. She and Vickie had been equally confused as the girl kept asking how she could have gotten her "numbah." Before they could figure out the mix-up, the girl had to run and the line suddenly went silent.

Luckily, answering was easier than calling. As she fumbled the black ley line from the pocket of her moss green trousers, the vibrating felt more insistent. She turned it around in confusion a few times; sliding her thumb across the glass. She was disappointed when a face framed with long silky black hair appeared in the mirror. It was her host family's teenage daughter, Indira, rather than Rose's older and much friendlier face.

"Mother wants you to come down for breakfast."

Fortunately, Vickie's phone was unable to project images. So while she was able to see the exasperated expression on Indira's lovely face, the teenager who refused to actually walk up the stairs to deliver a message couldn't see that Vickie was not, in fact, in her room.

"Sure," Vickie responded quickly. "I'll be right there." She slid her hand over the black glass and Indira's slim dark-eyed face vanished from the polished mirror surface.

After the freedom of being on her own for so long, Vickie still wasn't thrilled about being held to the same rules her host family felt was proper for a fifteen-year-old girl. Silly restrictions like not leaving the house without permission were a big part of her not being sold on the idea of trying to fit into family life. But she had to admit, the food went a long way toward making the loss of autonomy worth it. Indira's mom, Shivani, had a gift for making sure every meal was amazing. Regardless of having just enjoyed a yummy snack, Vickie saw no reason to miss out on Shivani's cooking.

With only a twinge of regret at having her peaceful morning interrupted, she grabbed her care package and popped back to her room before anyone had the chance to discover she had ever left.

CHAPTER 2

The chaos of a typical morning in the Chanda household greeted Vickie as she entered the dining room. She slipped quietly into a chair between Indira's little brothers who were continuing their never ending argument.

"Your clubhouse plans were all over my side of the room again," Rakesh complained to his older, but smaller, brother. "You know I hate it when I can't walk without stepping on crumpled papers everywhere!"

Nakul shrugged, his mop of overgrown black hair falling into his eyes. "If it bothers you so much, you pick them up."

Vickie caught Rakesh's eye and smiled sympathetically. Normally, the tall nine-year-old with the shoulders of future linebacker was an island of calm in his family's sea of volatile personalities. But Nakul had spent much of his thirteen years perfecting the art of pushing people's buttons, then using his angelic face and dimpled smile to charm his way out of trouble. The frown on Rakesh's broad, gentle face made it clear his brother's charms were not going to work this morning.

"Maybe if you would actually build something instead of just talking about it all the time," Rakesh taunted, "then I would get a break from your goofy face and your mess!"

Vickie winced as Nakul rose to the bait and began defending his current project. Before she had arrived, Rakesh had created a retreat in the attic where he could escape from his brother's constant chatter and activity. But after only two days of suffering through Indira's complaints about having to share her room with a "hippie," he had offered his sanctuary to Vickie. The small, cozy space was much more her style than the huge, bright room with all the windows and the fluffy beds had been. He had helped arrange her collection of bean bag chairs and knick-knacks from her lamp. They turned the attic space into the first room she could remember being able to call her own. This latest argument with Nakul made it clear just how much of a sacrifice Rakesh had made when he gave her the room.

"Boys, enough!"

Shivani's entrance into the dining room was preceded by the amazing aroma of potatoes and onions. Both boys immediately fell silent as their mother swept past with a platter of lightly browned dosa.

She stopped next to her husband's chair and cleared her throat twice, "Jai…"

Jai glanced up from his newspaper, his reading glasses balanced in the edge of his nose. One look at his wife's evaporating patience, and he showed himself to be as intelligent as his bright eyes and pencil thin mustache made him seem. He quickly folded his newspaper and stashed it under his chair.

"Mmmm, my favorite!" Jai sniffed at the platter of soft, crispy crepes Shivani placed on the table in front of him. "And, since I am by far the luckiest man alive, I bet there will be my beautiful wife's scrumptious mango chutney to go with it."

Shivani accepted his praise with the grace of a woman who knew every extravagant word was nothing more than the absolute truth. She glanced at the door leading from the kitchen. As if on cue, Indira entered the room, balancing a tray with three different dishes of chutney in one hand and holding her baby sister on her hip with the other.

Jai grinned, "Ahh! See? I was right. Luckiest man alive."

Shivani brushed a hand over the glistening black hair that was pulled back into a stylish braided knot at the nape of her neck and smiled at her husband's appreciation. Just like the elegantly embroidered black kameez she wore, not a hair or a thread was out of place. Everything in her life was held to high standards; her appearance, her cooking, her home – and most especially her daughter.

Vickie secretly marveled at the ease with which Indira deftly deposited the tray on the table before placing a squirming Maya into her high chair. The often arrogant fifteen-year-old might currently be an annoying slender shadow of her mother, but she was already showing signs of someday being as talented at running a household.

Maya gurgled happily and tangled a chubby fist in Indira's long hair as her sister buckled the safety strap that would keep the adventurous toddler from escaping. A familiar unease tugged at Vickie's heart before she turned her face away from watching the loving competence with which Indira untangled herself from Maya's grip. Vickie switched her attention to the selection of spreads available.

The clink of silverware and the hum of voices created a backdrop of homey noise as breakfast continued. Vickie passed on the pasty ginger chutney, knowing it was too hot for her taste. She was spreading a tart cranberry chutney on the other half of her breakfast when she realized part of the family conversation she hadn't been listening to was directed at her.

"… be a good opportunity to meet the other members." Jai smiled expectantly at Vickie.

She quickly swallowed a mouthful of dosa and cleared her throat as the silence caused five pairs of matching dark eyes to turn her way.

"Umm … sure?" apparently was the right thing to say. Jai smiled approvingly and patted her on the shoulder as he pushed up from the table.

"Good, good. We will pop down to the Plaza right after dinner tonight. Guild meetings are important, but they aren't worth missing Mama's cooking." Jai winked at his sons, sharing an inside joke that had his daughter rolling her eyes.

"Just so long as she doesn't miss her lesson with Zoya," Shivani insisted.

Vickie caught the glare Indira shot in her direction. Apparently she still hadn't forgiven Vickie for being able to swing homeschooling. Indira protested, but Shivani had pointed out how much Indira would miss being at school with her best friend, Alyssa. Nothing could get Indira past resenting what she saw as another example of the new girl getting to do whatever she wanted.

Shivani had been surprised by the otherwise accommodating genie's resistance to joining Indira at school. Every time the subject came up, the skinny little thing had somehow managed to wriggle out of the conversation. When her husband had suggested a home study program, she had graciously agreed to the compromise. Provided of course Vickie's education was overseen by someone appropriate. Shivani's Aunt Zoya, who worked at the local library and had never been married (poor thing), had volunteered. Shivani now treated the arrangement as if Vickie's lessons with Zoya had been her intention all along.

Momentarily distracted from wondering what she had just agreed to, Vickie smiled at the mention of Zoya's name. She wasn't sure just what sort of homeschooling program Shivani had had in mind when she enlisted her aunt's participation. Vickie was sure most of the instruction she'd had so far was not part of the intended curriculum. Appropriate or not, she loved lesson days.

"I wouldn't dream of interfering with Vickie's education," Jai assured his wife teasingly as he began his 'leaving for work' ritual.

He ruffled the thick black hair on both of his son's heads and growled affectionately at them to get haircuts. Then he brushed the back of his fingers caressingly across Indira's cheek. He leaned over to tickle Maya under her round brown chin, causing her to giggle. Finally, he turned his gaze on his wife where she sat trying to spoon applesauce into the toddler's mouth. Shivani might be a plump, benevolent dictator most of the time; but whenever her husband smiled at her each morning she blushed like a school girl. Every time. Jai leaned down and placed a lingering, yet very proper, kiss on his wife's cheek. As he turned and headed out the door, Vickie almost missed the slight tug on his sleeves that covered steel blue cuffs that matched the ones that were permanently fastened to her own wrists.

He seemed so normal, so middle-class America. It was easy for her to forget that Jai Chanda was also the treasurer of the local Djinni, Demons, and Efreets Guild. Of course! That must have been what he was talking about. Vickie stifled a groan. She had hoped she would be able avoid attending a meeting of the DDEG for a little while longer. She liked Jai, but it sounded as if the guild was nothing but old guys talking business. Boring meetings with suits and rules weren't really her scene. If going would make Jai happy, she supposed she could suffer through one night of hanging out with the establishment. Zoya was constantly telling her that it was what people didn't know that kept them trapped in prisons of their own making. So perhaps it was time for Vickie to put a little effort into learning more about the genie gig.

For years Vickie had thought she had it down. Someone rubs the lamp and they get three wishes. When not working on wishes, she figured she was supposed to just chill and wait for the next summons. With what she had seen of Jai's life so far, apparently there was a lot to learn about existing outside of the lamp. Given the nature of what her life had been like before becoming a genie, the idea made her a little nervous.

CHAPTER 3

While Shivani bustled her children off to school, Vickie managed to retreat to the familiar comfort of her lamp. Since she had arrived in Santa Fe, she had come to appreciate the benefits of living with a family that was accustomed to life with a genie. Everyone respected the sanctity of the lamp. She had seen the boisterous Nakul walk softly past the locked case that held his father's lamp. Even tiny Maya was being taught "no touch" with forceful consistency. This atmosphere of respect was new to Vickie. The power inherent as part of the genie gig was balanced against the vulnerability of having a piece of her soul tied to her lamp. In the past, her way of coping with the hold the lamp had on her had been to never venture far from it. Now, as she became accustomed to this newfound sense of lamp security she was also becoming more adventurous.

The household rules regarding lamps also meant that Vickie was able to spend part of each day in a blissful Zen state of amorphous meditation. Feeling safe from an unexpected rubbing of the lamp was a nice change. Unfortunately, that didn't mean she was safe from all forms of summoning.

Above the fireplace hung a beautifully engraved brass gong that Shivani had received as a wedding gift. The first time Vickie noticed Shivani pick up the felted mallet and give the gong and firm tap, she was confused by the lack of sound produced by the instrument. When Jai soon arrived full of apologies over being late for dinner, Vickie learned two things. First, was the fact that Shivani only used the gong as a means of last resort. Second, Shivani was serious about everyone being on time for dinner.

Vickie had assumed the gong was specially attuned to Shivani's husband, but she was mistaken. As she was chilling in her lamp a sudden reverberating sound imposed itself on her ears and made her entire essence hum insistently. She misted out of her lamp and began to search for the compelling source of the sound. What she found was a flustered Shivani standing in the living room with the mallet in hand. Maya was pulling herself up on one of the stacks of boxes that filled the living room.

"Oh good, it worked," Shivani said. "I am sorry for the imposition, but I need your assistance."

Vickie eyed the toddler warily, afraid Shivani was about to ask her to watch Maya.

"My book club has been collecting donations for the expanded children's section at Zoya's library. I had planned for them to be dropped off there today, but somehow signals got mixed and they ended up here." She looked at Vickie hopefully, "Do you think you could help me load them into the van? I know it's a lot to ask; some of them are quite heavy…" Her voice trailed off. Vickie sprang into action.

"No problem!" Vickie said. She would happily tote heavy boxes of books rather than take care of the toddler.

Once everything was loaded in the van, Vickie headed for the stairs and the safety of her room.

"Thank you so much, dear," Shivani called after her. "You did such a good job. It would be a tremendous help if you could come with me to unload them as well?"

Vickie was stopped in her tracks by the not-so-subtle appeal. What could be the harm? She climbed into the van.

"How about we stop and get Indira to help?" Shivani asked. "We can be finished and have her back to school before her lunch break is over."

Vickie cringed inwardly.

Surprisingly, at first Indira seemed happy to help. Her friend Alyssa had been absent for the past few days and lunch was boring without her there. With extra hands, unloading was easier than loading had been.

Vickie was amused each time Zoya tried to grab a box and help.

"Young backs are better suited to such work," Shivani insisted as she placed a restraining hand on her aunt's arm.

Zoya sighed in resignation and pointed toward a desk hidden beneath a mountain of paperwork. "Just set the boxes over there," she said.

Vickie started clearing space for the stacks of donations while Indira took a cart outside to the van and began piling boxes onto it.

"Hey, whatcha doin here?" A slender redhead with smoky eyes and bright pink lipstick leaned nonchalantly against the side of the van.

At the familiar sound of her best friend's voice, Indira glanced quickly to check on her mother's whereabouts. When she saw the two older women were absorbed in a discussion of the types of books packed into each box, Indira ducked around to other side of the van. She insistently motioned for Alyssa to move out of her mother's line of sight as well.

"Helping mama with book club donations. Why haven't you been in school lately?" Indira asked in an irritated whisper.

Alyssa shrugged her shoulders noncommittally. "I had better things to do."

Indira's expression as she noticed her friend's disheveled appearance was filled with confused worry. "Apparently not. Where did you even find those shorts?"

The normally perfectly-manicured Alyssa was dressed in ragged cutoffs, sneakers, and an oversized sweatshirt.

"Eh, they were in my sister's room. I needed something I didn't mind getting dirty." Alyssa acted as if her odd appearance was nothing out of the ordinary.

The thought of her fashionista friend planning to get dirty on purpose distressed Indira even more. "What's going on with you lately?"

"Nothing," Alyssa replied indignantly. "It's just a pretty day and I thought it would be nice to head out towards Eldorado and do a little hiking."

Indira was sure that was the first time she had ever heard the word 'hiking' escape her friend's lips in anything other than a mocking tone.

"That sounds like a pretty lame reason to skip school. I know your mom has been distracted since your dad left, but even she is bound to notice something eventually." Indira's discomfort over Alyssa's odd behavior was growing, along with her fear of them being caught by her mother if she didn't get back to work.

"Well, fine!" Alyssa sneered. "It looks like you'd rather do charity work with your mom's new pet project anyway. Since you obviously would rather hang out with her, then I guess there's no point in asking if you want to join us anyway."

Indira winced, knowing she meant Vickie, but she narrowed her eyes at the word us.

"Us?" She looked around, puzzled. "I don't see anyone but you."

Alyssa hesitated. "I was waiting at the park across the street for my... ride."

Indira arched one eyebrow slightly. This was not like Alyssa.

A scrawny gray and white hound with black markings around its eyes came trotting up to Alyssa and nudged her with its nose, making sure to keep a skittish distance from Indira.

"Even if I wasn't here with mama, I would think skipping school to go hiking in the desert was a bad idea." Indira said. Alyssa ignored the pointed suggestion and focused her attention on the dog.

A resentful silence grew between them. Indira fumbled for a way to break it.

"Where did you get the dog?"

"Oh, it's a stray I was just, umm, thinking of adopting. His name's Tony," Alyssa mumbled uncomfortably.

Indira squatted and held her hand out. The dog took a step toward her. It seemed to be ready to move close enough for her to pet when she heard footsteps approaching. The high-strung animal lurched away from her hand as if afraid she was going to try to grab him. He turned his head toward the sound and sniffed at the air. With a low growl he turned and ran back toward the park. He stopped once to bark insistently at Alyssa, before breaking into the long, ground-eating lope of a greyhound.

"What an odd dog." Indira shrugged. "What's wrong?" She quickly forgot the stray as she realized Alyssa was also ready to run away.

"Look, I gotta go," Alyssa said nervously. "I don't want anyone to realize I'm not home sick like I told the school when I called and pretended to be my mom."

"Wait!" Indira tried to catch her friend's hand, but Alyssa easily slipped away from her and began to run in the same direction the dog had gone. The girl and the dog vanished behind a stand of juniper trees. Vickie poked her head around the side of the van.

"There you are! Your mom was wondering where you were," she said.

Indira glared at Vickie resentfully and shoved past her to push the cart full of boxes toward the building. "I was taking a break. These things are heavy."

Taken aback by the sudden change in Indira's mood, Vickie quietly picked up the last box and followed her. It seemed no matter what she said or did around the other girl, it was always the wrong thing.

After they delivered the last boxes, Indira made a point of waiting in sullen silence to be taken back to school.

Shivani began the usual juggling act of holding Maya on one hip and attempting to locate something in the large purse dangling from her other shoulder. "Here. Hold her a sec."

Distracted by keeping a stack of boxes from tipping over, Vickie was not as alert as she normally was to the possibility of having the child thrust into her hands. She began to stammer a refusal, and instead found her arms full of giggling, dark-haired, Maya. Vickie tried to keep an awkward grip on the squirming little girl who wanted down with the single-minded determination of a toddler intent on exploration.

Seeing the girl's obvious distress, Zoya reached over and deftly plucked her great-niece from Vickie's arms.

"There's my pyaari beti!" Zoya smiled at Maya and planted playful kisses on the sweet girl's cheeks. Maya squealed and laughed, momentarily distracted from her escape plans by the exuberant display of affection.

"And here is the list of everything that was donated." Shivani waved an envelope in one hand triumphantly. "Let me know if anything is missing after you've had a chance to check in the books."

Shivani and Zoya traded envelope for baby. Once Maya realized she was back where she started and the game of 'pass the baby' was over, she resumed the determined wiggle that she was convinced would eventually win her freedom.

"How about we get some frozen yogurt after school as a thank you for your help, eh, girls?" Shivani asked. Distracted by trying to hold on to her younger daughter, she was oblivious to the brooding silence emanating from her older daughter. "We could make a girls' day out of it. Maybe even do some shopping?"

Vickie winced. She knew that last suggestion was aimed at the comfortable crop top and green trousers she always wore. Her lack of interest in all things fashion was a source of distress for the always impeccably-dressed Shivani.

If Shivani was unaware of the tension brewing between the two girls, Zoya was not. The older woman smiled. "Actually, I was going to suggest that Vickie stay with me. We could have some extra time for lessons."

Shivani hesitated as she tried to decide between her desire to get Vickie into a new outfit and the benefit of education.

Zoya sweetened the deal. "I promise we will make going to a store part of today's lesson." She cast a warning glance in Vickie's direction. "And Vickie will promise that we will come home with at least one new outfit."

Vickie sighed and nodded her agreement. She brightened considerably when Zoya whispered for her ears only, "As a reward, you will also get to go to Nambé Falls for P.E."

P.E. meant the yoga lessons. Vickie would transport them to some beautiful place in the mountains, far from town. They had been to several different spots, but Vickie's favorite was a grassy meadow near Nambé Lake. The trips also served as geography lessons. The genie was becoming quite knowledgeable about the mountains and high desert prairie that surrounded Santa Fe.

"That's probably best," Shivani agreed. "Come on, Indira. We need to get you back to school before lunch period is over."

The teenage girl let out an exasperated sigh and glared at Vickie resentfully as she followed her mother back out to the van.

"So, what was that all about?" Zoya asked as they watched the two depart.

"I honestly have no idea," Vickie said.

CHAPTER 4

"You know, if you would be more enthusiastic about finding a new outfit, we could finish much faster and have more time at the falls," Zoya admonished an obviously disinterested Vickie as they rummaged through a local consignment store. "I swear, getting you to do something you don't want to do is about as easy as nailing Jell-O to a tree."

"I like Jell-O," was the younger girl's only remark, but she smiled and began sorting through the nearest clothing rack that held skirts and pants in her size.

Zoya's vibrant laugh echoed from the shoe bin she had nearly emptied in search of something that would be just right for Vickie. "Of course you do."

Even if she was less than fond of clothes shopping, Vickie enjoyed every outing she had been on with Zoya. The middle-aged, flamboyant beauty was the exact opposite of her traditionalist niece. Where Shivani was plump, petite, and definite in her every thought and deed, Zoya was a statuesque free spirit. The family resemblance was evident in their flawless creamy brown skin, high cheekbones, large dark eyes, and somewhat prominent nose. However, the resemblance ended with their pretty faces. Shivani had a good heart and the best of intentions, but she also had an agenda. Zoya did not.

"When I think of all the things you missed while you were out of touch with the world," Zoya's voice sounded muffled as she tossed aside rejected sneakers, flats, and boots. "I don't know how I can manage to catch you up on all of it. I mean, you missed the early days of MTV, the space shuttle, Madonna, Star Wars…" As the list grew, Zoya's voice rose in disbelief until she emerged triumphant with a pair of silver sequined platform shoes dangling from one hand. "My word, you completely missed out on disco!"

From the look of the glittery path to a broken ankle in Zoya's hands, Vickie thought maybe it was best she had missed disco. She was relieved when the shoes went into the basket Zoya was carrying for herself rather than being added to Vickie's.

"What about this?" Vickie pulled a swishy cotton skirt with brightly colored geometric designs from the rack.

Zoya eyed it critically. "Hmmm, you know I saw a peasant blouse with some lovely bead work on it somewhere…" Her voice trailed off as she retraced her steps. "Ah-hah!" She waved a rust-colored blouse with a ruffled neckline.

Vickie admitted the two looked pretty enough to satisfy Shivani, and the cotton was soft enough to meet her own comfort requirements. "So, are we done now?" she asked hopefully.

"Not yet. We have to find you a pair of shoes that you will actually keep on your feet." Zoya moved to search through a different bin.

"I don't understand this obsession with shoes." Vickie glanced at the sneakers she was wearing and wiggled her toes. She preferred going barefoot whenever possible, but those worked just fine if shoes were necessary.

"That much is obvious, dear," Zoya chuckled.

"If you find me shoes, can we do P.E. next?" Vickie tried to keep her voice from sounding as bored as she felt.

Zoya smiled at her over her shoulder. "Yes."

Vickie sighed and looked around for somewhere to sit. But the store was so full of stuff, there didn't seem to be a clear spot anywhere. She shifted a pile of faded jeans to make room to rest on the floor. A flash of brown leather and turquoise beading caught her eye. She lifted the jeans enough to pull a Navajo sandal free from where it had been buried.

"What about this?" She held up the flat sandal with geometric turquoise stripes decorating thin brown leather straps.

"It's perfect!" Zoya exclaimed. "I hope it has a mate. Where did you find it?"

Vickie gestured toward the pile of jeans at her feet. "Under there."

A determined search soon located the missing shoe.

"Excellent!" Zoya said. "I will pay for them and we can go."

Soon the two of them were back in the convertible and headed north out of town.

As they approached the park, Zoya did a quick survey of her pupil's transformation from homeless waif to hippy chic.

"You look lovely," Zoya assured her.

When she had first met Vickie, she had worried that the bright New Mexico sun would do horrible things to the girl's milk-white skin. But Vickie seemed as oblivious to UV rays as she was to most everything else. Zoya was determined to uncover the pain that lurked behind the genie's sweet, vacant smile.

"There, arrived in record time!" Zoya announced as she pulled into a parking spot, turned off the car, and reached for the bag with their yoga mats.

They took one of the hiking paths that branched off of the public parking area. When they rounded the bend and were hidden from sight by a thick stand of fir trees, Vickie took Zoya by the hand.

"Ready?" she asked. Zoya nodded with a grin. The two vanished in a puff of dun colored smoke, positive that no one had seen them disappear.

A scrawny gray and white hound with black markings around its eyes emerged from the shadowed undergrowth and trotted over to where the women had been standing only moments before. He sniffed the ground, then growled low and menacingly in his throat before he turned and slipped back into the shadows.

CHAPTER 5

Vickie took a deep breath of fresh mountain air as they appeared in her favorite meadow near the still waters of Nambé Lake. A gray tumble of rocks from an old rockslide edged by a stand of tall, thin pines was reflected in the mirror-like surface of the lake. They took time to adjust to the sudden altitude change as they set up their yoga mats. She changed out of her new clothes. Zoya placed a small speaker on a nearby stump and connected it to her phone. The gentle strains of the music they used for warm-ups were perfectly suited to the beauty surrounding them.

They worked through sun salutations, stretches, and the obligatory downward facing dog. The music began to pick up tempo. Even though Zoya tended to select music with more of a driving beat for some of her yoga sessions than was strictly traditional, Vickie was still caught off guard when the steady increase in rhythm became a thumping pulse of bass and drums. They moved from the beginning mountain pose into a warrior sequence. As she inhaled and brought her arms above her head, she could feel the music vibrating through the mat she was standing on. The unexpected rhythms added an energy and intensity to the next poses that she found exhilarating.

By the time they moved to the relaxation sequence that ended their session, the music was once again a gentle composition of wind and strings. Rather than sitting and meditating as the music faded to silence, the two of them remained lying on their mats in a final savasana pose.

With her vision filled with white puffs of clouds against the bright blue sky, Vickie was conscious of how grounded she felt. Her skin tingled with a warmth and energy that kept the chill of the 60 degree weather from being uncomfortable. She could hear Zoya quietly shifting to reach for the light blankets and water bottles she had laid out before they began.

Vickie sat up on her mat and accepted the offerings with a quiet smile. She wrapped the soft fleece around her shoulders and enjoyed the feeling of peace that always followed a good session in the mountains.

"That was an unexpected music choice," she commented as Zoya copied her relaxed lotus position and slowly sipped her water.

"I have been experimenting with rhythms to enhance different energies. I like the way you can actually feel the pulse of these new songs." Zoya laughed softly. "I had the volume turned up so loud at home when I was editing the play list that the vibrations actually caused a photo of Maya to fall off the table next to my speakers."

"That is one way to decide if a song has enough energy I suppose." Vickie smiled and shifted on her mat to face the sloping ridge of Santa Fe Baldy.

A herd of mule deer made their way from the trees and approached the water's edge. One doe was exceptionally round and obviously pregnant. Her large ears flickered nervously in the direction of the two women before she risked joining the herd in their usual forage. Vickie watched the timid mother-to-be and sighed deeply.

"Care to share?" Zoya's typical invitation to conversation caught Vickie in a rare talkative mood.

"I had a baby once."

"What happened?" Zoya kept her voice light, and free of obvious curiosity.

"My sister took him. Said genies make bad mothers." Silence stretched for several heartbeats before Vickie continued. "She also said that since genies were the next best thing to demons, I was obviously evil...." Her voice trailed away to a faint whisper.

Sensing there was much more to the story than that, Zoya risked a softly prompting,

"So where is he now?"

"I'm not really sure," Vickie admitted. "I suppose they might still be living in Tennessee."

"Tennessee?" Zoya asked. "I thought you were from California."

"Oh, I lived there for a while, but my family is from the Smokies. Mama was pregnant with me when Daddy got sent to Korea. Linda, that's my sister's name, said Mama was never really the same after she got news of daddy's death."

Zoya wasn't surprised by Vickie's sad past. "Is your mom still in Tennessee too?"

"Oh, no, she died when I was about nine or so." Vickie's dry-eyed statement of fact was more heartbreaking to Zoya than a weeping emotional breakdown would have been.

"Linda was almost thirteen at the time, so she took care of us. She worked and found places for us to stay. She always had lots of friends whose parents didn't seem to mind having a couple of extra hands helping out around their farms."

The surrounding pines began to cast long shadows as the sky showed the first signs of approaching twilight. Not even the dropping temperature could break the spell of the story Vickie was sharing for the first time. They scooted closer together on the yoga mats and pulled their blankets tight.

"About a year after Mama passed, Linda met this guy who had a big farm. When he invited her to come and live with him, he said there was plenty of room if she wanted to bring me, too."

Vickie smiled for the first time. "The Smoky Mountains are beautiful. Sunrise was my favorite time of day. I loved the way the mists would drift off the mountain tops and mingle with the clouds until you couldn't tell where the land stopped and the sky started."

The smile vanished as less pleasant thoughts came to mind. Vickie grew silent, the easy words drying up in the face of long buried memories rising to the surface.

Zoya nodded encouragingly. "Go on."

"There were other people living there. It was actually more of a commune than a farm."

Zoya nodded and did a few quick calculations in her mind. Given what she already knew of Vickie's past, she figured they must have been living at the commune in the early to mid-60s. Having been a teenager herself at the time, Zoya could see how that would have been a logical place for a couple of orphaned girls to wind up.

Vickie shrugged. "Looking back now, I realize things were a lot nicer there than a farm in the mountains that didn't have any cash crops should have been. There were four big houses, with plenty of rooms for everyone, really nice bathrooms, a common area for dancing, and a big TV room. That's where Tony usually stayed, either in the TV room or his office." She grew quiet before adding, "or with Linda."

"Tony?" Zoya wanted to be sure she was keeping track of everything Vickie was sharing, "That was the man who owned the farm?"

"Yeah," Vickie nodded her head and grimaced. "He was this tall, hairy guy with a huge mustache. He always wore these awful paisley silk shirts and a gold medallion that was about as big as my hand." She shook her head as if trying to get rid of heavy thoughts, "We were happy enough I guess. At least, we were until I got called."

Zoya looked at her in confusion and Vickie tapped the blue steel cuffs that were so much a part of her wrists that Zoya often forgot they were there. "Ahh, I see. I've never heard it referred to as 'being called' before."

"That's what Tony called it," Vickie said. "He said the community was blessed with a guardian spirit that took the shape of a special lamp. Sometimes, when they had a need that couldn't be filled any other way, the lamp would choose someone to be its instrument for making sure everyone had what they needed."

Zoya reached out and took the girl's hand, sensing things were about to get painful.

"I didn't hesitate when he said the lamp had chosen me to bring special blessings to the farm. I felt honored as I put on the cuffs. I promised to swear eternal fealty to the spirit of the lamp and obey the words of my master. As soon as the cuffs clamped around my wrists I found out honor wasn't exactly the right word for my situation."

The first tear began to roll silently down Vickie's cheek. Zoya's tears soon followed.

"I also discovered what obeying the words of my master meant – when Tony was the master." Vickie spoke through clenched teeth.

Zoya's imagination began to fill in the blanks as the tears fell freely. Vickie's voice grew so quiet Zoya had to lean close to hear what she was saying.

"I'd always done what I was told. You would think being ordered around by a master wouldn't be that big of a deal. But there was just something so awful about being unable to stop my body from doing anything he said. My mind would scream no, even as I carried out his commands."

Vickie drew a deep shuddering breath and changed the subject, as though unable to continue putting some memories into words. "The wishes were easy. He really did use them to keep his little domain comfortable and running smoothly. He liked having lots of people looking up to him as if he was some sort of savior. No one knew what he was really like or that he was using magic to support the community. He held off on using his third wish. Tony enjoyed having Linda's baby sister in his thrall too much to let me off the hook."

Zoya couldn't keep quiet any longer, "Did Linda know what was going on?"

Vickie shook her head. "Not until I turned up pregnant."

Zoya was shocked. Vickie shrugged. "Things got bad when Linda found out just what sort of man she had hooked up with." Her voice shook. "To be honest, I expected him to take his anger out on me when she confronted him about cheating on her. Because he had ordered me to be silent and stay put, there wasn't anything I could do to help when he began hitting her for daring to question anything he chose to do. Linda managed to calm him down and convince him she loved him. She said she didn't care what he had done to me."

It was obvious Linda choosing Tony over her sister had hurt Vickie more than anything he could have done.

"Things got quiet for a while after that. At first, Tony was kind of into the idea of having a kid he knew was actually his. He also enjoyed watching my sister treat me like a leper. But then I got so huge and miserable that he would get annoyed just looking at me. Finally, one day, he lost his temper and yelled, 'I wish you'd just go ahead and have that brat already!'"

Vickie giggled softly through the tears, "You should have seen how furious he was when I immediately went into labor and he realized he'd wasted his last wish."

Her face took on a wistful expression that was barely visible in the gathering dusk. "He was such a pretty baby. I named him Paul. You know, after the Paul."

"McCartney of course," Zoya nodded with understanding. "Good choice."

"That's about all there is to tell, really." Vickie wiped the tears from her cheeks.

"But, how did you end up leaving?" Zoya wanted to get the entire story before Vickie went back to keeping everything bottled up inside.

"Oh, well. I'm not really sure." She bit her lower lip and tried to recall the events exactly. "Tony kept my lamp locked in his office. Even though I was technically free once he had used his three wishes, I just couldn't bring myself to leave the farm. My sister and son were my only family. Besides, I didn't know where to go. Bad as it had become, it was the only home I knew. When Linda and I had the fight where she snatched Paul from my arms and told me I was evil and a horrible mother..."

The silent tears returned as words momentarily failed. Zoya laid a hand on Vickie's wrist.

"I couldn't stand listening to her. I just dissolved into a mist so I could escape from all the mean things she was yelling at me. I hid in my lamp and hoped Tony wouldn't find me. I fell asleep, but I have no idea for how long. When I woke up, I was floating down a mountain stream. Most likely, Linda threw the lamp away so she could finally get rid of me. I figured Paul was better off without all the fighting, and I was better off anywhere other than stuck at the farm with Linda and Tony."

Vickie smiled halfheartedly. "When no one came looking for me, I just went back into the lamp. I figured I'd let the universe decide what it wanted to do with me."

Zoya sat in silence, absorbing the full impact of everything Vickie had shared. "Well, that certainly explains why you flinch every time you're around Maya."

Vickie nodded. "Yeah, it can just get to be too much. I don't know what to do with kids."

"It will get better, you'll see." Zoya patted her friend comfortingly.

"You know," Vickie said thoughtfully, letting a notion form in her mind that she had never dared explore before. "I've spent a lot of time meditating, thinking about all those things Linda said, and getting to know myself over the years. I just don't feel evil." She paused, searched for the right words, and took a deep breath. "I, umm, I think my sister was wrong."

"Well, of course you're not!" Zoya exclaimed. "There isn't an evil bone in your body!"

Vickie snickered at the older woman's vehement outburst. "Well, technically, sometimes there isn't even a bone in my body." She partially dissolved into a Vickie-shaped mist to prove her point.

"You know what I mean!" Zoya laughed and slapped her hand in playful irritation toward the place where Vickie's shoulder should have been. As the mist scattered into swirling bits of color before coalescing once again into the shape of her young friend she wanted to shout for joy. She had finally gotten Vickie to open up and begin literally pulling herself back together. Apparently, the girl's healing was even more overdue than Zoya had guessed. She bounced with happiness, silhouetted against the darkening sky.

"Oh, my word!" Zoya suddenly scrambled to her feet and began stuffing yoga mats and water bottles into her bag as she realized how much time had passed while they were talking. "Shivani!"

The genie wiped away all trace of tears and banished the painful memories almost as quickly. "We have to hurry or I'll be late for dinner!"

They packed hastily, and Vickie poofed them back to the waiting car in record time. When they pulled up in front of the Chanda house, Zoya risked a few extra moments to pull her young friend into a tight hug. She didn't know how to put into words how much Vickie's trust meant to her. All she could manage to say around the lump in her throat was, "You are not, and never were, evil."

"I know." Vickie gave her friend a grateful smile. She rushed into the house before Shivani was forced to begin brandishing a felt tipped mallet.

CHAPTER 6

Vickie stopped to magically shuffle her possessions as soon as she was safely through the front door. She pulled her new clothes from out of mid-air, changed, and tossed her familiar favorites out of sight all with one flick of her wrist. She ran from the hallway to the dining room and slid to a stop just in time to avoid colliding with Indira who had both hands full of dishes she was carrying to the table.

"Oh, you made it," Indira said in a tone of withering indifference. Vickie winced.

"Ah, Vickie, you made it!"

Funny how when Shivani said it, the comment had a completely different meaning.

Shivani gave the genie an approving look. "And look at you! Such pretty colors against your pale skin. Perhaps a bit out of date, but a definite improve…" she coughed as her inspection of Vickie's new look made it to her feet. "Well, making progress at least."

Vickie glanced down at her bare feet.

"Ooops, I forgot." She grinned sheepishly at Shivani and reached out to yank the leather sandals out of thin air and pulled them on.

Shivani successfully hid the smile that tried to escape. She patted Vickie on the arm affectionately.

Nakul grinned at her as she took her usual seat between him and his brother. "Nice shoes."

"Why, thank you," she grinned back, knowing it wasn't the shoes he liked, but the magic that kept her belongings always within reach.

After the day she'd had, Vickie was ravenous. The conversational buzz made a pleasant background hum as she enjoyed every bite of her delicious meal. When everyone had finished, Vickie stood and began gathering dishes to help with the cleanup. Shivani took the plate out of her hand and shooed her out of the way.

"Don't keep Jai waiting. He likes to get to his meetings early." She placed the plate on top of the stack Indira was carrying past them and smoothed a lock of light brown hair back from Vickie's face. "You go have fun and listen carefully to what the men have to say." She leaned close and whispered conspiratorially in the young girl's ear. "They like it when you make them feel wise and important."

Vickie snickered softly, and went to join Jai in the foyer.

He held out his hand with a flourish. "Care to join me?"

She placed her hand in his and the two of them dissolved into a silvery mist that vanished from the hallway and emerged beside a tall stone monument in downtown Santa Fe. They solidified without any of the dozen or so people strolling past the Plaza noticing.

Vickie looked around in surprise. "Oh wow, no one is even looking at us."

Jai dropped her hand and gestured toward the pointed obelisk that stood in the center of the plaza. "There is an old magic surrounding this monument. It draws the eye not only because of its clean lines and precise placement, it actually commands attention. You would have to set off firecrackers while appearing out of a scented cloud to get anyone to notice. So long as you are quiet and discreet, this is the safest place in town to materialize."

They walked past the empty band stand and passed a group of tourists bickering with a sidewalk vendor over the price of a brightly colored Indian blanket. After walking several blocks, Jai halted in front of a beautiful adobe building tucked inconspicuously between a café and a shop selling silver and turquoise jewelry. Vickie stumbled to a stop beside him; her attention focused more on the art galleries and the music spilling out from brightly lit doorways they passed than on where she was going. The dark brown stain of the carved wooden doorway in front of them created a sense of exclusivity that discouraged casual entrance.

"Are you sure it is okay for me to be here?" she asked Jai as the "members only" feeling increased the moment they walked through the door.

"I'm positive," Jai assured her.

"Wow," was the only thing Vickie could say as she stood open mouthed, gazing up at the crystal chandelier casting flickering candle-lit shadows onto the polished wooden floors.

Jai glanced at the masculine elegance of the great room with both pride and chagrin. "Yeah, it is a bit over the top. But we like it."

He steered her toward his waiting guild members. The small group of men was gathered in front of an oversized fireplace with a hand-carved wooden mantel. On the far side of the room a highly polished bar was well stocked with amber liquids. A hint of expensive tobacco perfumed the air.

"I wasn't sure what I had been expecting, but it certainly wasn't this," she said.

"Don't let the respectability fool you. We aren't all a bunch of old stuffed shirts," a voice assured her from the curved stairway. A tousle-haired young man wearing tailored black jeans and a black suede blazer over his Navajo-patterned cotton shirt thumped down the stairs and moved to Jai's side. He draped one arm familiarly over the distinguished gentleman's shoulders. "So, this is the mysterious Vickie we have heard so much about."

"Don't scare her off, son," a deep voice called out from the group of men standing near the fireplace.

Vickie found herself facing five pairs of curious eyes. A large man with deep wrinkles fanning out from sky blue eyes set in a deeply tanned face stepped forward. "I am Editon, guild master of DDEG local 2-01. It is a pleasure to meet you, Vickie."

The accent was difficult to place. The thick snow-white hair combined with the impressive amount of silver he wore reminded her of the Choctaw natives back home. He motioned for Vickie to make herself comfortable on one of the oversized leather chairs gathered in the center of the room.

"Get her a drink, Ricky," Edition ordered the young genie who was continuing to hover near Vickie. Ricky tossed the guild master a saucy salute and headed to the bar.

"Just water, please," Vickie called. Ricky was back and placing a glass of ice water in her hand before she had a chance to get herself settled. The others each took a seat while Jai conjured a new chair and placed it next to Vickie for himself. Feeling overwhelmed by the opulence and the power of the room, Vickie was grateful to have someone familiar close by.

"I suppose before we get started, introductions are in order." Editon motioned to the impeccably dressed man with thinning blonde hair man seated to his left. "Gregory is our recording secretary, and also happens to run a fantastic bed and breakfast off Canyon Road." Gregory lifted his wine glass in her direction and smiled.

"Next to him," Editon continued, "is Frank." A quiet man in a tan western suit tipped his hat and nodded his head. "Frank is a bit of a craftsman. He did most of the woodwork in here."

A short, dark-haired man with glasses spoke up before Editon had finished introducing Frank, "And I am Huan. I do Make-a-Wish."

"Uh, don't all of us?" Vickie asked.

Huan's grin of pride faded. Editon explained. "Our guild is more civic minded than some DDEG chapters. Huan is a board member for the local Make-a-Wish Foundation. As such, he also functions as our guild liaison to the charity and makes it possible for us to be discreet with our contributions. After all, who better than us to ensure the more difficult wishes happen?"

A broad-shouldered man with a long thick mustache that shook when he talked spoke up next, "My name is Santiago. Welcome to Santa Fe, senorita. Our city is made lovelier by your presence."

Jai chuckled and rolled his eyes. He leaned close to Vickie and confided in a loud whisper, "Santiago thinks himself a ladies' man. Unfortunately, the only ladies he is used to talking to are the mares on his ranch."

Santiago laughed and was quick with a comeback. "Ah, but is not each and every one of them the picture of perfection? I know beauty when I see it!"

The laughter that followed his extravagant boast helped Vickie relax. She turned to Ricky who had taken the seat on the other said of Jai. "And what do you do?"

"As little as possible." He winked at her. The others made comments targeting the young man's complete lack of redeeming qualities before he admitted, "Actually, I am a ski instructor."

"So you see, his first statement was correct." Editon smiled down at the girl before clearing his throat in a very official sort of way. "Now that we all know each other..."

"Well, not really," Ricky interrupted. "We don't know anything about Vickie."

Once again she felt the weight of curious eyes. She was grateful when Jai came to her rescue. "You know she is a visiting genie who is a guest of my family." His tone made it clear that to ask anything further would be rude.

"It is the visiting part we wish to discuss." Editon turned his attention to Gregory who set his drink down on a convenient table that suddenly appeared beside his chair.

"Miss Vickie, I have done a thorough search, and I can't seem to find you listed in any active guild charters," the secretary said.

"Oh, well," Vickie bit her bottom lip nervously, "I don't suppose I ever officially joined a guild. Definitely never anything like this," she gestured toward the elegant room. "I, uh, met a guild master once, from Ventura. Only he seemed more interested in surfing than organization."

"Ahh, Kent." Editon exchanged a significant glance with Gregory. "That explains a lot. He was removed from office for incompetence a while back."

"Hmm, that could explain the silence when I tried to ask him a question recently." Vickie smiled.

"Since you seem to currently be without the benefit and protection of a functioning guild," Editon glanced around the circle and received slight nods of agreement from the six other members, "we would like to offer you an invitation to join ours."

Vickie blinked in surprise and choked on the sip of water she had just taken. "I, umm, don't know what to say."

"Undoubtedly, you would need to know what sort of benefits you would receive by joining," Jai prompted her helpfully.

"Oh." She thought about it a moment and shrugged. "Yeah, what he said." She smiled at Jai before turning her attention back to Editon.

"Well, as you should know," the elder genie began, "when the djinn, demons, and efreets organized four hundred years ago, it was for the purpose of protecting our interests. Our inability to protect ourselves and the magic from greedy, thoughtless, or even abusive masters was taking its toll on our dwindling numbers. More and more people were finding it preferable to renounce the power than to have no control over their lives. So, the founders came together and unionized. Now we help one another and use our powers for each other's good in addition to granting wishes for carefully-screened masters."

Jai leaned forward and whispered in Editon's ear. The older man nodded and smiled down at Vickie. "Our ever-diligent treasurer has reminded me that we are in a position to offer you a joining bonus of sorts."

"A bonus?" Vickie asked.

Editon nodded and Jai scribbled something in a large book with columns of numbers that suddenly appeared in his hands.

"There," Jai seemed quite pleased, "you now have two wish credits listed in your name."

His words did nothing to help Vickie understand what they were talking about. "What sort of wish credit?" she asked.

"Haven't you ever had bonus wishes before?" Ricky asked incredulously.

"No! Really?"

"This is why it is important for us to vote for guild reform," Gregory grumbled. "There are too many efreets in djinni clothing running around giving the DDEG a bad name. This is why we have a difficult time recruiting new members. Most djinni never experience the benefits of guild life."

Jai took pity on Vickie's rising confusion. "One of the benefits of guild membership is the sharing of residual wishes. Whenever a guild member successfully completes a three-wish contract with a master, the guild receives an extra bit of magic. It is up to the guild master to determine how that extra is put to use. Occasionally, we vote to spend it on the guild hall."

Vickie nodded, realizing where the opulence surrounding her had come from.

"Sometimes we divide the extra among the membership in the form of bonus magic that we can spend however we like. These bonus wishes aren't nearly as powerful as the magic we use for our masters, but if spent wisely they can make life very nice." Jai winked and Vickie found herself thinking of how often she had heard him say he was the luckiest man alive. She wondered if his wishes had anything to do with his luck.

"And, now, I have wishes, too?" She wanted to be sure she understood what they were saying.

"Oh, yes, my dear." Editon smiled. "Just think of the magic, and you will sense them."

Vickie closed her eyes and thought about her magic. "Oh, wow!" She could feel two warm pulses in the steel cuffs on her wrists that she'd never felt before. "It tickles!"

"I don't think I've ever heard it described that way." Santiago laughed and the rest of the guild joined in.

Vickie blushed. She wondered how she might spend her newfound wealth.

As the laughter died down, she cleared her throat. "You mentioned djinni, demons, and efreets, but all I see are genies." She motioned toward the blue steel cuffs visible on everyone seated around her.

"Yes, well." Editon cleared his throat uncomfortably. "There was more diversity among members in the early days. Unfortunately, it is rare that you find a demon or an efreet who is interested in anyone's welfare but their own."

"They also tend to move around a lot. Not exactly what you could call community-minded," Ricky added. "They don't avoid people or anything. They just aren't likely to want to be a part of something unless it benefits them exclusively."

They were so kind about answering, Vickie found it easier to ask more questions. When Jai cleared his throat and tapped his watch, everyone reluctantly agreed it was time to end the meeting.

Editon stood and shook Vickie's hand. "I am glad you decided to accept our offer of membership. I think both you and our organization will benefit."

"Thanks. You've given me a lot to think about." She followed Jai as he made for the door Santiago was holding open for them.

"I will walk with you to the Plaza before returning home," Santiago offered.

"Some of our membership actually lives here," Jai said, pointing out a carved glass case with heavy silver locks that held three antique lamps. "When we built the hall, we included accommodations for members who wanted a more secure place for their lamps than living alone offered. It would be rude to just pop in and out of their home, so those of us who live elsewhere make an effort to be respectful."

"If you want, we could add a room for you upstairs too," Ricky called out with a wink.

"She has a room," Jai reminded him as he placed his hand protectively on Vickie's back and escorted her through the door.

CHAPTER 7

The following evening found the Chanda family indulging in one of their weekly traditions: green chili cheeseburgers from the food truck that was at Alto Bicentennial Park every Saturday. While she normally wasn't very fond of meat, even Vickie had fallen prey to the local culinary obsession. She enjoyed trying different ingredient combinations. The only problem was there were too many choices.

"Come on Vickie, hurry up." Indira's petulant whine sounded from behind Vickie as she stood contemplating the menu options. "If you don't know what you want, just come back after the rest of us order."

Vickie stopped trying to think of something new and settled on her favorite, "I'll have a buffalo burger with provolone, avocado, roasted green chile, and chipotle mayo on a cheddar brioche bun."

As soon as the cook handed her the overflowing burger wrapped in brown paper, she joined Shivani and Jai where they had snagged a couple of picnic tables under the pavilion near the new playground equipment. Until recently, Vickie hadn't been fond of spicy food. Now she relished every bite. The seasoned curly fries and an ice cold coke made the meal complete.

Once hunger had been satisfied, rather than rush to the climbing wall, Rakesh glanced hopefully at Vickie. "So, can we try again?" Nakul halted in mid-stride, waiting to see if she was going to say yes.

Vickie shrugged. "Sure. Why not?" She pulled the ley line out of her pocket and laughed as both boys scrambled to sit on either side of her. Each of them were talking at once and telling her what to do.

"Let me show you how to watch videos."

"I wanna find more beta game downloads."

She was surprised when Indira slid down the bench till she was sitting opposite Vickie, "Have you been able to listen to music on it yet?"

"Yeah, kinda." Vickie looked down at the black glass and swirled her finger over it experimentally. "If I just say 'play music', it will play something but I never know what I'm going to get. See, watch."

She swiped her finger over the glass and spoke directly to the screen, "Play music." Immediately, the pavilion was filled with the high pitched twang of sitar and tabla. She tried again.

"See?" Vickie shouted over what sounded like a garage band trying to play an up-tempo version of Norwegian Wood. "At least that is better than the screaming that happened last time. I thought someone was dying."

Indira reached over and slid her thumb along the side of the device and the volume immediately reduced to a bearable level. "Well, at least you know it has good speakers."

Vickie nodded her head along with the tambourine that was only slightly off beat. "That's even better."

"Here, let me try." Indira held out her hand for the phone.

Vickie handed it over hoping the lure of a magical phone might be enough to thaw Indira's cold shoulder treatment.

"Open Pandora," Indira spoke clearly into the round black mirror.

A terrified face appeared on the screen. Suddenly, the line went blank.

Vickie took back the ley line and tried to get it to respond again. "Well, that's odd. It never did that before."

"Maybe you have to be specific," Indira suggested as they continued to try and figure out how to make the phone do what they wanted. "Ask it for something by both title and artist, like "play Bruno Mars, 'Just the Way You Are'" or something."

"Eww, no!" Nakul protested, "Play 'Animal' by Neon Trees!"

"Or 'Dynamite' by Taio Cruz," Rakesh chimed in with his favorite song.

"Personally, I like 'Born this Way' by Lady Gaga."

Alyssa's sudden appearance behind Indira caused all four of them sitting at the picnic table to jump. Vickie shoved the ley line into her pocket. Alyssa stared at her intently.

Indira stood up awkwardly. "Oh good, you're here!" I was hoping you'd show up so we could play a few sets of tennis." She grabbed her bag, then frowned. Alyssa was dressed in skinny jeans and hiking boots, and wasn't carrying a tennis racket.

Without removing her intense gaze from Vickie, Alyssa shrugged off Indira's hand. "Yeah, about that. I haven't got time to play. But since you're here, I want to talk to you about something."

Her face became a mask of greed. A chill ran down Vickie's spine as the redhead turned and walked off. Indira ran to catch up with her friend. The two stopped near a stand of aspens and began to have an animated conversation that involved a great deal of arm-waving.

The boys quickly lost interest in their sister's girl drama and ran off to play. Vickie sat by herself and felt increasingly uncomfortable as several pointed gestures made it obvious the two girls were fighting about her. Occasionally their voices grew loud enough that pieces of what they were saying could be heard.

"… wouldn't share something like that with me?!" Alyssa shouted.

"…Not what you think…!"

"…Know what she is…!"

"…Can't talk about…."

"… Don't trust me…?"

"…There are rules…."

"…Thought you were my friend!" As Alyssa shouted that last line at the top of her lungs, she shoved Indira away and ran toward the parking lot. A dog that Vickie hadn't noticed before followed quickly on the girl's heels.

A tearful Indira called after her friend, but Alyssa refused to listen. Finally giving up when the redhead vanished from sight, Indira returned to the pavilion and slumped onto the picnic bench.

"You okay?" Vickie placed her hand comfortingly on the other girl's shoulder, but Indira pulled sharply away from her.

"Leave me alone! It's all your fault," she glared resentfully at Vickie. "Everything was fine till you came!"

Vickie sat back, not sure what she had done to deserve such hostility.

"Look, I'll say I'm sorry if that helps. But I don't know how your friend's behavior is my fault." Indira refused to look at her. Vickie gave up. "Fine. Whatever."

She walked across to the playground to Shivani.

"I don't feel well," she told her. "I'm going back to my lamp."

Secure in the familiar isolation once again, Vickie attempted to clear her mind and focus on her breathing. This living in the real world was hard. There were so many emotions and rules. She wondered how long she could make the remains of Rose's care package last if she decided to never leave her lamp again.

Outside, a petulant redhead fidgeted nervously on the driveway as she worked up the courage to go and get what she'd been convinced was hers for the taking. "You're sure you can keep their weird alarm system from going off when I open the door?"

The dog at her side sat down. He stared up at her in exasperation and bared his teeth.

"Okay, okay!" Alyssa rubbed her palms on her jeans one more time. "We need to do this before the family gets home. I'll do my part, but you better know what you're doing."

The dog licked his lips and growled, even as his tail thumped noiselessly against the grass. Alyssa strode purposefully toward the door.

CHAPTER 8

Jai hastily folded his newspaper and stashed it under his chair when he heard the abrupt clink of breakfast dishes hitting the table.

"What's the matter, dear?" he asked just as he caught sight of Vickie's empty chair. He quickly began trying to soothe his wife's ruffled feathers, "Remember, she said she wasn't feeling well last night."

Shivani sniffed thoughtfully and considered the possibility that Vickie might be unwell rather than rude. "Very well, I will go and wake her then."

Jai winced, knowing firsthand how jarring the gong could be. He hoped the poor girl wasn't actually sick, or being woken that way wasn't exactly going to help her feel any better.

The family waited as the gong vibrated silently. When several moments ticked by without an apologetic Vickie appearing, they began to exchange nervous glances. Shivani struck the gong again. Her expression shifted from one of annoyance to genuine concern.

"Rakesh, be a good boy and check on her." She gestured. The boy ran toward the stairs, taking them two at a time. She called after him, "But, remember, no touching her lamp!"

Maya began to whimper hungrily as the food sat untouched on the table. Shivani hurried to the toddler's side and began putting small pieces of oat and carrot idli on her plate. "Come on, everyone, no sense letting one lie-abed spoil breakfast. Eat something before it gets cold and is ruined."

Everyone reached for platters of food at the same time. Their hands touched, and they chuckled softly, the tension easing. They were eating when Rakesh appeared alone in the doorway. Shivani was surprised.

"Where is she?"

"She's gone!" he exclaimed.

Shivani glanced at her husband worriedly, "You don't think she could have run away from us…?"

Rakesh shook his head vigorously. "No. Her lamp is gone from the attic. Her stuff is still there. Only the lamp is missing."

"Oh, Jai!" Shivani sat down abruptly. She pulled Maya onto her lap, holding her youngest tight.

Her husband pushed away from the table, threw his napkin down on his practically untouched breakfast, and headed out the door. "Don't worry, Shivani. I'll let the guild know right away."

The family sat in stunned silence as his voice echoed from the foyer. "Editon? We have a problem. My home has been compromised."

Moments later, a cloud of swirling silvery mist filled the living room and six serious genies stepped out of it.

CHAPTER 9

Vickie was surprised when she felt an insistent tug on her mind. She had a moment of disorientation as she realized someone was rubbing the lamp. Confusion replaced meditative serenity: no one ever touched lamps in the Chanda home. Forces swirled around her as she was compelled to leave her sanctuary and bow to the wishes of a new master.

Smoke gushed from the lamp, swirling and expanding as Vickie brought her hands together beneath her chin, already in mid-bow when her body solidified.

"What is your will, my ... Alyssa?" Vickie looked around in confusion. Instead of her cozy attic, she was standing on a mountain overlook. She shivered as the bite of cold mountain air brushed against her arms. The clearing was full of dancing shadows as the pine trees rustled in the wind. The form of a lanky greyhound slid from the shadows and circled both girls, growling.

"He was right. It's all true," the stunned teen muttered as she took a step back from Vickie. She held Vickie's lamp clutched to her chest like a lifeline. Her boots, jeans, and sweater were much better suited to the cold night air than Vickie's thin blouse and skirt; but she matched Vickie shiver for shiver.

"You stay put! I um, I have this," Alyssa shook the lamp in Vickie's direction like a lion tamer with a whip, "so you have to do what I say!"

Vickie wasn't sure who was more frightened by the situation they found themselves in, her or Alyssa. She tried to calm the trembling redhead by adopting the traditional stance and language. "But, of course, mistress." Regardless of her personal opinion of the girl, rules were rules and there was no doubt that Alyssa had rubbed the lamp. "So what is your first wish? You get three of them you know." Vickie tried to keep her voice calm and friendly.

"Oh, I know a lot more than that." Alyssa's smug smile was not the least bit attractive. She knelt down and held the lamp out to show it to the greyhound. A dark mist with blood-red sparkles suddenly swirled around the dog and grew into a man-shaped form.

"She's had a very good teacher."

The voice that echoed from the swirling cloud turned Vickie's blood to ice. She remained still as a rabbit hypnotized by a snake, watching as an all too familiar form took shape before her incredulous eyes. With the same self-satisfied smirk on his face Vickie had once been fooled into thinking was a charming smile, a tall angular man draped one arm carelessly around Alyssa's shoulders.

"And now, look at the lovely gift she's brought her teacher." He leaned over and rapped one knuckle against the side of the lamp in Alyssa's hands. The resulting vibrating hum scraped down Vickie's spine like nails on a chalkboard.

"Tony." Vickie's voice cracked as she choked out his name.

The greasy black hair was tinged with gray, and his awful silk shirts had been exchanged for Navajo cotton and a dark suede jacket; but the drooping mustache and gaudy medallion hanging against the thick, curly chest hair was definitely the same. So was the cruelty in his voice.

"What is it dear? Spit it out!" His mocking tone caused the girl next to him to snicker. He grinned down at her and winked before moving toward Vickie in a slow, menacing glide.

"What are you..? I thought you were... How did you...?" Vickie tried to come up with a coherent thought through the fear and disbelief.

"What am I… doing here?" he prompted. "Why, the mountains are lovely this time of year. And, besides, this delightful young lady and I have big plans for a new community."

Remembering how Tony had treated the women in his last 'community,' Vickie began to fear for Alyssa almost as much as she was worried about her own safety.

Tony began to circle Vickie, his soft voice purring in her ear, "You thought I was what? Still in Tennessee with your stupid sister? Please!" He snorted derisively before trailing one sharp-nailed finger down her cheek. "How did I find you?" He leaned close and sniffed at her hair.

Vickie flinched away from him, closing her eyes as a shiver of revulsion ran down her spine.

"Serendipity. Believe me, I was just as surprised as you when I caught whiff of a familiar scent, in Santa Fe, of all places. Amazing how you still look as young and innocent as the last time I saw you. Must be all that clean living." The leer in his voice was a physical assault.

She just couldn't bring herself to fully believe the reality of her situation. The dog was Tony? She opened her eyes and strained to catch a glimpse of steel cuffs glinting in the moonlight on his wrists. But that didn't make any sense. How had she never seen them before?

"You were a genie all along?" It still seemed impossible to her that he could have hidden his true nature so well.

He sneered at her. "Do I look like a genie to you?" He tugged the sleeves of his suede jacket over the cuffs, hiding them from sight. He paused for a moment and shrugged, "Though I will admit to a passing similarity, in power if nothing else. But as an efreet, I have more, let's call them options, than that ridiculous 'let's help each other' gentlemen's club you visited."

"You've been following me?" She was horrified at the thought of him lurking on the edges of her life.

"Everyone knows about the Plaza being a safe zone for popping in and out of town. Sometimes knowing where to be is better than being lucky. Made it easy to know what certain types were up to while I needed to lay low."

He turned and walked toward the edge of the scenic overlook they were standing on, "But, now that I have you to indulge my creativity, things are starting to look up."

"Sorry to burst your bubble, but only three wishes to a customer," Vickie was surprised to hear the defiant tone in her voice, "and you already had your turn."

"Ahh, but haven't you ever heard the phrase, 'rules are made to be broken'?" Without turning around he pointed at the still stunned and silent Alyssa, "My dear partner is eager to have me coach her on the best use of her wishes."

"Which means you are stealing her wishes." Vickie was furious.

Alyssa blinked at Vickie and glanced down at the lamp in her hands. "I really get wishes?"

Tony turned sharply at the tone of wistful greed in Alyssa's voice. He crossed to her and ran his hand caressingly down her arm to where her hand clutched the handle of the lamp. His fingers intertwined with hers as he covered her hand with his own, then tightened their unified grip.

"We get three wishes, pet," he said through the clenched teeth of a predatory smile.

"Oh, yes. Of course. We," Alyssa agreed quickly, even as she cast a speculative glance in Vickie's direction.

Tony reached up with his other hand, caught the young girl's chin in a bruising grip and forced her to look at him instead of the genie. "You wouldn't be thinking about doing something foolish, would you?" His voice growled low in his throat, and he tightened his painful hold on Alyssa's face.

Tears gathered in Alyssa's terrified eyes. "Never," she managed to say clearly enough to satisfy him.

Tony released her jaw and patted her cheek mockingly. "Good girl." He deftly snatched the lamp from her grasp. "But I think I will hold onto this. Just to be safe."

The sight of her lamp once again in Tony's hands made Vickie nauseous.

"Now, we have to make sure you get the wording just right. Wishes are literal things, and they can't be taken back once you make them." He drew Alyssa toward the edge of the overlook and turned her forcibly to face the valley spread out below them. "Now, focus on the details and the layout of the buildings. Speak clearly, just like we rehearsed."

The realization that she really could wish for anything made the girl less willing to simply do what she was told. Alyssa shook her head. "Wait. This doesn't make any sense. We can have anything, live anywhere! Why wish for some crummy farm in New Mexico when we could be millionaires and live in France?"

Tony's jaw clenched. His hands tightened on Alyssa's arms. Alyssa gasped. Vickie feared for the girl's safety as she realized how easy it would be for the efreet to simply throw the teen off the cliff if she became too troublesome. He managed to keep his voice light, with the threat of violence thinly-veiled, while he spoke to her as if she were a half-witted child.

"You obviously weren't listening when I explained it to you before. Matter can neither be created, nor destroyed. It can only be changed. When you make a wish, the magic draws the substance for that wish from other places. A wish that requires lots of change, like millions of dollars or a mansion, would pull lots of substance. It would cause ripples in reality that other magic users can sense."

He shifted his attention back to the valley floor, "Oh, no, believe me. I have a lot of experience with this. Small wishes that require the least amount of change and are hardest to trace are the way to go."

Oblivious to the danger she was in, Alyssa continued to protest, "But, you aren't wishing small. Buildings are big and you want us to create several of them. If we want buildings, why can't they be pretty and somewhere much nicer than out in the middle of nowhere?"

"Listen closely, dear." The threat in the growled endearment finally registered with Alyssa. She cowered before the increasingly angry man looming over her, "The trees and the isolation are important. One provides substance and the other keeps busybodies from noticing." Tony's non-existent patience vanished. "So, are you ready to make the wish exactly as we rehearsed? Or, do I need to find someone else to be my partner? After all, anyone can rub a lamp and make wishes. Maybe your little friend would be a better choice anyway. After all, she was smart enough to hide the magic from you."

"No!" Tony had finally found the right button. Alyssa couldn't stand the thought of Indira being better than her at anything. Her false friend had been keeping secrets from her; now it was Alyssa's turn to have a secret of her own. She grabbed the lamp from him and whirled to face Vickie. "Genie, I wish for a homestead to be placed there," she indicated a thick stand of pines beside the stream in the valley below, "that has a grand main house and the typical outbuildings of a working hacienda."

"That is truly your first wish?" Vickie gave Alyssa one last chance to change her mind.

"Yes! Do it now!" the girl commanded angrily.

"To hear is to obey," Vickie answered sadly. She folded her arms at shoulder level; the steel bands on her wrist clinked together as she closed her eyes and let the magic build. A cloud of muddy-colored smoke swirled around them, picking up speed before it descended on the valley below and obscured the stand of trees from sight. Lights and multi-colored flashes dotted the murky funnel of misty magic as it picked up speed. The points of light became streaks of color just before the cloud exploded upward and vanished, leaving behind four buildings and a corral.

"Excellent work as always, Vickie." Now that he was getting what he wanted, Tony once again oozed urbane charm. He turned to Alyssa with a smile. "So, shall we go explore our new domain?"

The young girl nodded, unable to take her eyes from the rancho that had appeared from out of nowhere. She was eager to see the adobe buildings and wooden railings up close.

"Ah, but first," Tony pointed to where Vickie stood, "how about you put away your toys like a good girl? We wouldn't want her thinking she's free to just roam about wherever she pleases."

Alyssa hugged the lamp close.

"Back in the lamp, genie," she pointed an imperious finger in Vickie's direction, "and stay there until I call."

"I hear and obey," Vickie whispered dejectedly. She dissolved into mist and returned to what had always been the safety of her lamp. The shiny curved walls suddenly felt more like a prison than a sanctuary.

CHAPTER 10

Indira lurked in the hallway, trying to overhear what her father and Uncle Editon were saying in the living room. When she'd first heard that Vickie was gone, she had been relieved. After the fight with Alyssa, all Indira wanted was for the stupid genie to vanish. Her dad's overreaction to Vickie leaving took her by surprise. When the members of the guild appeared, and she heard words like 'breach of security' and 'possible threat to the family,' she began to worry.

The good looking guy with the dark hair was talking now. "…just doesn't make any sense. With the wards on this house, it should be impossible for a stranger to just waltz in here and walk off with a lamp."

"Not if they used magic," the short guy in glasses contradicted him. "We found residual traces, but outside in the yard. Not actually in the house."

"We shouldn't just assume this was the actions of a stranger," Uncle Editon spoke up, "Jai, who has been through the wards often enough that they would no longer set off the alarms? Wards are excellent, but familiarity can mean exempt."

"Goodness, Editon, we've lived here for years. That could be a long list." Jai began counting possibilities on his fingers, "Shivani's Aunt Zoya practically lives here. But she would never do something like this. She adores the girl. There are the guys from work, Shivani's book club, plus the kids and their friends are always running in and out."

"Do any of them know about the magic?" Uncle Editon asked.

"Of course not! That has always been rule number one: 'Never talk about the magic.'"

Indira felt nauseous as she suspected what may have happened. She stepped into the room and cleared her throat to catch her father's attention. "Daddy?"

Jai barely acknowledged her. "Not now, Indira."

"But, Daddy…" Her voice broke as she fought to stay brave enough to say something rather than just run to her room and pretend she knew nothing about what was going on.

"I think you may want to listen to her." Uncle Editon spoke with quiet authority. Jai turned and faced his daughter.

"What is it, dear?"

"I…" Indira swallowed and tears welled up in her eyes as she suddenly found herself the center of attention of all seven men. "I didn't tell her. She just knew."

What began as a whispered confession picked up steam and got louder as the words began tumbling out. "She said I was an awful friend to have kept secrets from her all these years. Best friends are supposed to trust each other, and she said that since I didn't trust her enough to tell her the truth, even after she called me out on all my lies," she paused to swallow the tears out of the way of the words, "then obviously we were never friends to begin with."

Jai knelt down in front of Indira and held her hands as he caught her lowered gaze. "Alyssa?"

Indira nodded miserably. "But I swear I didn't tell her, Daddy. I never said anything about the magic."

He hugged her close, "I believe you, kitten."

"Well, regardless of how she found out, at least now we know who to look for," Editon said. One by one, the guild members vanished in puffs of smoke.

"Let me know if you find anything," Jai told the last one before he left.

"Of course," the tall man with the mustache replied, "but you know as well as I that if Alyssa's already rubbed the lamp, there isn't much we can do until she finishes making her wishes."

Jai sighed and nodded. "True. But at least the sort of frivolous wishes that are common among fifteen-year-old girls is sure to make a splash that will be easy to trace. Keep your eyes open for sudden instances of fame, beauty, and wealth."

Indira winced as her father stood up and turned his back on the trail of smoke that lingered for a moment after the last of his guild members departed in search of his missing ward. He motioned for her to take a seat on the couch. "In the meantime, I think the two of us should have a little talk about responsibility."

CHAPTER 11

There had to be some way out of this mess. Vickie tried to dematerialize, but any attempt at magic felt like holding water in her hands. No matter how hard she tried to gather the energies and focus her will, it all slipped away. She tried in vain to use the wishes she had been so excited to receive from the guild. All she felt was a warm tingle, a surge of power, and then the wish dissipated against the barrier of her mistress's will. No matter how she tried to rephrase each wish in her mind they all boiled down to the same basic thought: for someone to please come and save her from Tony.

She still couldn't believe the horror of her situation. For some reason, the thought of Tony leaving the commune in Tennessee had never crossed her mind. He had enjoyed lording it over the other members of the community too much to ever leave there willingly. But, here he was, trying to create a new power base from which to manipulate, use, and abuse gullible victims. Vickie's train of thought spiraled into darker territory as she began to worry about what may have happened to Linda — and Paul — if Tony's previous kingdom had collapsed.

No matter how awfully her sister had treated her, Vickie couldn't bear the thought of something terrible happening to Linda and the baby boy she'd left in her care. She had always believed that Linda could handle anything. Never once had the thought crossed her mind that Paul may not be safe. Now she couldn't stop thinking of all the horrible things that could have happened to them at the hands of a deceitful efreet.

She needed to do something, but she had no idea what. Vickie had never thought of herself as the hero type. She couldn't even get out of her lamp, so how could she possibly save her sister from some event that could have happened any time during the past decades?

She slumped to the floor in a dejected lotus position. Any attempt at clearing her thoughts just filled her mind with an ever increasing list of horrible 'what ifs.' She shook her head and felt frustrated tears sting her eyes.

Vickie shifted uncomfortably as a lump dug painfully into her hip. If she ever got back to her room, she was going to make sure to move some of the pillows back into her lamp. Having to remain solid was making things much less comfortable than she remembered.

She froze in mid thought and then slowly reached into her pocket. Her ley line! Of course!

With shaking hands she swiped one finger across the screen and said as clearly as possible, "Call Jai!"

A question mark appeared on the screen as the ley line attempted to make a connection. She was simultaneously disappointed and relieved when she saw Indira's face appear.

"Vickie?! Vickie where are you?" Indira shouted incredulously when she heard Vickie's voice. "Everyone in the guild is out looking for you and Alyssa. She is the one who took your lamp, isn't she?"

Vickie tried to stop the rush of Indira's frantic babbling, "Yes, she took my lamp. Where is your father? I need help."

"He is talking to the guild on his phone." Indira's face became fuzzy as she turned her head and yelled "Daddy! It's Vickie!" She came back into focus. "They got a lead on a wish, but it wasn't the right kind or something. Has she rubbed the lamp yet? Apparently, if she has already rubbed the lamp, the guild can't do anything until she finishes making all her wishes. Something about master's rights and autonomy or something. They have been arguing about it for hours," Indira concluded.

It was all Vickie could do to keep from crying. She had been so sure if she could just call for help, then this whole ordeal would be over. She had hoped there would be some sort of loophole in the guidelines that would allow the guild to save her from Tony.

"Then, there is nothing they can do to help me?" Vickie asked dejectedly.

"I wouldn't say nothing." Jai's image replaced his daughter's on the screen. "We are limited, but now that we know you are safe..."

"...And being held by a thief." Ricky's indignant face crowded close to Jai's.

"...We have options," the sound of Editon's deep voice in the background filled Vickie with relief. "However," the significant pause caused Vickie's joy to be short-lived, "we need to know where you are being held."

"Most importantly, you have to get her to use up her wishes. Once she has made all of her wishes we can demand she turn over the lamp," Gregory's voice added from off screen.

Vickie sighed, that would be easy if she had only Alyssa to deal with. The girl would be a fountain of wishes if Tony weren't keeping her in check. Tony!

"Oh!" Vickie exclaimed. "You don't know about Tony!"

"Tony?" Jai's voice dipped ominously.

"Alyssa's dog?" Indira asked.

"Yeah, but no," Vickie said. "He isn't just a dog. He's an efreet and he has Alyssa completely under his spell."

The disappearance of all the faces and the long silence that greeted this news caused Vickie to shake her phone frantically, afraid the silly thing had somehow managed to drop the call. She was relieved when Editon's voice drawled menacingly. "Well now, that means we are playing a whole new ballgame."

Santiago's friendly accent joined the conversation. "Can you tell us anything about where you are located, senorita? Tracking efreets can be tricky business."

Vickie was grateful for her sunrise meditations and yoga excursions with Zoya. She knew exactly where she was!

"Yeah, we are on the northeast edge of the Pecos Wilderness, up in the Sangre de Cristo Mountains. Look for a hacienda in a high-altitude valley."

Frank's quiet rumble came through the ley line, "There aren't any haciendas up that way."

"There's one now." Vickie chuckled.

"Ahh," chorused through the line as everyone realized what she was saying.

"You're doing great, Vickie." Jai's image dominated the screen once again. "Just get her to make those final two wishes. We're on our way."

The ominous promise hovered in the air as the line went dead.

Relieved, Vickie began dancing the most exuberant celebratory jig the cramped space inside the lamp would allow. She was amazed at how energizing knowing she had support could be. She was still trapped in her lamp, still needed Alyssa to make her final wishes, and Tony was still in control, but now she knew she wasn't alone. It made all the difference in the world.

She stopped dancing in mid-cavort as she heard Tony and Alyssa approaching. Vickie stood on tip toe, tilting one ear toward the spout opening above her head and tried to hear everything they were saying.

"No, you can't have horses until after we have recruited people to join our new community," Tony growled, obviously tired of repeating himself. "I have no intention of mucking out stalls. Me working is not part of the grand scheme of things here."

"But, you're magical too. Can't you just make it all vanish, or something?" Alyssa whined. She was growing equally as frustrated over having all of her wish ideas vetoed.

Tony's hand clenched into a clawed fist as he resisted the urge to grab the girl by her scrawny neck and throttle her until she finally understood. "I've told you. Magic doesn't work that way. I can do some small things, but without the power of the wish I can't make anything."

"Don't you have a lamp or something? I could just wish on you too." Alyssa was getting bored with his refusals. Vickie held her breath. The girl had no clue as to the mine field she had just stepped in the middle of.

"No one. Wishes. On me." The threat in Tony's voice was nothing compared to the hatred shining in his eyes.

Alyssa backed away. "Okay. I get it. You don't do wishes." She collapsed on a leather sofa that was part of the furnishings in the new hacienda. "But, can we get something to eat? We've spent hours checking everything out. It's really cool, but I'm starving and that new kitchen doesn't have a speck of food in it."

Pacing agitatedly around the room, Tony glanced at the lamp sitting on the high window ledge, safely out of reach of any hand but his own. Just the sight of it calmed his nerves. Logic had no impact on Alyssa. He changed tactics and turned a charming smile on her.

"How about I pop into town and get us something to eat, and maybe a few beers to celebrate what a perfect setup we have here?"

Alyssa wasn't sure she saw anything worth celebrating, but the thought of unrestricted access to beer was an effective distraction. "Sure, but maybe don't be gone too long? I don't like the thought of being up here by myself."

Tony smiled through clenched teeth. "I'll be gone as long as it takes. You stay put and don't do anything stupid." He dissolved in a cloud of oily black smoke.

Alyssa flinched as he vanished from the room. She was never going to get used to the way he could appear and disappear so quickly. It made her feel as if he was always watching everything she did. Her eyes flickered nervously around the room as she curled up on the couch and waited anxiously for him to return.

Vickie resumed her happy dance when he left. Alyssa was alone! Vickie had no idea how much time she had before Tony would return. Now all she had to do was get Alyssa's hands on the lamp. Even the slightest rub could technically be called a summons. Shouting would do no good; Alyssa would never hear her. But what if she could move the lamp? She tried throwing her body against the wall. The best she managed was a brief wobble before the lamp settled back solidly on its base.

She needed more weight, more energy, more something! She thought of calling Zoya; after all, two heads were better than one. Thinking of Zoya and energy gave Vickie an idea. Scrambling to her feet, she held up her ley line and spoke very clearly and specifically. "Play Zoya's warrior mix."

The pulse of the driving bass and drum mix filled the air. Vickie slid her thumb along the side of the ley line, just as she'd seen Indira do when she turned down the music. But this time she slid her thumb in the opposite direction, turning the music up as loud as it would go. She clapped her hands over her ears and winced, but the discomfort was worth it as she felt the floor beneath her feet begin to vibrate.

Vickie danced and bumped against the wall in time with the heavy bass beat. The lamp began a bouncing slide along the ledge, flirting occasionally with the possibility of toppling over the edge before wobbling back to safety. When the music built up to a climatic crescendo, Vicki jumped and threw herself at the wall. The lamp slowly teetered off the ledge and fell. It landed with a bone-jarring smash against the Saltillo tile floor.

When she saw the lamp fall, Alyssa screamed. She ran to where the brass vessel lay on its side. She reached for it, then remembered Tony and snatched her hand back. Then, she thought of the genie inside and worried about losing her wishes if anything had happened to Vickie during the fall.

Greed overcame her fear of Tony's return. She snatched up the lamp and looked for any sign of damage. Alyssa ran her finger anxiously over a huge dent in the side, and then nearly dropped it again as a dun-colored mist issued from the spout. Vickie stepped into view.

"You called, mistress?" The skinny girl smiled and bowed.

Alyssa distrusted anyone who was that happy. "No, I didn't. And you know it."

"Oh, I was sure I felt a rub of the lamp." Vickie shrugged and looked around curiously. "Do you know what you want for your second wish? A trip to Paris? Maybe a new wardrobe?"

She kept her voice light and cheerful as she listed some of the things she thought a girl like Alyssa might want. If she could just get those final wishes out of her, there was a chance she could be free of Tony before he even knew she was out of the lamp.

Alyssa's eyes lit up at the thought of walking the streets of Paris in a Joanna Mastroianni dress and Louboutin stilettos. "Ooohh, what a lovely thought." She grinned at Vickie. "I wonder just how many pairs of red-soled shoes I could fit in my closet."

"Why not get a whole new closet just for your shoes?" Vickie grinned back.

Alyssa laughed at the idea. "That sounds much better than the thought of living in this nowhere hacienda."

Vickie nearly cheered. It was working!

"But, I also like the thought of having my own horse." Alyssa glanced out the window to the empty corral.

"What kind do you want?" Vickie led the girl to the window so she could get a better look and possibly imagine the pen filled with horses. "Do you prefer Arabians? Morgans? Quarter-horses?"

"I've always wanted a leopard Appaloosa. You know, with lots of huge black spots all over."

"Just say the word, and it will be all yours," Vickie said, encouragingly. Alyssa opened her mouth.

"SILENCE!"

Tony's voice thundered from the roiling black cloud that suddenly appeared in the room. He stepped forward, threw the pizza and beer that he had been carrying to the ground and snatched the lamp from Alyssa's hands. "I should have known that the moment my back was turned you would try to steal my wishes!"

As terrified as she was, Alyssa was still willing to fight for the dreams Vickie had been dangling before her eyes. "They aren't your wishes, they're mine! You've already had yours. I heard her say so!"

Tony's hand lashed out with the quickness of a viper. The back of his bony fist slashed across her cheek with the full force of his fury.

Alyssa never even saw the blow coming before she was sliding across the floor. She pressed a trembling hand to the gash on her cheek from where his knuckle had cut the tender skin. She sat in stunned silence with the furious efreet standing over her.

"You... you hit me!"

"You foolish little idiot! The only thing that was ever going to be yours was a pair of steel cuffs and a lamp – if you were lucky!" He sneered down at her. "But you're not even worth enslaving."

Vickie took a step toward the fallen girl.

Tony whirled on her. "You get back in your lamp! You're no part of this!"

Vickie hesitated, expecting the swirl of force to pull her back in the lamp just as it had always done when Tony had ordered her around. But there was nothing. He had no power over her. A smile lit her face as she stood before him defiantly. "It's not your lamp anymore, Tony. My magic is hers now, not yours!"

"Silence!" The fury at having his order ignored caused the veins on his skinny neck to bulge. "I control her, so I control you! The magic is always mine!"

"No!" Alyssa shouted, clenching her fists. "I wish you would just shut up, leave me alone, and stop keeping all the magic to yourself!"

Now that was something Vickie could work with!

"Granted!" she shouted with glee. Feeling far from her usual indecisive self, she threw up her arms. The magic surged forth in answer to the intensity of her desire.

Two pairs of shocked eyes turned in Vickie's direction as a silvery-gray cloud enveloped Tony. The lamp hit the floor with a clang as his hands began to shrink. His yell of protest choked into a furious howl as he was completely obscured from sight. Alyssa scrambled away from the swirling cloud that grew darker as it spun faster and faster. Vickie kept her will focused on the mist, shaping the wish with a determination she had never applied to the magic before. This was one wish she wasn't going to just leave up to the universe.

The cloud burst apart in a bright white explosion and a battered, skinny, greyhound stood growling where Tony had been. The dog lunged viciously toward Alyssa and was brought up short by an invisible force.

"Tough luck, Tony," Vickie smiled triumphantly. "She wished for you to leave her alone, so guess what? You can't ever touch her again."

The dog stood panting, its eyes tinged with red as it began to slowly advance on Vickie.

"Oh, really, now, what good do you think that's going to do?"

Just as the dog made a leap for Vickie's throat she vanished in a silvery mist and materialized beside the terrified girl sitting on the floor.

The dog writhed and growled as if trying to scratch at a thousand fleas all at once.

"Figured out the rest yet?" Vickie taunted him. "You might as well stop trying to shift."

"What did you do?" Alyssa asked in frightened whisper.

"You wished for him to stop keeping all the magic to himself," Vickie replied innocently. Alyssa looked at her in confusion.

"Soo…" Vickie waited for Alyssa to catch on and sighed when it seemed beyond the reach of the girl's imagination. "So now he doesn't have any of the magic."

"You mean he isn't an efreet anymore?"

"Oh no, he's still an efreet." Vickie spoke clearly, making sure the dog heard and understood every word she was saying, "He is just an efreet who can't do magic."

She reached out a hand to help Alyssa stand. "The 'shut up' part was easy. Kind of difficult for a dog to speak clearly."

The dog gathered himself to leap again, but when clouds of mist began to appear between them, he turned tail and bolting out of the room.

"Vickie!" Jai rushed to her side, followed by Ricky and Editon.

"You found me!" Vickie grinned.

"You gave good directions." Frank said, with a smile.

Huan pushed his glasses back into place and frowned at Vickie in concern as he noticed the blood on the other girl's cheek. "Are you okay?"

"I'm fine," Vickie assured them all. "Really!" she insisted at their combined attitude of concern and disbelief. "Better than fine."

Santiago paused in his examination of the room. "But that lousy efreet got away."

"Oh, no, it will be easy to catch him." Vickie smiled smugly.

"I told you, efreets are hard to track," he insisted.

"Well, this one won't be." Vickie giggled softly. "He has a glowing red arrow hovering over his head that is visible to any magic user who looks at him."

"What?" Editon demanded.

She smiled sheepishly, hoping she hadn't done something wrong. "I just sort of slipped that into the wish under the 'leaving her alone' criteria. I figured it would be kind of hard for him to mess with her if it was easy for everyone to spot him from a mile away."

Ricky burst out laughing and clapped Santiago on the back. "What say we go enjoy a little efreet-hunting?"

Santiago grumbled. "More like shooting fish in a barrel at this point. Where's the challenge in that?"

Editon called after the two as they headed out the door, "Bring him to the guild hall when you catch him. We have a few violations of protocol to discuss with him." The words sounded innocent enough, but Vickie shivered. She didn't think she would care to be on the receiving end of a discussion of guild violations with the elder guild master.

Alyssa whimpered and tried to hide behind a chair. Frank glanced at her.

"What about her?" he asked.

"She has one more wish," Vickie said.

"I'm sure we can help her with that." Jai moved toward his daughter's ex-friend. He shook his head in fatherly disappointment as he kicked a beer can out of his way. "If she words it just right, she might manage to erase the worry she has caused her poor mother." He leaned close as Alyssa flinched. "She might even do something to make amends for all the trouble she has caused."

Alyssa sighed and nodded her head. Obviously, new clothes were not going to be part of her last wish.

CHAPTER 12

When Vickie and Jai stepped out of the swirling mists and into the Chanda living room, she was completely unprepared for her reception.

"Shivani!" Zoya yelled as she caught sight of Vickie and ran to throw her arms around the startled girl. "She's back!"

"Did Alyssa really steal your lamp?" Nakul demanded to know as he ran down the stairs.

"Are you okay? They didn't hurt you, did they?" Rakesh hovered behind his aunt trying to make sure Vickie hadn't come to any harm.

Shivani came running into the room with a crying Maya in her arms. She didn't bother handing the toddler to someone else before she pulled Vickie into a bone crushing embrace. "Maiṁ tumhārē bārē meṁ bahuta cintita thā!"

Vickie hadn't learned enough Hindi to be sure of Shivani's tearful words, but Shivani's concern needed no translation. Vickie was touched.

Maya didn't mind being squished between her mother and Vickie. She reached out and cupped her tiny hand against Vickie's cheek.

"Vee back!" Maya exclaimed.

Vickie stiffened at the touch of the tiny hand, and then tears began rolling down her cheek. She lifted her arms to return Shivani's hug and rubbed her cheek against Maya's hand.

"Yes, Vee is back," she agreed softly.

The entire family laughed and made a fuss over Maya's new words.

Indira's approached Vickie shyly. "I'm sorry that my friend," she searched for the right words, "stole you?"

"It wasn't entirely her fault," Vickie assured Indira. "But, before I tell you all about it," she looked at Shivani apologetically, "is there possibly something to eat?"

Shivani sprang into action as if launched from a rocket pad. "Oh, my dear, you must be starving!"

She reappeared moments later with platters of chicken curry and fried rice. The family followed Vickie into the dining room, anxious to hear all about her adventure.

"Let her eat first!" Shivani insisted as she piled a plate full of spicy chicken and set it in front of Vickie.

Vickie caught Zoya's eye when she mentioned Tony's name the first time. Her friend understood the significance, but refrained from asking questions she knew Vickie would rather not answer in front of everyone.

By the time Vickie finished telling them everything, a much-humbled Indira had already helped her mother clear the dishes from the table.

Two days later, when Zoya swept into the house to resume their lessons, she found Vickie sitting in the middle of the living room floor with Maya. Vickie was building block towers and laughing at the little girl squealing with delight as she knocked them over.

"Look at you!" Zoya smiled down at the sight of Vickie and the toddler.

Vickie shrugged and tried to pretend finding her alone with the baby wasn't a big deal, "I'm trying to keep Maya entertained while Shivani gets some rest. She's been cleaning as if that will somehow make it impossible for anyone to ever steal anything from her house again. I swear she has some sort of magic of her own. She's even managed to find a way to polish my lamp without rubbing it."

Zoya snickered. "How does she do that?"

"I have no idea! But after Frank got the dent out of it, she became obsessed with making sure there wasn't a speck of dust anywhere near it."

"That sounds like a very Shivani way of coping," Zoya nodded as she made herself comfortable on the couch. "And, how about you? How are you coping?"

"I'm fine," Vickie insisted as she rose from the floor and sat next to her friend. "He never laid a hand on me."

"That's not what I meant." Zoya waited.

"I have been thinking about Linda and Paul," Vickie admitted reluctantly.

"Understandable." Zoya nodded.

"It's just," Vickie exhaled and rushed through the thought, "he would have never left the setup he had in Tennessee unless something awful happened."

"And?" her friend pushed gently.

A long silence stretched between the two of them as Vickie struggled to make sense of her churning emotions.

"And, I'm worried about them."

"Peace only comes when reason rules," Zoya translated the Hindi quote stitched on her yoga bag, pushing her friend yet again.

Vickie chuckled softly, "You know, when they said they had a place for me with an Indian family in Santa Fe – you are not at all what I expected."

Zoya laughed and Maya chimed in, wanting to be part of the fun. She toddled over to the couch and climbed up between the two of them. Vickie ran her fingers though the little girl's dark baby curls and sighed.

"Okay. I give in. You're right."

"Me? I didn't even say anything," Zoya responded with serene innocence.

Vickie raised one eyebrow at her friend.

"Do you mind watching Maya? I won't be gone long."

"Are you sure?" Zoya asked, pointedly.

"Yes, I'm sure." Vickie stood up with determination. "Let Shivani know I will be back in time for supper." She took a deep breath, and vanished in a puff of silvery smoke before she could change her mind.

CHAPTER 13

Just as Vickie remembered, the road leading to the homestead traveled over a hill and vanished in the misty distance. She probably could have saved herself a lot of walking if she had simply appeared at the main house, but she preferred to take this visit one careful step at a time.

Vickie wasn't sure what she was hoping to find. It had been so many years since she had been here; there were forests of pine trees growing where there used to be fields. She began to wonder if the homestead would still be standing or if it, too, had been abandoned and overtaken by the trees. If it was there, would there be any people? If the people were there, would any of them want to see her? Coming might have been a mistake, but Zoya was right. She was never going to be at peace unless she finally knew the answer to all the 'ifs.'

It looked as if the dirt drive leading through the split rail fence was used frequently and in excellent repair. That was a good sign. She hoped.

She passed through the gate and caught sight of the main house. The wooden exterior was gray and weathered, but the roof looked like it had fresh shingles. On the far side of the compound, a large kitchen garden showed signs of activity. A wagon overflowing with green leafy vegetables stood silently, but there was no one in sight. As she rounded the corner of an old dilapidated barn, she saw a thick-set woman in faded overalls bent over a broken tiller.

The woman caught sight of Vickie. She pushed strands of grey hair that had escaped from her ponytail out of her eyes as she stood to get a better look. Vickie was unable to see her face clearly, but there was something familiar about the way she stood with one hand on her hip. The woman went completely still, her hand still raised to her brow. As Vickie drew closer, the woman walked away from the tiller. She reached the edge of the field and stopped, both hands now covering her mouth as she stared in shock at the young girl walking across the yard.

They were face to face before Vickie could see similarities between the woman with long grey hair and the pretty girl she remembered. Her face was round and blemish free, her eyes were as green as ever; but sun and hard work had etched lines around the eyes that spoke more of the hardships than the years that had passed. It wasn't until she heard Linda's voice that she was sure this stranger was her sister.

"You haven't changed at all," Linda whispered in disbelief. "You look exactly the way you did the last time I saw you."

Vickie glanced down at herself, not sure how to react to the drastic change in her sister's appearance, "Well, I did finally get some new clothes last week." She plucked at the pleats of her swishy skirt and tried to think of something else to say.

Linda broke the uncomfortable silence. "Nice to see you're finally wearing shoes."

"Sometimes," Vickie agreed.

Linda reached up and tugged nervously on her ponytail, extremely conscious of her grey hair the longer she looked at her sister's light brown locks that the years hadn't touched.

"So, what brings you here after all this time?" Her resentment of Vickie's youth and beauty made her voice steadier and stronger than it had been.

"I didn't actually realize how much time had passed," Vickie answered honestly. "It's easy to lose track of the days when you spend most of them meditating inside a lamp."

"You've been inside that lamp all these years?" Linda asked.

"Well, not all of it. But, mostly. Yeah, I guess."

"Wow," Linda whispered, "that's a lot of sittin'."

Vickie shrugged awkwardly and turned her attention to the homestead. The neatly manicured flower beds and the chickens pecking in the yard were new. A line of white wooden rocking chairs sat in the yard, facing the view of the mountain and the hill sloping to the distant fence line. Two of the old houses looked to be in good repair, but one was nothing but weeds and a crumbling chimney. There was no one in sight; she wondered where everyone had gone.

"The others are out berry-picking," Linda answered Vickie's unspoken question as she followed the direction of her gaze.

Vickie could sense the pride in her voice as Linda added, "Not as many of us here as used to be, but we do all right. I suppose being stuck on the homestead all this time wasn't so bad after all. A lot better than being cooped up in a lamp."

"Stuck?" Vickie asked, puzzled. "Why stuck?"

Linda inhaled deeply and grimaced before speaking of events she'd long since buried in the past. "Turns out you weren't the only genie around here. After you left," Linda glanced at Vickie and coughed, "I found three other lamps hidden in Tony's office. I was furious. So I rubbed one of them and made a little wish of my own." The dry chuckle held an echo of remembered fury, "I wished Tony would leave the homestead and never be able to come back or bother us again."

Vickie nodded in understanding. "The magic took what you said literally."

Linda nodded, "Yep. I didn't realize then just how specific magic could be. As long as we never left the homestead, he couldn't get to us. And believe me, he wanted to pretty badly for a time. If anyone so much as stepped off the place, they were snatched up in a cloud and we never saw them again."

The horror of watching friends vanish and never knowing what became of them shadowed Linda's eyes.

She glanced down at her callused hands, "It was hardest on Paul. We had to home-school him. He never got to leave and do any of the things other boys normally did." She grew fierce, "But don't you think he wasn't happy. 'Cause he was! He has a good life here. He's married and has a little girl. Cute as a button. So, don't you go getting any ideas about trying to take him back. It's too late!"

Vickie took a step back in the face of her sister's vehement declaration. "I wasn't thinking of anything like that."

"Then, what did you come back for?" Linda eyed her suspiciously.

"I… I don't really know." Vickie admitted. "I guess I just wanted to make sure you were safe."

Linda snorted. "A little late for that, don't you think?"

"Yeah." Vickie searched for the right words. "But, um, I guess under the circumstances, I actually have some good news?"

Linda folded her arms and waited. Her aggressive stance evaporated as Vickie took a deep breath and began to tell her all about the run in with Tony. They both chuckled over the fact that Tony was brought up short by yet another woman wishing he would go away.

"Wait a second," her sister interrupted as Vickie listed in detail all the things the wish had done to him, "you're telling me that that SOB is now permanently stuck in dog form and is facing some sort of genie guild justice?"

Vickie nodded. "That about sums it up."

The change in her sister was a magic all its own. Years vanished from her face as she started laughing and actually pulled Vickie into a fierce hug. "That is the best thing I've heard in more years than you can count, baby girl!"

Vickie's eyes misted at the sound of the pet name she hadn't heard since before their mama had died. The quick hug ended with both of them standing in awkward silence, neither knowing what else to say.

Vickie began to back away. "So, yeah. I just wanted to make sure you were safe. And umm, now I know." She ran a nervous hand through her hair and sighed. "So I think I'll head on back, now."

Linda shifted uncomfortably. "Where are you going? You just got here. You haven't even seen Paul."

"Yeah, I know." Vickie cleared her throat. "Maybe next time I visit."

"Why not just stay?" Linda offered hesitantly.

"I can't." Vickie looked around and took a deep breath of chilly mountain air. "I promised I wouldn't be gone long."

"Oh." Linda paused a moment, then enveloped Vickie in a tight embrace. "I'm sorry for everything," she whispered.

Something wound tight in Vickie finally let go. She swallowed past a sudden knot in her throat and managed to speak around the threatening tears. "I know. I forgive you." She was surprised to realize she really meant it. She hugged Linda and stepped back with a genuinely warm smile on her face. "I'm not mad or anything."

Linda searched her sister's face and saw she was speaking the truth. She, too, released decades of tension in one long deep sigh. "So, you'll come back and visit again soon? Stay long enough to meet Paul next time?"

Vickie nodded and gave her sister's hand a squeeze. "I promise. I will visit soon. But, for now, I have to get home for dinner."

She folded her arms and smiled as the silvery mist obscured Linda from sight. Vickie realized how much the sound of the words 'going home for dinner' sounded surprisingly right.

And it wasn't just because Shivani was such a good cook.

www.ingramcontent.com/pod-product-compliance
Lightning Source LLC
Chambersburg PA
CBHW031939240626
47153CB00003B/785